The Book that Made Headlines in Chicago!

"THE TAKE PROVES SAFE BET FOR SUCCESS"

A CRIME THRILLER AS EXP
AUTHENTIC AS
THE POPE OF GREENWICH

THE TAKE

EUGENE IZZI

ST. MARTIN'S PRESS/NEW YORK

THE TAKE

Design by John Fontana

Library of Congress Catalog Card Number: 87-16386

ISBN: 0-312-91120-3   Can. ISBN: 0-312-91121-1

Printed in the United States of America

First St. Martin's Press mass market edition/July 1988

10 9 8 7 6 5 4 3 2 1

To my wife, Theresa, who inspires me

Acknowledgments

I would like to give my deepest thanks to Philip Spitzer, the best agent in the world; Jared Kieling, the best editor I've ever known; Chris Heaney, the best friend you could ever have; and Bill and the Doc.

Without these five men this book would never have been published.

E.I.

1 Dr. Javier Chacona had six hours to spare before he had to be at the free clinic. He felt a mixture of erotic excitement and terror, not an altogether unpleasant feeling, as he injected the coffee-with-cream-skinned young woman lying on his couch, smiling at him, her face a mirror of pleasant anticipation. Her long jet-black hair smelled pleasantly of strawberries. It shone brightly in the dim light escaping through the heavy purple draperies running floor to ceiling, covering the wall of glass that was Dr. Chacona's living room window. She licked her lips as the jolt of cocaine and heroin entered her bloodstream directly, coursed through her veins, *whack,* right to her head it went, warm, hot, even. She *felt* it race through her, making her safe, making her forget everything bad, making her feel on top of the world.

Chacona hadn't wanted to do this; it wasn't part of the deal.

"Lucille," he had near begged her, "your brother will *kill* me if he thinks I had anything to do with needle marks on your arms."

Lucille Ortiz had smiled, exposing her perfect teeth, white and small, a beacon in her dark face, her eyes sparkling with deception, an expert at manipulation about to ply her trade once more.

"He will kill you more slowly if you do not do what I say," she told him. "I will tell him you tried to rape me." And Chacona had shivered with fear at the thought of her brother, Francisco Ortiz, thinking even for a minute that Dr. Chacona had tried something funny with his sister.

"I will tell him you tried to rape me," Lucille said, "instead of making slow, long love with you, as I plan to, after."

And that had been what had broken Chacona's will. Looking at her, her perfect breasts jiggling loosely under the silk hot-pink shirt she wore on this freezing winter morning, the tight round ass squeezed into the white jeans, so tight he could see her pussy there, etched into the fabric as she sat casually on his leather couch, the deadly package next to her, still in the flight bag. The thought of this girl with the full red rich lips, the straight-narrow nose so uncommon among the women of his homeland, the light-skinned Puerto Rican girl whose brother would kill him for even thinking of her in a sexual way, that had broken Chacona, and he had no way of knowing that her simple lush charms had broken dozens before the very same way.

So he had taken some of his personal stash—after putting all the pure fresh stuff in the flight bag into his safe—and mixed it with ether, expertly, with shaking fingers not good enough for surgery anymore but certainly dexterous enough to mix a batch of freebase.

They smoked it, and this calmed him down some.

Looking at her next to him, her greed naked in her eyes, he suddenly knew why his homosexuals still refused to use rubbers, still took unprotected cocks into their mouths, still took it up their asses, knowing full well that AIDS was knocking them off by the thousands, and the list was growing larger every day. He'd see them at the free clinic, Monday and Friday evenings, six hours he donated twice a week. Their lesions, their swollen glands, death in their eyes, wondering, hoping and praying that they would only have a case of the flu.

"Safe sex," Chacona would tell them, over and over again, until the words lost their meaning to him, became one single sound, *safesex*. "Don't you know about safe sex, about *rubbers*, for God's sake?" Losing his cool, very unprofessional, but they were breaking his heart, these young men were. Dying in agony, without dignity, abandoned by lovers, parents, friends, they would slink away, feeling so terribly sorry for themselves, in shock, most of them, never thinking it could happen to them.

But that wasn't it now, Chacona knew. It wasn't ignorance, nor disbelief in their own mortality, that drove them into sexual encounters with strangers. It wasn't the well-it-won't-happen-to-*me* bullshit that kept other people smoking while hundreds of thousands of other smokers kicked off each year of cancer and heart disease, it wasn't that at all. And he only figured it out now, staring at a pair of coconuts jiggling inside a tight pink silk blouse.

It was the excitement of mixing sex with the thought of death.

For he had never, in forty-seven years of life, been as aroused as he was at this moment. He had had girls, many, many times. Hundreds of them. Some, even lovelier than the one next to him here now. White girls, black girls, Puerto Rican girls, Chinese girls, Mexican girls, Japanese girls, Scandinavian girls, some of them so breathtakingly lovely that he had to smoke freebase two, sometimes three times to be able even to *think* about a hard-on. And more girls than ever, now that Carmie was gone. And his practice was going to hell. And the word was spreading around the paranoid and suspicious and disgusting gossipy medical community that maybe good Dr. Chacona was drinking a bit too much, maybe even writing prescriptions for himself, because he had had two malpractice suits filed against him in the past year, and the nurses who had worked with him in the operating rooms during both surgeries had almost had to be fired before they would calm down and swear not to go to court and testify against him. He had lost his visiting rights at Mercy and was keeping office hours only three days a week. Of course, on the good side, he was donating twelve hours a week at the free clinic in Uptown.

So the women were now a diversion, and if it hadn't been for Lucille's brother Francisco, why, Dr. Chacona would probably be broke and hungry instead of rich and horny and able to do something about it.

And Francisco would have Chacona's nuts cut off at the base if he ever even suspected that the good doctor was having sex—safe or not—with Francisco's twenty-two-year-old sister.

But she had threatened him, had she not? Left him no choice. And he was feeling more erotically excited than he had ever been before in his life.

The thought of this girl here, under him, moaning with pleasure, maybe screaming as she came around his thick brown cock, ahhh, the pleasure, the danger, the excitement of it!

And so he understood why some of his homosexuals did the things they did. Because now he was doing the exact same thing, or planning to, and the chances were good that his actions would yield the exact same results. Death, slow and horrible.

He forced the thought from his mind and stared again at the jiggling going on under that silk blouse, his mouth forming in a seductive, man-of-the-world smile, unconsciously reaching up and lightly stroking his thin black mustache, raising his eyebrows, thinking that if he had to die for this, he was sure going to do whatever the hell he pleased, then casually asking Lucille if she was ready for a speedball yet.

As Dr. Chacona was injecting the sterile needle into Lucille's arm at eleven that Monday morning, Fabrizzio Falletti was stretching and rubbing his eyes, feeling next to him in the bed, wondering where in the hell the woman was. He was still half-asleep, crabby and angry. He was always this way the morning of a score.

He felt confident, sure of himself. He was the best safeman in Chicago, now that Safeman Willy was dead. He could divert alarms, open locks, get into vaults as well or better than any of the so-called professionals in the Midwest. And he never thought about getting caught. It wasn't in his game plan. But still, the day before a score, after all the planning and backbreaking hours staking out the score, writing it all down, getting all the tiny little details right, when he was ready to go, he'd start getting just a little bit mean. A few days before the score he'd get surly, aggressive, and the only person who could even approach him in safety was his partner, Doral Washington. Which did nothing to calm him down, because Doral was always supremely confident, going into a score as if he were going to dinner with his family, in charge, capable, unflappable. Doral's only sign of nervousness would be falling into ghetto slang before a job, so badly that Fabe could barely make him out. His fearlessness was one of the reasons Fabe had chosen him for a crime partner; that and Doral's casual approach. Out of a cityful of pretty good thieves to pick from, he'd chosen Doral to be on the inside with him. The other reasons were numerous, would take Fabe a week to sort out in his mind; the physical condition Doral pushed himself to sustain, like Fabe himself a perfect physical specimen, working out every day, even between scores, to keep the edge. That came to mind right away. But mostly it was the supreme self-assurance Fabe was

5

drawn to. Not cocky or arrogant, but not ignorant, either. Doral knew they had a chance at being busted on any score they went out on; after all, they had met in prison. But he also knew that the odds against a bust could be knocked down so low that it could be compared to having four aces in a poker game; some fool might pull a straight flush, but you couldn't let the possibility stop you from betting.

They both knew that when the time came to go out and do it, the odds were in their favor. They were holding all four aces. Only fate or an unkind god could interfere. All the details had been worked out, all the mischances wiped out as much as possible. Fabe knew that Doral could be counted on to do his part coolly, professionally, and Fabe knew that if fate did intervene and the heat came down, they'd go down together; none of this business of running off and sending the other guy commissary money while he fought the El Rukns in the joint. They were a team, all for one and one for all.

Fabe stretched, smiling as he thought of Doral. He rolled out of bed and padded naked to the bathroom, took care of business, and came out in a well-worn plaid bathrobe that hung past his knees. He walked to the balcony of his apartment on the ninth floor of the Armitage Building on the corner of 71 West Huron Street on the near North Side, unlocked the sliding glass door and slid it silently on its track. He stepped into the bright sunshine and the bitter December cold, feeling the gooseflesh rise up all over his body.

Thirty-one degrees out here, not much wind, the high rises all around him pretty much blocking it off, but the skin of his scrotum still contracted as the cold air found its way up his bathrobe and he stood there leaning on the railing, taking deep breaths, doing the breathing exercises that Doral had taught him years ago in the joint when they'd celled together and Doral had been into Yoga, bald heads, black power, and political muscling to free the enslaved black man. At least in the yard, he'd been into it.

Fabe looked across the street, noticed that the Chinese joint had been closed and now an Indian restaurant was announcing its grand opening. He wondered if he'd have the guts to walk in there and order something. He hoped the menu was in English. With his luck, he'd probably get an order of spitting cobra or something, if he wasn't careful. The restaurants in the area were opening and closing every month or so, catering to the neighborhood's tastes. Owners taking a big chance while they scratched their heads trying to figure out what would make them money in a neighborhood diverse and strange, yet monied. Fabe had known when the Chinese joint opened that it was a mistake; yuppies weren't into Chinese. Probably not into Japanese either, now that they'd learned that their beloved sushi was really raw eel and carp. Probably into Indian cuisine these days, and that was why the joint across the street was opening up. Or Thai food. Maybe Vietnamese. Fabe hoped they were, standing on his balcony smiling, getting an image of some character in a three-piece suit with a fifty-dollar haircut chewing on a piece of doggie, telling his girl how delightful it was.

Fabe looked directly ahead and saw the Sears Tower rising up into the clouds above, thinking how he hated heights. Really hated them, but this was the main reason he had chosen the apartment, instead of one on the other, quieter sides of the building. He wanted to be able to get up every day and step out onto his balcony in his bare feet wearing a bathrobe and stare up at the biggest building in the entire world. Simple as that.

He saw that people were driving by him down there and looking up. Pointing. He wondered if they could see his balls hanging down. Well, it was *his* balcony. If they wanted to look they could look. But he'd be damned if he'd go inside just because some peeper was gaping at him.

He imagined what they were looking at and he smiled. He was a tall man, six feet three inches, and weighed just a little under two hundred and fifty pounds. He had a forty-eight-inch chest and a thirty-two-inch waist. His hair was black and a little on the longish side; he went out to Ken's Silver Shears in Sauk Village once every other month or so for a regular man's cut, but with the score coming up here, he hadn't had time. Kind of a big honker, a Roman nose, he referred to it when he was feeling kindly. High forehead, high cheeks. Born here and labeled with a silly-ass dago old-country name so his father's pride could be assuaged. Dumb. But he never even thought about having it legally changed. He smiled broader, thinking of the folks in their cars driving by looking up at the big guy in the bathrobe with nothing under it, taking in big, deep, long slow breaths of freezing air, shivering in the December morning air. He stamped his feet to make sure they still had feeling in them, and went inside.

He was feeling a lot better now.

Thirty-eight years old and a millionaire, almost, already, how could he not feel good? Tonight would be the last one. If they had any luck at all, it would put him over, put him past the goal he had set for himself six years ago when he and Doral had teamed up. One million dollars, cash, locked up, his take, less nothing; cars, rents, none of it coming out of what he had stashed away. There had to be a million dollars sitting there, his to do with as he pleased, and then he would be done. Get out before the odds caught up with him. Give it all up and go another route. Not take any static from anyone, that was out of the question, but with a million dollars in liquid cold hard cash put away he could really go to work. Turn it into ten before he was forty-five. Make more money than he'd ever make if he scored every week instead of four or five times a year.

And tonight would put him over. He plugged in the coffeepot, wondering if he'd miss it. The almost narcotic thrill of going into a well-protected place where you didn't belong, with the express intent of taking everything that wasn't nailed down.

Deciding he could live without it. He'd tempted fate long enough, he and Doral. Hell, Doral claimed to be a millionaire already, investing in real estate in Old Town, making his secret deals, wearing suits when he wasn't with Fabe—a real businessman. Fabe wondered why Doral even went out on scores anymore, if he was so well set. Wondering if it might possibly be because he didn't trust anyone else to go in with Fabe but himself. Or because of the kick he got out of it.

Fabe poured himself a cup of hot coffee and lit his first cigarette of the day, looking at it funny, wondering why it was that he only smoked on the three days before a score and the three after. He couldn't be nervous, could he? He didn't feel nervous.

Well, maybe just a little.

There was the familiar tightening in his chest, a set in his shoulders, a warmth in his belly, maybe a slight quickening of the pulse that he wasn't used to. But hell, that didn't mean he was *nervous*. How about the big shots in the banks, they probably felt this exact same way when they watched the interest rates slowly creeping down, meaning more and more people could get their money, but meaning, too, that they couldn't pick and choose from among the best prospects anymore either. Fabe wondered if they could be considered to be nervous.

And guessed they probably were.

So, okay, he'd settle for nervous. But not afraid, definitely not scared. They could never make him show fear, not even in the joint those first few months when the word got around that a cop was jailing on the block and every convict with a score to settle seemed to crawl out of the woodwork trying to turn him out or beat him to death. He'd fought so long and hard that even all these years later his hands were misshapen and scarred. But they hadn't scared him into dropping his drawers, not then, not ever. Which was a rarity for any white guy in the joint down in Joliet, and a near impossibility for a cop. If all that hadn't made him afraid, then going out on a score with all the cards in his hand was a piece of cake.

The only fears he would admit to were of heights and fire, and he'd beaten the heights by going down to Marseilles, Illinois, on Sundays and leaping out of airplanes with the sky divers until now he could stand on the top floor of the Sears Tower and not get sick at all, maybe just a little belly tightener. Conditioning himself, preparing himself.

How many times, over the years, had the only way to get in been from above, he and Doral rappeling down from unguarded and impossibly high rooftops, like a couple of spiders in the dead of night, up in the clouds together spinning black webs, way up there, seemingly miles above the street, and they would hang there, next to each other, not looking down, not speaking, as Fabe worked on the window from the outside, slipping in like ghosts, opening safes with smooth steady hands, hands that did not tremble no matter how long it had taken them to open the window, or cut a hole in it big enough for them to fit through—a dozen times, maybe?

The fire was something else again. He didn't think he should start burning houses down so he could stand in them until the last minute, feeling the flames licking at his clothes before he ran from the building, uh-uh. Fabe wanted no part of fire. Which was the reason he had moved only onto the ninth floor of his twenty-five story building. He knew that the Fire Department snorkel equipment was useless past the ninth floor. It was a fireproof building. Ha-ha. *Nothing* was fireproof. Not if an arsonist wanted to brown it badly enough. Like nothing was burglarproof. They could slow him down, but they could not stop him. And so he would stay on the safe floors, where the firemen could save him if some crazed terrorist decided to ash the Armitage Building, teach the imperialist running dogs a lesson.

He finished his third cup of coffee, sort of timed it so he'd finish his fourth cigarette right along with it, and headed for the shower to get clean and shaved and dressed and ready to meet Doral at one, after his usual Monday breakfast with his ex-partner.

They had a big day ahead of them.

2 There wasn't a day that went by that Police Inspector Jimmy Capone didn't get down on his knees and thank God that his brother had been born first instead of the other way around. Their father had been a hardworking, taxpaying leather tailor with a drinking problem and a warped sense of humor, and he had thought it would be very funny indeed to call their firstborn son Alberto. And so it had been Jimmy's older brother who'd had to explain to the teachers every year, who had to take the taunts in the schoolyard, who had to fight a dozen bloody battles at the beginning of every new school year, and who still had to face the indignity of walking into their home every single day of his life, until he was seventeen and ran away to join the Army, and hear their father's drunken yet cheery holler of "Hey, Al Capone, how's it going?"

Not to mention the rare occasion when they had been busted for some childhood bullshit, the cops acting tough, throwing the fear of God into this gang of pretty good kids, shake them up a little bit so that they wouldn't get any worse than they were. Catch them drinking a little beer, maybe, or playing cards on the sun porch at the park after school, line them up against the nearest squad car, frisk them, and shout into their faces, *"The fuck's your name, boy,"* and oh man, when they got to Jimmy's brother and the other boys would be stifling their laughter in spite of their fear, and Al would be terrified, knowing better than to lie but scared to death to tell the cops the truth. How many times had the both of them been taken home for some crappy little thing, when every one of the other kids had been let go with a good chewing out?

And their father, standing there in the doorway of the family home, looking at the cops who'd grabbed them, listening to them explain that they had stopped the kids for some reason and that this little wise guy had told them that his name was Al Capone.

Old Pa, he sure had some laughs at Al's expense, no doubt about it.

Across the street from the Armitage Building, Jimmy Capone was sitting alone in a booth, positioned so he could see Fabe's building and the corner of the Indian restaurant opposite. Jimmy was on the third corner, in the Iron Horse Café, waiting for Fabe, as he did every Monday and Friday when they were both in town. Not ordering yet, waiting for Fabe. Sipping his black coffee and looking around.

Noontime crowd not in yet, just a black guy in the booth behind him, two giggly girls sitting at the counter talking in whispers, an old bag fella, smelly and bearded, jealously guarding his last drops of coffee in the front booth next to the door, knowing he'd have to leave soon, walk out into the cold and merciless day as soon as the lunchtime working people came in. A lady in a fur coat sat two booths behind the old fella, gazing at him with fear and mistrust as she took proper little bites out of her club sandwich. She glanced around and caught Jimmy's eye and smiled at him, rolling her eyes at the drunk, and he looked away, angry. He had no use for compassionless folks. Which was sort of funny, being as Jimmy was a Chicago Narcotics Investigator, a species not generally well known for their trust and kindness toward their fellow man.

After getting out of his blue suit, Jimmy had been assigned to the elite Organized Crime Squad, a top-notch killer unit of top men who kept their eyes on the mobs around town, not only the Mafia but the bikers, the Puerto Rican gangsters, the black gangs, anyone who ran a tightly knit, continuing criminal enterprise. But mostly, they set out to get, and spent most of their time trying to break, the Mafia.

Which caused Jimmy more than a little grief, since he was of Sicilian heritage and the constant butt of his cronies' jokes and only half-kidding insinuations.

As it turned out, Jimmy Capone was one of maybe four honest guys on the entire team, and when it hit the fan, like it always did with those elite squads of answer-to-nobody super-cops, the unit had been disbanded and heads had rolled. Jimmy, clean as a whistle, came out on top. He got transferred to the Narcotics Division, was eventually promoted to inspector, and then took over leadership of the entire unit. As if the promotion and transfer had been some kind of jive-time reward for being honest, for living up to the oath he'd taken and sworn to on the last day of Academy training all those years ago. He'd take it, though.

And the best thing about being on Narcotics, the very best thing of all was, for the most part he no longer had to deal with a bunch of Mafia guys, most of whom he considered to be class-less scum and cowards with no imagination or backbone. He still pictured them as fat guys with napkins tucked into their collars, spooling spaghetti, listening to Caruso records.

Contrary to popular belief, the mob does not operate the narcotic action in the city of Chicago. Any rookie cop could tell you that. But the Mafia is such a prize catch to all the print and

TV folks that they haven't yet decided to let the general public in on this secret. It would hurt everybody on slow news nights.

Which is why a half dozen guys wind up every year in the trunks of their cars over at O'Hare airport, stinking the place up until someone finally calls the law and they come and pry the lid open and try to figure a cause of death.

That wily old man, the Swordfish, had known years ago that heroin was hot, way too hot, and it would bring them down if they dared run the stuff. And besides, he had children of his own, and then grandchildren. He had never allowed any of his people to deal in drugs, and those who dared to step outside their authority—those greedy hoodlums who weren't satisfied with the massive profits from loan-sharking, prostitution, gambling, porno movies and magazines, those very few who stepped outside of the law of the head man—these men were dealt with efficiently and mercilessly.

Which was to say they would wind up in the trunks of their cars, in the parking lot at the airport.

Unless they got lucky, that is, and the feds or the Narcotics Division got them first, in which case they would generally spend between ten and fifteen years in the joint, that being generously considered by the mob to be punishment enough, and they could get out and return to their old business if they had what it took to take it away from whoever had taken control of it in their absence. If they got nailed on a narcotics bust, there was no money for the family while they were away, and no guarantee they could get out and return to their old business. Narcotics were off limits to them, and if they didn't learn one way, well, they'd find that it was dog-eat-dog out there.

But that didn't stop them, not at all. The chop-shop guy would look at all the big dough he was making, and it didn't take much imagination to figure it tripled, and before you knew it he was into junk in one form or another. And from there into his carpeted trunk. Or into a cell in Atlanta. Or, if Jimmy got him, Joliet, which was a little bit tougher than your average federal prison. Like maybe a thousand times tougher. Guys in Joliet ate you and swallowed you whole and didn't care whom you knew.

And a month didn't go by where one of Jimmy's snitches didn't give him a good solid mob bust. He guessed that maybe, at times, the information was fed to him by rivals in the Outfit, guys who wanted what the druggie was hanging on to on the side. Jimmy couldn't have cared less. A drug bust was a drug bust, and it didn't matter a bit to him if the crook's mother had turned him in. A collar was a collar. The guy would go away and do his time and the only problem was there was always another piece of scum to take his place.

But still, after seventeen years on the force, at thirty-eight years of age and after having served as a bluesuit on the North Shore and then as an aggressive and talented Organized Crime Detective supercop, and now a big shot, the boss of the entire Narcotics Division, he could look at himself in any mirror he wanted to and tell himself that the light was never too harsh because he'd never ever taken a penny in graft from anyone, not even a free lunch or a cup of coffee. And this made Jimmy feel very good indeed.

There he is, Jimmy thought, as Fabe slid into the booth next to him, elbowing him a little for fun, saying something Jimmy didn't catch.

"What?" he asked.

"You getting hard of hearing or what?" Fabe said, then said, "Watch my lips. How do they know Christ wasn't born in Italy?" Jimmy thought about it. He had a logical, orderly mind. He could see no reason why Christ hadn't been born in Italy. He shook his head, waiting for the punch line, but Fabe was already smiling into the eyes of the shy waitress who had been hanging around since Jimmy arrived. Fabe ordered his eggs and bacon, with buttered toast and coffee, and the doll waitress lowered her eyes and smiled at Jimmy, asking him what he wanted, and he ordered lunch. She left, managing a quick look back at Fabe, sitting there looking like a million bucks without a care in the world. And there he himself was, the same age as Fabe, going bald already and running to fat. He fought a bubble of resentment and smiled at Fabe.

"She's got eyes for you, you know it?" Jimmy said. Baiting Fabe now, he said, "Just your type, too. Nice ass, big tits. You ever notice how she always seems to get our table, no matter where we sit?"

Fabe looked honestly surprised. "Come on, Jimmy, she's just a kid."

"Twenty-two, twenty-three. Old enough. You playing around with the kid, Fabe?" Jimmy grinned, knowing he was getting under Fabe's skin.

Fabe changed the subject. "What's new?"

"Missed you at the game yesterday, buddy."

They held season tickets to all Bears' home games, and it was a rare occasion when either of them did not show. Even today, with the Bears having won three out of four Superbowls and the stadium filled with yuppies, they still managed to enjoy themselves. Jimmy watched Fabe and decided that he wasn't going to answer. So he continued.

"You know the kid sits behind us, got the Walkman for listening to the game and the Watchman for seeing the instant replays? Some guy, walking down the steps there, he stepped on a mustard packet somebody dropped, and it squirts all over this sucker's pants, and the kid jumps up, drops his TV set on the concrete, and shrieks, 'There's *mustard* on my Argyle socks!'"

This got a laugh from Fabe, a no-bullshit gutbuster as he remembered the kid who sat behind *him* at the games, probably twenty-five, a commodities broker with a daddy rich enough to buy him a seat, who brought a different model-type to the game every time the team was in town. He settled down, caught his breath. The waitress set his coffee down and Fabe looked up, turning on the guinea charm now, thanking her, thinking about what Jimmy had said, really *see*ing her for the first time.

She was on the tall side, which he liked. Maybe five-eight or -nine on the outside, nice body, what he could see of it, covered up with that stupid railroad-engineer uniform they made the girls wear. Blue eyes, which he favored. Brown hair. He liked brown hair. Had had enough of the phony blondes with the black snatches. Deep eyes, staring at him now, the shyness gone as they connected, looked at each other with meaning. Fabe felt as if he had swallowed boiling coffee in large gulps.

She took her eyes away before he melted and muttered something about bringing his order as soon as it was done, and he wanted to call her back, ask her her name, but Jimmy was sitting there, and he would never let Fabe live it down, hitting on waitresses, for Chrissakes.

"I remember that guy," Fabe said, getting back to the yuppie at the game before Jimmy said something wiseass. He thought he might belt Jimmy in the mouth if he said another word about tits or ass in connection with the dark-haired waitress whose name he didn't know.

"Same guy, last year, he's impressing this chick, he tells her he's on way to Las Vegas, Reno, that weekend."

They laughed some more.

The food came and God in Heaven she did it again, impaled him with that look, and he could not drag his eyes from her face, not until she broke the spell once again, said something he could not even understand, as he was staring *into* her instead of at her. He noticed little tendrils of hair wrapped around her ear, old-fashioned style, out of style maybe ten, fifteen years. That endeared her to him.

"Pardon me?" he said to her.

"I said, is there anything else?"

"Yeah," Fabe said, ignoring Jimmy, not caring how much grief he would have to take about it, plunging right in there. "What's your name?"

"I've been serving you for weeks, every Monday and Friday, and you don't know my name?" She said it sociably, just kidding around, trying to stay at the table while the place filled with lunchtime local workers.

Fabe just smiled at her.

"It's Sally," she said, and her shyness seemed to drop onto her again, as if it had been lifted for one magical minute there, waiting above her, just waiting for the moment when she might even be ready to say yes to a date. She walked off, hurrying, pulling her pad out of her engineer outfit's wide pocket, spilling some loose dollar bills, tip money, onto the threadbare yellow carpet. Bending down to retrieve them, she gave Fabe and Jimmy a good shot as the striped coveralls stretched across her firm supple behind. She picked up the bills and shoved them into her pocket, staying down there maybe a second or two longer than she had to, then getting up, not even looking back at them, confident that he was watching the show she was putting on for his benefit.

Jimmy gave a low whistle. "How about *that*?" he muttered, then looked back at Fabe. "And you're tellin me she ain't on the make for you? How many guys you think she gives *that* show to? And I'll bet you: If she did it more than once in her life, then I'm a fag."

Fabe sure as hell hoped she would never do that kind of thing for anyone else.

"How about that?" he said to Jimmy. "She likes me."

"Yeah, well, what's wrong with that? I mean, you ain't ugly, you're rich, you live in that fancy joint across the street, come out every morning, I mean after*noon*, almost, with your shlong hanging out, shit, what woman could resist?" Knowing that he had very little time to spend with his friend this day, only enough to eat his hamburger and run, he said, "Look, I got this new guy in; you, of all people, you'll love this.

"Kid comes in, fresh off the street, wearing a blue suit four years, makes a few good drug busts, the Department in its infinite wisdom gives him plainclothes and gives him to me. First day out, this kid, what's he show up in?"

Fabe looked at him now, smiling a little, the waitress in the back of his mind, knowing where Jimmy was heading. He made a guess. "A silk dago undershirt under a three-hundred-dollar sport coat."

Jimmy burst into laughter. "Bingo!" he said. "Not to mention the wraparound glasses and the pointy-tip guinea shoes. Looked more like a nigger pimp than a Narcotics cop."

"Hey," the big black guy behind them said, "watch that nigger shit, man."

Jimmy turned to him, honest regret on his face.

"Hey, sorry. Figure of speech, ya know?"

The black man nodded, accepting the apology, seeing the two swarthy, beefy guys sitting there, staring at him. "Forget it," he said.

Jimmy was still turned toward him, trying to smooth it over. "You know something? Since we been sitting here, I've said guinea, dago maybe ten times, and we're both Italians. So do me a favor, don't take it personal, it's just a term, bro, ya know? Just an expression. I mean, how often you ever hear somebody say, a 'Negro pimp,' huh?"

The black man was getting confused and a little anxious, even though Jimmy sounded sincere enough.

"I mean it, man," Jimmy said, "honest to God, I didn't mean nothing by—"

And the black guy was nodding his head, getting out of the booth, grabbing his check, signaling Sally, dropping a tip on the table, and now Fabe was smiling a little, then chuckling.

Jimmy stared at the big black guy's back as he made for the door. He turned to Fabe, a confused look of "What'd I say?" on his face. And Fabe broke into laughter.

"Nice going," he said to Jimmy, "Henry fucking Kissinger."

"Some guys, you can't say nothin' to 'em." And then, thinking back, remembering, making a connection after what had happened at the table there a minute ago, he said, "Remember, back, Jesus, almost thirty fuckin' years now, when we was kids? Your pop?"

Jimmy was staring at him, putting it together, smiling still, then broke into laughter that caused some heads in booths to turn their way.

"I come over to your house." Jimmy was rolling now, laughing so hard he could hardly talk. It came out, "I—hahahahahcomeahahahah overhahahahaht-t-t-tohahaha—your h-h-hou-house." And everyone was looking at them now, even Sally, the other waitresses, and the cooks, as they spilled coffee, pounded the table with their fists, stomped their feet, remembering Fabe's old-fashioned father, sitting Jimmy down at their kitchen table, telling him solemnly that he would always be welcome at their house, even though he was Sicilian, and therefore more nigger than Italian, since Sicily was closer to Africa than it was to the little town in the north where Fabe's pop was born. Later, as they grew older—became best friends,

21

in fact, joining the service and flying to Vietnam together—the old man would often come upon them hatching some sort of adventure and would rub their heads affectionately, telling Jimmy, "Youa a gooda boy for a nigger," which never failed to crack them up. And Fabe reached over with a shaking hand and rubbed it across Jimmy's head, saying, "You'sa gooda ni-nig——" and broke off as he collapsed again with laughter, there in the restaurant with his oldest and dearest friend, making a scene with all the patrons looking on.

It took a while, but they got themselves under control, rubbing their eyes and patting their aching guts. The other customers returned to their own lunches, as maybe the best thief in the city and the head man of the second-largest Narcotics Division this side of the feds mastered themselves and took careful sips of coffee, trying to calm down.

"So's I tell him, this stiff, I says, 'Look, kid, you guys, you watch too much television, for Chrissakes. I see you coming down the street, to meet me, I'm sellin drugs, say, I'm gonna figure you for a North Side faggot.'" And Jimmy looked around at the next booth, now empty, half-expecting a couple of gays to be sitting behind them, asking him to apologize again. "'Or else, all I got left to figure you for is a copper, seen that asshole show about Miami too many times.'

"By now the kid, he's almost in tears. Gentle as I'm bein', too. First day in the majors, his boss comes down on him, so I go to plan B, I says to him, 'Look, you know what vice guys do, right? They hang around the park, late at night, tryin' to get some fairy to offer them money to blow 'em. That's what vice does, whether it's here or in Miami.

"'We're Narcotics.'" Jimmy shook his head, a pained expression on his face. "'Man, we are it,' I tells him, 'we are the guys supposed to stem the traffic, bust the pushers, get some of the shit off the street, and if we're real, real lucky, maybe get a big break, put one of the big guys, a supplier, in the joint.'" He stopped and waved for a warm-up on his coffee, and a puzzled-looking Sally brought it, smiling slightly, giving Fabe a glance as she poured.

"I send him home to change," Jimmy was saying, "and I start only for maybe the millionth time to wonder if I'm in the right racket.

"TV guys, Fabe, they set the mark for these young guys today. Half the kids on the job today, they forget about busts. Nowadays everybody gets *popped,* popped or *nailed,* instead of arrested. Every suspect, he's called *pal* at every opportunity, they never blow a chance to call a bad guy *pal.* I don't even remember the last time I heard *pinched,* for Chrissakes."

Fabe said, "Hey, Jimmy, I was you, I'd be wondering where this kid, just got out of a car, he gets the money to buy those fancy clothes."

Jimmy looked up quickly and their eyes met, locked.

"Don't let's start this again, okay, Fabe, just one time, please?"

Fabe ignored him. "Look, since I been out, what, six years now, I been pulled in and had my head busted four times. Four *times.* And these guys weren't looking for a confession, man, they weren't even looking for a bust. They wanted, Jimmy, to come in partners with me. *Partners,* Jimmy. I don't even go partners with the mob, and they *kill* people who say no. And these're supposed to be the fucking cops." Just looking at Jimmy told Fabe he'd gone over the limit. They'd been over this ground before. Jimmy didn't care what the facts were or how many cops were found dirty every year by the Office of Professional Standards; got arrested by the State's Attorney's Office or even the U.S. Attorney. To Jimmy, a cop was a cop, and no matter how close they were, Fabe wasn't one anymore. Fabe held his hands up in a placating gesture.

"All right, all right, shit. Just one question." He fixed Jimmy with a hard stare, looked right into him, and everything else was there going on around them—people with Walkman radios on their ears were eating lunches of salads, waitresses and busboys scurried past—but not to them. All that was gone, and they were locked in together, alone, just the two of them.

"You got six guys, in the entire fucking department, you can trust?" Fabe said.

Jimmy broke the look first. Sat back in the booth. "Yeah?" he said. "How many guys you meet in prison you can trust?"

Jimmy didn't miss a beat. "Just one," he said.

Now that the subject had been approached, Jimmy felt free to tug at the string a little bit, see what unraveled. "You ready to retire yet?"

"Just about."

"Don't let me catch you, Fabe."

"You won't. I don't mess with drugs. Never have, never will."

"That's not what I mean, and you know it."

"I know." He took a quick sip of his coffee, then looked at Jimmy again. "Sorry," he said.

"Hey, Fabe, I put up with a lot, you know? Guys calling me, wanting to know how my buddy the safeman is doing. I tell 'em, call you up, ask. They can't fucking figure out why we're tight. And I don't give a shit.

"But I got my ass in a sling the last time you was gone; I always came, every month, to see you in there. Now I'm an inspector, Fabe, the shit hits the fan, well, the politics, it gets heavy. I'll never not be there for you, don't misunderstand, but I can't go to bat for you."

"Hey, I didn't ask you to last time either, did I?"

"That was different." There was heat in Jimmy's voice.

"I gotta go," Fabe said.

"How's Doral?" Jimmy asked, getting up from the chair, grabbing the check. He paid on Mondays, Fabe paid on Fridays.

"Doing good."

"Look, I can always tell, Fabe, you know? I know something's about to happen. You get testy, a little bit mean. Don't take it personal, I sit have coffee with a guy I know two weeks, he puts his coffee cup down wrong, I know something's up. You I've known all my life. And I want to know you the rest of it. So stay healthy, retire, huh?"

And Fabe did something he'd never done before and would never do again: He told somebody about his business who wasn't involved in it. He looked at Jimmy standing there, hands in his coat pockets, his collar turned up on his old-goddamned-fashioned trenchcoat and a toothpick sticking out of the side of his mouth, and he said, "Starting tomorrow, Jimmy, I'm officially retired."

Jimmy's eyes widened, but just for a second. "Good," he said simply, and turned to leave, then came back, looked down at Fabe sitting alone staring into his coffee cup until he noticed Jimmy's presence and looked up.

"Hey, Fabey, how *do* they know that Christ wasn't Italian?"

And Sally walked up, hot coffee in hand, and Fabe smiled, his face going from dark and gloomy to happy in a second. He said, "Because they couldn't find three wise men and a virgin, Jimmy." And he turned his head away from Jimmy, looked up at Sally, and moved his lips silently along with the words Jimmy spoke as the cop said, "You sick son of a bitch." And then Jimmy was gone.

"How'd you know he'd say that?" Sally said.

"Got time to sit down?" Fabe asked her.

"Yeah, well, I'd like to join you, sir, but I am kinda busy

right now.'' She waved her hand around the room as she poured him his last cup of coffee, then looked up, and their eyes met again.

Fabe felt silly, radical, like a little kid in high school again. He wasn't used to girls like this. She seemed, seemed what? Innocent? Yeah, innocent. He fought the fear, reminded himself that he was a big boy now.

"You got a phone number?" he asked, then hurriedly added, "Or I guess I oughta ask, you got a husband?"

"No, I mean *yes*. Oh *dammit,* yes, I have a phone number and no, I'm not married.'' She was blushing and Fabe wondered when was the last time any of the women he knew had done *that*.

"Can I have it?"

She tore his napkin in half and scribbled her name and number across the front of it, pushed it toward him, and before hurrying away said, "Maybe you shouldn't call me, I'm probably not at *all* like the girls you know.'' And she was walking, head down, embarrassed as all hell, and Fabe had time to raise his voice and say, "Hey, that's what I'm *hoping*,'' before she reached the door and sped into the kitchen.

He took the napkin and spread it out carefully on the table, got out his pen and pocket phone book, and carefully wrote her name in under *S*. He didn't even know her last name. Well, time enough for that. He had other plans for this afternoon and evening.

He dropped a five-dollar bill on the table, on top of the two Jimmy had left, hoping he wasn't being too much of a showboat, maybe scare her off, make her think he was trying to buy her, then put his things back and hurried off into the cold winter wind.

He didn't give her another thought for over sixteen hours.

3 Fabe walked out of the Iron Horse Café and stood looking at his apartment building across the street, feeling excited, up, *ready* after months of careful planning. He took deep breaths and smiled into the wind, watching it grab the plumes of white mist from his mouth and swirl it away into nothingness.

When he started to walk north on Clark, it would begin. Within half an hour he would be in Doral's mansion, and from that point on the question was moot; the thing would happen, the score would be a go. He always savored these last few minutes before setting the plan in motion. Always savored the freedom of choice. Go across the street, into the nice warm apartment, get undressed, into bed, fuck it, it would be all over with. Or turn right, head up Clark, head for Old Town, and risk life in prison. Easy choice, you would think.

Tight, wound up, ready, Fabe turned and started walking slowly up Clark.

One of the things he loved the most about his neighborhood was the mix. A dirty old woman in a shabby old wool coat stood waiting for the light to change, a shopping cart with all her worldly possessions held in a steel grip as the wind whipped her filthy, lice-infested gray hair into her eyes. Snot ran down her nose and onto her chin, from there to land on the front of her ratty coat. The front of her cart was nearly touching a parked black Cadillac, whose owner was leaning on the right front fender wearing a long, nearly ankle-length coat made of camel's hair. His neat, fifty-dollar razor-cropped hair stirred fashionably in the breeze as he checked his watch impatiently, and Fabe could see even from the middle of the block that the thin piece of gold on his right wrist would probably feed the bag lady for six months.

Unbathed winos waited on the bus benches, as if they had someplace to go, making the power-lunching career women stand in the wind as their slit skirts whipped around their legs and their striped gym shoes tapped impatiently on the curb.

Fabe paid $5.50 a day for parking rights in the public garage next to his building, and an extra $2.50 a day to keep it on the first level, washed and ready to go. Not for purposes of making a quick getaway; if the law wanted him, he could have a helicopter on the roof and they'd find a way to get him. But for convenience. As he passed the garage he thought about going in and driving the Eldorado over to Doral's. In the summertime he kept the Cadillac in the open-air garage for WLS-TV employees over on State and Clark, a short walk from the apartment. He had a friend inside, got him the pass, and he left the car there under guard six months of the year when the weather was nice. But the Chicago winters were brutal, and so he paid the $8.00-per-day fee, and felt lucky at that. He brushed the thought off for a couple of reasons. He wanted to see his city again this cold wintry afternoon, just in case. Wanted to taste and savor his freedom, wanted to look at the winos and the bag ladies and the gang teenagers skipping out on school and fur-coated rich women and the rabbit-coated overly made-up hookers in the leather miniskirts trying to act hot in frozen winds, and look one more time at the fleets of Cadillacs and Mercedes Benz sedans making their slow sure way down Clark in traffic that made them snarl behind Ramblers and fifteen-year-old Chevrolets and Fords—ancient Cadillacs filled with young and hopeful black faces staring arrogantly at rich men who turned their heads away.

Less than two blocks away was the Lawson YMCA, in a neighborhood where the apartments went for a hundred grand to start. Jewelry stores with nationally known names stood next to secondhand shops and an AMVETS. Street hustlers, artists, pimps, yuppies, hookers, and thieves commingled peacefully in his area. Passing a boutique with a phony trendy name, he came next to a four-dollar-a-night flophouse, where the few of the homeless who could afford the tariff would sleep on old army cots and catch lice, if they did not already have them, and listen all night to the broken asthmatic coughs, wheezes, and farts of the damned.

Two homosexuals walked hand in hand, unmolested, down the other side of the street, and Fabe smiled when two pimps standing on the street in front of a pawnshop hollered good-naturedly at them, telling them that any one of their ladies was good enough to turn them all the way around, and they shook their heads, smiling, saying "No thank you brother" without opening their mouths.

Fabe walked quickly, trying to remember whether he had smoked in the restaurant, knowing it would have been a dead giveaway if he had. Jimmy liked to tell him that he had just gotten lucky on the promotion, liked to lay his status in the department on the fact that he had been one of the few honest officers—the old unit, but Fabe knew better. There wasn't a shrewder cop on the force. And he would, if he had to, bust his best friend if he was caught with his hand in the cookie jar. But he would *not* put a stakeout on him due to suspicion. If Fabe told him what he was up to, where he was going this afternoon, yeah, there'd be a bust, no doubt about it. He could never slap

Jimmy in the face with what he was and expect it to be ignored. But Jimmy would never go out of his way to pinch Fabe, either. Unless, of course, Fabe got into narcotics. Then it would be all systems go, and Jimmy would put him away, right now, no questions asked, no quarter given.

He plodded past the Chestnut Station Theater, with its old-fashioned barred ticket booth, watching for tourists for fun, knowing how to spot them. If a pedestrian stepped high while approaching the curb, he was a native, simple as that, expecting the eight inches of concrete step before regaining the sidewalk. On Michigan Avenue, of course, and State Street, and down VanBuren, for the most part, the city had installed ramps for the handicapped, but down here the funding didn't reach too far. The out-of-towners, the suburbanites, they would expect low curbs or handicap ramps. That's the way things were in the suburbs. And in New York, and in Bumfuck, Idaho. So they'd trip, stumble, look up sheepishly, maybe even smiling, before remembering where they were, the big bad city of Chicago that had no heart or mercy.

Another way to spot them, right *now,* was under the El tracks. If they jumped at the hurricane roar of the passing trains, odds were good that they didn't come from the city. As a kid, doing muggings, purse snatchings, smash and grabs, Fabe would always look for out-of-town plates on cars, the newer the better, or for people who stepped into the high curbs, or who ducked when the El went by overhead. Always good pickings, there, tourists or suburbanites with cash in their pockets, instead of locals, playing the game, fighting so damn hard to keep up with the Joneses that they didn't have two nickels to rub together.

The farther north Fabe walked on Clark, the higher-classed things got. No longer any beggars around, that's for sure. The Astor Street matrons got a little upset when the winos pissed on their driveways. And the cops, who enjoyed their Christmas bonuses and who knew good and damn well that just about any resident on North State Parkway could pick up the phone and call the mayor at home, rousted the undesirables and the gang-bangers and the winos and the bag ladies in a most unconstitu-tionallike manner, keeping the folks happy, allowing them to pretend that they were the monied upper class; better than the rest, a cut above most. And they could forget that a six-block-walk west would bring them smack-dab into the middle of Cabrini Green housing project, where the *badass* gangbangers lived.

Now he saw mostly foreign cars on the street, men with trim beards walking arm in arm with tipped-blond ladies, fash-ionably slim, in fur coats, bareheaded so the wind would whip their hair just so, while the men adjusted their overcoat collars, proud of themselves and the women they'd acquired, pulling on their dead pipes in the bitter wind, pretending they weren't as afraid and insecure and frightened of the unknown as the rest of us.

The younger people all jogged, with little radio speakers stuck in their ears.

And then he passed the score, and turned his head away as he did so, it didn't exist yet, it wasn't there. Not until he was with Doral and the thing was ready to go down.

Farther up Clark was the gigantic, blocks-long Sandburg complex, the world's greatest monument to urban paranoia. Even the children's playgrounds were surrounded by eight-foot-tall security fences. Fabe likened it to being in a luxurious fed-eral joint, or like in that old TV show, *The Prisoner,* where the guy who used to play Secret Agent got sent to the island where every luxury was provided except freedom. He shivered and stepped quickly as he went by. Security was one thing, but *Jesus.*

Turn left, down to Wells, already stoking up for the night, Monday or not. As a kid, Fabe had loved Wells Street, sneaking into the Earl of Old Town's, having a few brews and listening to Steve Goodman and Bonnie Kolac singing about things that made no sense to Fabe but sure did sound good, and he'd nod his head and clap politely at the end of each set, trying to act as if he belonged, wondering if someday, sometime, he'd ever feel he belonged *any*where. He had been big, heavy, muscular, and mean-looking, and no one ever made him feel uncomfortable except himself.

The smells assaulted him, pizza and spaghetti, bratwurst and beer, and he took it all in happily, wondering how many assholes would pay good money to go into the Ripley's Believe It or Not Museum or the wax museum, when the very same dough they were throwing away could be spent in Piper's Alley at Uno's on the best deep-dish pizza in the world.

A group of young professionals, men and women, stood in front of a sports emporium bar, the current fad, in leotards and shorts, wearing headbands and Chicago Bears wool hats, some with jerseys with number 34 or 9 on them, for Walter Payton or Jim McMahon. They were stretching, doing warm-ups, ready to go on their daily lunch-hour run, in a group, right on the god-damn *side*walk, for Chrissakes, and Fabe hoped they'd start out in his direction, hoped and almost prayed that they would, so he could knock one of the arrogant bastards on their ass; teach them a few things about being in shape. Run a hundred miles a week and think they're bad, for God's sake.

He stopped himself, knowing it was the score making him resentful at these people who made their fifty grands a year and worried about having everything they saw advertised in *GQ* magazine. He did not stop to think that maybe he was jealous, or even a little bit lonely. He turned his head away and looked up the street, where Morrie the newsguy was leaning against his stand, his ancient cracked face looking introspective, as usual, the philosopher of Old Town, in his suspenders and filthy green work pants, combat boots, and long army-green coat. He was looking at a pigeon perched on his thumb, pecking at the kernels of corn in his palm, and Fabe buried his head in his collar, not wanting to stop and shoot the shit, not today, not when he'd be pretty poor company.

West on North Park Avenue, then two short blocks to Doral's place, and suddenly, without announcement or preamble, in another world altogether.

Cobblestoned sidewalks, wide and roomy, reminders of a simpler past when the North Side wasn't what it was today. Big, big houses, some four floors, some five, none less than three, which at one time had been the homes of the rich. Single-family mansions with barred windows and many fireplaces and old, claw-footed bathtubs in one of six bathrooms, now cut up into condos and apartments, bringing down two grand a month rent, up to a million five to buy. And right there, smack-dab in the middle, surrounded by empty land that any realtor would die to subdivide and build on, was Doral's place.

Six levels, which had *not* been cut up into apartments. The first was under the street level, with barred windows protecting it from prowlers. Blackout curtains on the first three floors, where you could see in from the street if they had not been put up. Doral enjoyed his privacy. Fabe knew that each floor had two stone fireplaces and a full bathroom. Doral had paid seventy-five thousand dollars for the house and the surrounding five lots four and a half years ago, which was a *steal,* but he'd had cash and had forgone the title search, doing the business in the back office of the home of the previous tenant's attorney, who whisked his client immediately onto a flight bound for Costa Rica. A seven-foot wrought-iron-and-steel fence surrounded the entire property, with large, sharp tips on the ends honed to razor edges and painted matte black by Doral personally.

Fabe used his magnetic card, inserted it into the recessed slot in the stone gate pillars, waited while the iron gate slowly opened, then stepped through and turned, watching as the gate swung closed and clicked behind him. He walked to the door and unlocked it with his own key, then stepped into the chilly reception hall with the closed-circuit camera mounted on a bracket just above arm's reach. On the doorframe directly above was the push-button alarm system that would give him access to the house. He punched out six different sets of three numbers, and the inner door clicked open. He entered the hallway, watched Doral bounce up from the lower level, his hands wrapped with tapes, his naked torso sweating.

"Ooooie," Doral said, sweating, breathing heavily, a gigantic grin breaking his ebony face in half, "didn't *you* dress for Yuppieville." He eyed Fabe closely, as if seeing him for the first time. "All you needs, Fabe-babe, is a pair of steel-clasp galoshes, maybe a wool, long-billed winter cap, with earflaps."

Fabe was wearing a winter-weight lumber jacket, red and green, a pair of Levi's, and a pair of arctic army combat boots.

"Yeah, well, lookie here, Doral, I done forgot I was coming to the haunts of the very rich. And besides, my valet, the poor man, had to hurry home to England for the week, personal troubles, don't you know."

Doral chuckled, as if he were not about to embark on a score that could net him fifteen years in Joliet. "Better take off the lumber jacket, man, before one of the local homo*sex*-uahls comes breaking down my door, get a look at the big ugly stud dressed so pe*dest*rian."

Fabe took his advice. Already he was beginning to sweat in the overheated place. He followed Doral down the stairs to the first level.

It smelled like a gym, which is what it was.

Universal equipment stood against every wall: abdomen machines, fly machines, lower-back machines, jogging treadmills with heartbeat hookups, tricep machines; a thirteen-position steel monstrosity Fabe never could figure out; an inversion bar with unbuckled boots hanging from it in two spots; chrome solid dumbbells and barbells with chrome plates piled neatly on a mat. In one corner, off all alone, like a relic of times long gone, was what they headed for.

Over to the bags.

Two leather hundred-pound heavy bags, two kidskin brown speed bags. A couple of jump ropes hung from hooks on the wall, next to a dozen pairs of boxing gloves, ranging from sixteen-ounce practice mitts to striking gloves, lightweight padded mittens to protect the hands while hitting the bags.

"You eat yet?" And in Doral's pre-score twang Fabe heard, "Jeet Jet?"

"Had breakfast with Jimmy."

A pained expression crossed Doral's face. "Man, why you gotta break bread with a cop on the morning of a score?"

"Look, Doral, as long as we aren't moving drugs, he won't pinch us."

Doral turned to him, smiling softly, as if at something long forgotten and now faintly remembered. His long, fine-boned hand moved to the crotch of the purple satin Everlast boxing trunks he wore. "He can pinch this, he want."

Fabe smiled. The only sign of nervousness Doral ever showed was falling back into the speaking patterns he had learned on the streets, years ago, on the South Side. As the time to go and do it neared, he would fall back into slang and words not used by street-smart blacks in fifteen years, spoken in a slow, Southern, badass drawl. Sometimes, by the time they entered a building and were working on the safe, Fabe could not understand Doral at all.

He said, "He will, he catches you talking about him like that."

"You gonna warm up some?"

"Yeah," Fabe said, nodding his head, a look of concern on his face. "I'm tight as a drum." He saw the look on Doral's face and added, "But ready." The machine that was his body would not, *could* not be allowed to be controlled by emotion or even ordinary logic for the next several hours. He would have to be a cold, non-thinking thing, doing his job, programmed by experience, preparation, and belief in himself.

He stripped and hung his clothes on a hook, where they would stay with all his money and identification until after the score. Hanging on a hook next to the gloves were his own personal trunks, a leather boxing jockstrap, headgear, which he would not be using today, and his own tapes and Ace bandages for wrapping his fists before putting on a pair of gloves. He could not afford to harm his hands this day of all days.

It was an old ritual with them, going back since the time Doral had bought the house and filled the ground level with tons and thousands of dollars' worth of weight-lifting equipment that they never used, except for the abdomen machines. As Fabe dressed, Doral shadowboxed, warming up, getting ready, working up a sweat, watching himself, in the mirrors that filled this corner of the room's walls, with a clinical, wary eye, seeing his lithe, tight muscles working under the near-black skin, jumping and wriggling, watching to see if maybe they were a little flabby, or a little slower-moving than the last time, two days before.

Which was a joke. Doral was two inches shorter than Fabe, but probably stronger. A product of the street, taught from birth to take what he wanted when he wanted it, he had learned the

36

value of a sound body while serving his first term in St. Charles Correctional Center for Boys, where the bigger guys raped the younger guys their first day in. Thousands of push-ups had tightened the triceps until they looked like stones in a stream. Large, yet light, his biceps muscles popped as he pulled his arms in and struck them out at nothing. His chest and belly looked like armored plating. But best of all, to Doral's way of thinking: dressed, he looked almost skinny. All that sinew and strength hidden under the best tailored clothes money could buy, the average man on the street would take one look and think, Skinny sucker, which was just fine with Doral. Gave him the element of surprise when he had to explode in a second's violence, ending the whole thing with barely a lightning-quick strike of either hand. He had been the heavyweight champ in Joliet five years running. And he had beaten Fabe in the finals every single year, or at least the four that Fabe had been locked up.

Fabe, on the other hand, was a big lummox. In Doral's opinion he lacked style, grace, and class. Which did not make Doral love him one ounce less. As he slapped at the air with motions so fast as to almost appear as blurs to the human eye, he started kidding Fabe, knowing he'd piss him off, have a laugh or two before the work began.

"You wanna know what I think? I think old Jimmy, he be *jeal*ous of me, my re*lat*ionship with ya'll." He ventured a side-long look at Fabe, saw he was smiling, shaking his head. He grinned.

"Yeah, Jimmy, he see this big pretty black stud, now, to-day, current, hip down and about it, he say to hisself, 'Now dat dere niggah, he be corruptin' the *mo*-rals of my war buddy and ex-partner, Fabrizzio, big dumb suckah, don't even be knowin' all niggahs, they fuck anything warm, deep and round!'"

"You asshole," Fabe said, chuckling a little, "he

probably thinks I'm your daddy, after making you a bitch in the joint.''

"Bitch! *Bitch*! Why, the night they brought you over to my cell, all scared and shakin', I knew right then, I waved the big black cobra at you, you'd eat it right up, you was so scared.'' This was a running joke with them. His first night in prison, Fabe had beaten to near death a couple of studs who had made the mistake of thinking they had landed a scared fish who would tremble and be made on the spot. After three weeks in the hole, he had attacked and torn into the leader of a local tier gang, who had suggested that he would favor Fabe and treat him like a son if he just did what he was told, starting with right now falling on his knees; and after two more weeks in the hole, the administration had stuck him in a cell with Doral, who was widely known to be sexless. Neither a jocker nor a jockee, not interested. He had somehow just turned it *off*. And Fabe had spent the first hour that night leaning against the wall, staring at Doral, who lay casually on the lower bunk, staring back, shaking his head from time to time. Doral had at last broken the ice.

"You gonna stay in my house, sucker, you're gonna see a lot of me. Now if you can drag your eyes off my beautiful face for a second, I want you to know: I want no part of your booty, and you *better* not want any part of mine. And if you fucking snore, better plan on getting evicted.''

Fabe had nodded, removed the stuff from his cardboard box, and, careful not to violate the rules of prison protocol, put them on his shelf, watching Doral, making sure he wasn't claiming any of Doral's space. It took six weeks before they got comfortable with each other, and then it had only been a case of territory protection, when the punks who pushed into the cell intent on hurting Fabe forgot or ignored the fact that they were entering Doral's goddamn *house*. Doral came off the lower bunk with a speed and fluidity that startled the four would-be rapists, and it was that second's hesitation that cost them. Fabe was already swinging, and Doral moved to the entrance of the cell, blocking escape, setting up an effective crossfire, Fabe in the corner, his back to the gray brick walls, Doral eight feet away, and the four tough guys had to split up to cover them both, two on one, good odds maybe elsewhere in the prison, but against Fabe and Doral, not anywhere near good enough.

And a beating wasn't good enough either. A message had to be sent to the entire prison population, the whole main line, that Fabe was off limits. Doral had had his share of cellmates, some okay, some whacked out, some he had been forced to slap the hell out of daily in order to keep them in line, others who fell on their knees when he entered the cell, offering themselves humbly, figuring that Doral would be a great old man and protect them from the badasses out there who were taking them off daily. But none had impressed him as the big silent white boy had, even if he *had* been a cop once. And so the terrible beating began. When it was over, one of the men was blind for life, another had both his arms and legs broken, one had somehow miraculously gotten by Doral and had raced down the steel-grated tier screaming, a flap of skin ripped from his forehead and most of his teeth gone. The fourth, the well-known leader of the gangbangers intent on turning Fabe out, was thrown from the third-story tier, screaming a final terrified scream, his arms flapping, his eyes bulging, the knife he had carried into the cell buried in his own chest.

Doral did not wait an instant. After heaving the man over the rail, he raced back into the cell, grabbed one of the two men left, and was dragging him to the rail when Fabe grabbed his arm, shouting something at him, and Doral dropped the body, spinning into Fabe's face, ready to battle *him* if he had to.

"Don't," Fabe was saying softly, breathing hard, staring directly into Doral's eyes.

Doral did not have time to argue. The screaming guy going over had attracted attention, prisoner and guard attention both. It was either fight it out with his cellmate and then, after kicking his ass for him, throwing the other two men off the tier, or let it go. He did not have time for the first, but if he went for the second, the big white guy might figure him for a mark, might think he'd rolled over and shown him his ass. But he had no time to play around, the screws would be coming.

Doral got the blinded man to his feet and pushed him roughly from the cell, toward the iron stairway, and he and Fabe then rolled the other broken body out onto the walkway. They'd then hurriedly cleaned the blood from the floor as best they could, and by the time the riflemen and the other guards were shouting for a lockup and a head count, they were lying in their bunks, getting their breathing under control, each wondering about the other.

"It'd been the yard, sucker, you'da been on your own," Doral said finally. "And don't you never, *ever* put your hands on me again."

Fabe had kept silent, knowing the man was just blowing wind now, getting back the face he thought he had lost by buckling under. He wondered how many years you had to serve before murdering another con became the easiest solution to your problem with him.

And he wondered if they'd get beefed for the murder.

They were questioned, as were all the men on the tier, and no one, not one convict, had given them up. Not even the men they had nearly killed. Later comparing notes, Doral told Fabe that he had told the warden's investigators that the man had committed suicide, he figured. The guy had been a little des-*pon*dent-lately. . . .

Now, warming up on the floor there in Doral's new home, a far, far better one than the one they'd shared before, stretching his arms and legs and back, leaning forward until his forehead touched his knees, Fabe smiled inwardly, remembering that beginning to their friendship, how the tightness had come, the trust. How they'd started talking a couple of days later, then hanging out together. How the entire prison, including the officials, had known within the week what had really happened, but had no evidence to convict them of another beef with. How, later, much later, he and Doral had really become friends, going against every prison rule book ever written, breaking the race barrier, black and white as friends instead of jocker or jockee, ignoring the race difference and bonding to each other as buddies.

And later, as partners.

Fabe got up and grabbed one of the jump ropes, began skipping it away from the mat, on the highly polished hardwood floors, warming up still, watching Doral do push-ups on the mat, effortlessly, slowly, getting the maximum benefit. Remembering the many faces of Doral he'd seen.

Walking in Water Tower Place on North Michigan, on the sixth level, and seeing a couple of New Wave types coming toward them, the guy wearing a spike haircut extending into the air above his head perhaps a full foot, a gold ring in his nose, wearing a shabby old army greatcoat with *Smash the State* written on the front of it with Magic Marker, the girl with a waterfall hairdo, wearing pink and brown and gold and gray and yellow, her hair swooped up above her head and sprayed in place, the two of them staring smugly at the people they passed, enjoying their obvious discomfort as they dropped their eyes and hurried past, playing the part of the rebels, the outsiders, knowing that in staid Water Tower Place no one was going to accost them.

Except for Doral, who stood with his arms crossed, his forehead wrinkled as he raised his eyebrows at the two of them approaching, then speaking in a voice maybe three decibels louder than normal.

"Well, look at these two motherfuckers here!" he said in obvious wonder, astonishment, as if he were witnessing the approach of the first extraterrestrials from their spaceship, no anger or reproach in his voice, just a curious joy. People were smiling openly now, eyeing the two punkers. Doral's words had broken the ice. *They* were safe now; if the punks were to attack, it would be the smiling black man they'd get. Doral got louder yet, enjoying himself, getting off at the sudden looks of discomfort on the faces of the two kids.

"Hey, hey, motherfuckers," he shouted at them, still smiling at them, buddies, the obscenities just a brotherly gesture, not to be taken as insults, "why the fuck ya'll *dress* so funny?" And people were laughing openly now, stopping to stare at the two misfits, enjoying their red faces and their downward glances as much as the two punks had enjoyed their straight anguish minutes before. The entire sixth level seemed to stop moving, shuffling, shopping. They all just stopped and watched, knowing something was about to happen.

Doral ate it up with a spoon. He slapped his knee now and held his belly, laughing like hell, his eyes never leaving the face of the male punk, who was staring knives at him now, coming closer with each step.

"Hey, motherfucker, how you sleep with that ugly unwashed bitch you with?" he shouted, and the crowd now guffawed along with him, while the two punks stopped dead in front of Doral, breathing heavily, their eyes brimming with tears. Fabe watched with a detached humor, knowing he was witnessing an event, a Doral special. He grinned widely at the two punks, shaking his head, being a slightly annoyed adult, knowing he was pissing them off to no end with his amused disapproval.

"Well, hell, it was attention ya'll *wanted,* right?" Doral said, laughing right in the boy's face now, getting into it, onstage, his audience all around him. "Well, you got it now, brother!"

"You dirty *nig*ger," the girl hissed, and her companion looked at her as if she were insane, fear apparent in his eyes, stamped on his face. But it did not seem to bother Doral a bit.

"*Nig*ger," he shouted, cracking up, rolling his eyes and slapping his knee again. He turned to the assembled crowd. "Woman done called me a *nig*ger!" he shouted, and they laughed with him, and Fabe noticed two well-dressed young men elbowing their way through the crowd, security, obviously.

"I can't help being a *nig*ger no more than you can help being ugly, bitch!" he shouted, getting an uproar from the assembled shoppers. "But at least I know how to put on my clothes!" And now the crowd was closing in, shouting things at the two punks, together at last, voicing their disapproval at the racist remark the girl had shouted, crowding them onto the down escalator, jeering at them, giving them *hell,* and the two kids began to run down the steps of the escalator, getting to the bottom a couple of steps ahead of the angry crowd, and Doral grinned broadly at Fabe, began walking away innocently, as if he were not at all involved in what had just happened, and Fabe followed, shaking his head, smiling, thinking that a day with Doral might be a lot of things, but it was, by God, *never* dull.

Sweating now, he put up the jump rope and went and did a couple of fifty-rep sets on the ab machine, feeling his gut tighten more and more with every exertion, feeling things jumping around inside his belly, tight muscles bunching and loosening, getting harder still, his breath coming in huge gulps as he strained against the Nautilus machine, the pin stuck in number 10, as high as it would go, using the maximum the machine had to offer. When he finished he felt as if his gut had been beat on with a medicine ball. Push-ups now, then pull-ups using the handgrips ten feet above ground on one of the metal contraptions against the walls. Here the ground was carpeted with indoor-outdoor stuff, so the hardwood floor would not get scratched from the metal finish. At last, warmed up, *ready*, his muscles pumped up, he went and taped his hands, then wrapped them with Ace bandages. He stood before Doral, who had been waiting and watching him for several minutes. And then they began.

Slowly at first, very slowly so they could get used to it, they began to throw long, looping punches at each other's chins. The other man would slip it, get his balance, then counter with his own. Then again, slipping the punch and returning it, then again, a little more speed behind the punch now, quicker, a little more pepper on it. Until their hands were blurs and their heads bobbed with lightning speed, and the punches became shorter and tighter, six-inch uppercuts and jabs, all aimed at the head, no fair below the chin, the punches never touching, never hitting the mark.

Doral had tried, years before, to explain his philosophy to Fabe. Fabe seemed to believe that might made right, that the stronger man would always win. To Doral, this was all wrong. Speed, timing, balance, quickness, hand-and-eye coordination, footwork, conditioning, and *intelligence* would beat brute strength every time. Especially if the stronger man was throwing punches that were not connecting. This gave the other man the edge of undermining the strong man's confidence, not to mention wearing him down, since a punch missed takes twice as much out of you as a punch landed. And that's what they were doing now. For a full half hour, they threw punches and unblinkingly slipped them, never doing more damage than maybe clipping the top of an ear or the hair once in a while. *Discipline* won the fight titles in prison for Doral as much as anything

44

else—having the discipline to slip the best punches his opponent could throw, frustrating the opponent, making him mad. Doral knew a man who used to spar with Victor Galindez, at the time the light-heavyweight champion of the world. When Galindez was a little bit winded, a little tired, he would clinch, and whisper in a strong Spanish accent, "I fucked yo' mammy last night," and his opponent would push away, come at Galindez like a bull, throwing wild, choppy punches, trying to knock the champion out, which was against strict orders, and Galindez would have him. There would be a couple of minutes' break while the unconscious opponent would be attended to. And in those minutes Galindez would get another wind, and be ready for another sparring partner. Doral believed the best tool he had in a fight was anger, if it was the other man's.

When the digital clock buzzed and their half hour had ended, they gratefully stopped punching and walked around the gym, hands on their hips, breathing in gasps, chests heaving, sweat pouring from them in rivers. Minutes later Doral confronted Fabe, face to face, unsmiling now, breathing normally, shaking the sweat from his short-cropped hair, razor-parted on the right.

"Ready to go to work?" he asked softly.

"It's time," Fabe said.

"Let's hit the shower."

Fabe took his time, savoring the hot water, standing there letting it pour over him, stinging him, while his heartbeat slowed and his breathing returned to normal. When he emerged, Doral was already waiting for him, sitting on one of the press-machine benches, his face a mask of calm, staring off into space, as if searching for a word to complete a poem. Sensitive-looking bastard, Fabe thought. There were long underwear and heavy woolen socks outside the door, and as Fabe dried he marveled at his friend's thoughtfulness. Maybe he simply didn't want him to catch pneumonia. Maybe, a far-out thought, but maybe, Doral really *did* care about something other than money. Not that he'd ever say anything to make you think otherwise. Fabe put on the heavy underwear, and they got down to business.

The *real* reason all the weight equipment was in the room was for cover.

Doral hoisted one end of the Olympic-sized lifting bar resting on the bench he was sitting on, Fabe the other. Five hundred pounds all together. They hefted it to the floor and set it on the carpet next to the bench. Doral moved the bench aside. A tiny layer of carpet was overlapped, and when it was turned back, a small zipper, holding together a three-by-one-foot piece of carpeting, was exposed. Doral unzipped it. Underneath was hardwood floor, three sections of it, looking to the naked eye like any other three-by-one patch on the part of the floor away from the carpeting. Doral crossed the room, Fabe right behind him, and went to a stationary built-in weight machine with stacks of black rectangular iron weights attached to cables and pullies behind it. The top of the machine was bolted to the cement wall. Doral lay down on the DynaPower bench, pulled the handlebars to him, while Fabe went to the back of the machine and stuck the pin in the bottom weight slot, six hundred pounds. Doral gave a mighty heave, and Fabe reached over, with both hands, standing slightly away from the weights in case they fell, but directly behind them. Heaving and pushing, they managed together to lift the weights up, and Doral's arms were at last all the way extended, trembling, holding the impossible weight. Fabe walked around to the front of the machine, took a grip, and relieved some of the pressure for Doral. Slowly, Doral lifted his right leg, put it on the right handlebar, then did the same with his left. He began to push. By infinitesimal amounts, the weights began to creep higher still. Slowly, Doral pushed harder yet, his arms now on his ass, the veins sneaking into his forehead in stark contrast to the usual unlined black skin there. He breathed in deep puffs, and as he let out each breath he pushed harder. Finally, his legs were extended. Fabe had taken his place behind the machine again, and as he heard a metallic *click,* he stuck a long, thick hunk of metal under the weights, said, "Okay!" to Doral, and Doral rolled off the bench.

"Your turn, my man," he said, and Fabe got onto the exact duplicate machine directly across the room from the one Doral had lifted. They changed positions, and when Fabe rolled off the bench, and the weights were steadily in the air, twelve hundred pounds of weights pressing into the two circles built under each weight machine at the same time, the one-inch spot being pressed down with the combined weight, on the exact right spot due to the help of the thick hunks of metal the men had placed over the round eyes hidden under the machines, the hydraulics fell into motion, the counterbalances collapsed, and the three-by-one piece of hardwood floor popped open on a hinge, straight up.

Inside were the tools of their trade.

Burglar clothing on top, which Fabe quickly pulled out of the way. His lock picks and drills and sound enhancers and suction cups and pulleys and clothesline and rappeling lines next. He took what he knew he'd need for tonight's score, wound them tightly together, then taped them. The entire bundle would fit perfectly under his left arm now, under the special navy peacoat they'd had made for him.

Under the tools were Doral's pistols, any one of which, if ever found in the possession of a convicted felon like Doral, would bring him an automatic three years in a federal joint. Under the pistols was Doral's ready cash, several thousand dollars, in case they ever had to take off quickly. The three-foot-deep hole in the foundation was cement-lined, and solid. The piece of floor that popped up was cement-lined underneath. It was better and safer than a conventional wall or floor safe, and was virtually undetectable if you did not know where to look. And, like the numbers for Doral's elaborate alarm systems, only he and Fabe knew where to look and how to open it.

They dressed quickly, closed and relocked the hole, zipped the carpet back up, put the weight bench and the bar with its heavy load back where it belonged. They took their time, not looking at their watches, knowing instinctively how soon they had to move, but still going slow, being casual, making sure they made no mistakes.

Leaving the house, Doral set the alarms, opened and closed the barred gate leading to the street, taking along only the magnetic card that would gain them entry on the way back in. And even that would be hidden under the floorboards of their safe car, the one they would switch to after using one of the stolen getaway cars hidden on the streets near the score. Along with ten thousand dollars that they would use for grease money, if by some unknown and unforeseeable quirk of the gods they were arrested.

All was in readiness, and they had no need to speak. Fabe felt the familiar tightening of the bowels, the primal terror trying to creep up his spine. He fought it down, although it was not an entirely unpleasurable feeling. But it could make him panic if left unchecked. And he could not afford panic. Not even the sound of it in his voice. From this time until they returned, he planned to be a machine, emotionless, cold, hard. Uncaring. If Doral ever got shot at the score, Fabe knew he could get out, go it alone, without any heroic acts even in his mind. He would not go back for his friend's body, wouldn't even think about it. Although he would carry him on his back a million miles before leaving him for the police alive, which was a different thing altogether.

They were ready now, a couple of cool, calm professionals, getting ready to ply their trade, unstoppable. All the planning had been done, all the legwork. Now it was them against the establishment, which was what it was all about in the first place.

And, as usual, Fabe felt more alive than he could ever remember being before, knowing that each time lessened the odds, brought him closer to a collar. The realization that this was the last one for them didn't diminish anything. It sweetened things, in fact. It was the last time they would ever go out into the evening with larceny intended. Fabe felt an almost nostalgic sense of longing, then fought it off. He got into the safe car next to Doral. This wasn't like going to work, as he'd heard some guys in the joint describe it. No, each job was special to Fabe, each one filling him with such a feeling of power that he now regretted his decision to quit at a million, wished he'd made the goal two million. But he knew this was it. He'd said a million, and he'd stick to it. No sense, he figured, smiling inwardly, taking any chances.

4 The phone jangling next to his head awakened Dr. Chacona, and he snapped awake immediately, blinking his eyes, wondering if the heroin he'd smoked had made him miss his night at the free clinic. With the blackout draperies drawn he could not tell what time it was, or even whether it was day or night. He grabbed at the phone, clearing his throat as he did so, testing his voice before trying to talk into the receiver, just in case it was the other doctor at the clinic. He had enough trouble without making his last remaining loyal co-worker begin to doubt his trustworthiness.

"Hello?" he said, clearly, professionally, smiling there in the dark, naked with the lovely nude body of Lucille next to him, smiling because he'd pulled it off, had somehow gotten his voice to sound strong, even a little annoyed at being bothered.

"Where the fuck you at?" the gravelly voice demanded, and Chacona immediately lost all his cool. It wasn't a doctor. He wished fervently now that it were.

"Roland! How good to hear your voice! I was just about to—"

"You dumb beaner son of a *bitch*," Roland DiNardo said. "You use my name over the *phone*?"

"I'm sorry, I'm sorry, Ro——I mean, I'm sorry, all right?

I was just on my way over, Ro——I mean, I was just about to leave here—"

"Hey, you ain't here in an hour, bean, I'm sending some people over to get you."

"Don't do that!" Chacona shouted. "I mean, I'll be there, everything is okay, I got the stuff—" And the phone went dead in his ear. Roland had hung up on him, probably mad for real now because he'd said "stuff" over the telephone, too. But, Holy Mother, the man was paranoid. Shakily, Chacona hung up the phone and reached out and shook Lucille's shoulder.

He knew something was wrong even before he tried gently to rock her awake. Some instinct, honed from years as a surgeon, told him something was not right. Something was indeed very very wrong.

Cold.

That's what it was, she was cold. And stiff.

He rubbed her harder, hoping that his apartment's heating unit had broken down, that she was on the satin sheets and cold because it was below freezing outside, that that was all it was, because surely he could not have lain there beside a dead body for hours, could he?

When he finally realized that he indeed could have, he began to moan loudly, stuffing the edge of the satin sheet into his mouth so he would not scream, terrified, his eyes unable to leave Lucille Ortiz beside him on the bed, her eyes wide open, her mouth frozen in a faraway smile.

Chacona reached out a shaking hand and pushed her roughly, feeling the icy-cold skin and then seeing those once remarkable breasts jiggle stiffly as she rocked on the bed. He pulled his hand back and made a loud frightened noise. He took the sheet out of his mouth and stepped naked from the bed. He walked around to her side of the bed and threw the sheet up over her head, covering her. Chacona began to cry, knowing that he was a dead man.

He went into the living room and sat down, holding his head in his hands and rocking back and forth on the couch, trying to get himself back under control. Not doing too good a job of it. Also not seeing any way out of it for him this time, he'd sunk as low as any man possibly could. Lucille's insane brother would kill him now, of that he was certain.

And it would not be a fast or merciful death. If he'd simply been caught sleeping with her, with the sister of Francisco Ortiz, he might have gotten lucky and been given a bullet in his head, if Francisco happened to be in a good and forgiving mood. After all, the woman was in her twenties! But her *death*; Mother of God, her death would have to be repaid ten times over. He would be made to suffer terribly, suffer a slow and undignified death. A terrible, unworthy death. Better that he go to the safe now and mix up a batch of speedballs, shoot them into his asinine veins, the veins with the stupid hot blood in them, the blood that had made him think he could fuck and give dope to the sister of his homeland's most powerful criminal. But no, to do that right would take several hours, if he were to do it with pleasure, and that classless B-movie gangster Roland DiNardo would have his baboons breaking down his door in an hour.

Chacona made himself calm down. Going berserk now would solve nothing. Best to meet your fate calmly, like a man. He wandered the living room, his mind racing, and slowly made his way over to the far wall, to the safe hidden behind the picture of the bullfighter that his wife's Mexican mother had given them many years ago. The heavy burglarproof safe Roland DiNardo had had installed in his house behind the picture that was a reminder of happier times.

Snorting lines from his own stash of near-pure cocaine

made him feel a little better, a little more creative, a little more hopeful, and gave him a powerful desire to live a long and happy life. Thirty floors down, he thought, snorting more than he usually would at any one time. Right, okay. Thirty floors down. Obviously he could not carry the girl down on the elevator. Even if he got all the way to the first floor without seeing any other tenants, which had never happened since he'd lived there, he could never smuggle a lifeless person past the security guard, not after all the tenants had voted to bring in a more expensive security company than the surrounding buildings had, to give them better and safer places to live. No, that was out. So, all that was left to do, he knew, was to carry her the thirty flights down the fire stairs. She could not weigh more than a hundred and ten pounds, even with those enormous tits. The question was, could he do it? At one time, many years ago, he had been a serious health addict, lifting weights, running before it became fashionable, playing handball. He might be able to do it. The service doorman went home at four-thirty because he was a full-time college student at night, and he could not even be bribed to stay over and wait for an important delivery such as new furniture or a catering service come to deliver dinner to one of the many parties in the building. And there *was* a service elevator, after all, he had forgotten about that. He would not have to carry the girl all of the way after all! But did he have a key to it?

Chacona raced to his dresser and searched through his keys. Front door, outer door, service door, yes, yes, there it was, next to the slim bronze mail key. A round key almost exactly like the one he used to turn his alarm system on and off with. It would automatically bring the elevator right to his floor when he inserted it in the hole next to the elevator door, and the door would stay open until he removed the key and hit the button inside, which only went down. He searched his memory for the spiel they'd given him when he'd moved in, what they'd told him about the service elevator as he snorted two more huge, wide, long lines of cocaine, refining his plan, getting it down tight.

Yes, for security reasons, only the highly paid guard at the front desk had another key for the elevator. They could not be made at a locksmith's without authorization from the security company and the condominium board. They were numbered, and he'd had to pay a five-hundred-dollar deposit for it, which he would forfeit if he lost it. When a delivery came in, the service man would buzz the front desk, leaving the delivery man outside the back door, and he would tell the guard what floor the man wanted, what the delivery was, and the name of the tenant to whom it was to be delivered. The guard would then send one of the roaming security agents, of which there were always two on duty, over to open the elevator after he had checked with the tenant, verifying the delivery.

Did the guard know when the elevator was in service? Was there a light that would beep, or flash, telling him that it was in use?

Chacona checked his watch, cursing drug-induced paranoia. Hoping that was all it was. Deciding that it was now or never. It was nearly five already.

Okay. DiNardo, the son of a whore, would have no idea of what had happened. He would never suspect, probably, that someone as lovely as Lucille would ever want anything to do with a middle-aged man such as himself. So, no problem there. He would tell DiNardo that Lucille had made the delivery as planned, and he'd fallen asleep before bringing the twenty kilos over at the appointed time of four-thirty. He would decide what to do with Lucille's body later, *after* he got her out of the apartment.

He had a brainstorm then, as he snorted two more last

lines, all that was left of the rock he'd brought out of his safe, which had to have been all of a full gram and a half. An idea that would not only solve any problems he might have with security, but which would also throw the light of suspicion away from himself, and, in the process, enrich him more than fifty such middleman jobs could do.

He would make it look like a rip-off.

He had absolutely no illusions about DiNardo's opinion of him, or of Ortiz's. He was a realist, a survivor. He knew that they thought him to be less than a mule, much less, as a mule at least takes great risks. He was, to them, only a down-sliding loser, taking the drugs and paying off the delivery person as a buffer, and he knew without doubt that if the police ever caught on to him or even suspected him of being a major drug dealer, that DiNardo would, without a moment's hesitation, wipe him off of the face of the earth. This was a chance he was willing to take for the fifteen hundred dollars they paid him for each twice-weekly delivery. He was to take the dope, hand over the money, and deliver the drugs after waiting a decent interval to make sure that the delivery person had not been followed.

So if the delivery person were to be robbed and murdered *after* making delivery and collecting the money, could they possibly blame him? No, they would be looking for bigger fish, perhaps the New York Colombians, or even the Mafia itself, and would not that be wonderful, if Ortiz decided that DiNardo himself was the culprit and had decided that he did not need to pay Ortiz any longer?

His mind racing, his thoughts coherent and to him, at least now, brilliant, he raced to dress himself in the clothes he always wore at the clinic, to which he would be just a little late today. A somber black suit with a white shirt and black tie; a heavy, well-insulated London Fog topcoat. Simple black shoes. He whistled while he dressed, then took the time to pour himself a triple shot of Metaxa and drink it in one long pull. He went to the living room and grabbed the wooden handles of the cedar chest he used for a cocktail table, which had once been his Mexican ex-wife's hope chest, so many years before, and which he'd threatened to turn into kindling when she'd disappeared on him. The bitch. Thank God in Heaven that he hadn't. He carried the near weightless trunk into the bedroom and put it by the foot of the bed.

Lucille had stiffened, and that would be a problem. He would have to do something distasteful. Expertly, using his medical knowledge, he broke the bones and cartilage at her knees, elbows and neck, so he could fold her over and put her in the bottom of the chest. As he'd guessed, she was very light, especially naked. He closed the lid, then opened it again and threw in her purse and clothing. He had to sit on the trunk to close the hasp this time. He'd have to stop at a hardware store to get a padlock. And chains. And something to weight it down with.

He took two deep breaths, bent down and grasped the wooden handles, and hefted it. Doable. He could manage it now. The perfect crime. He carried his bundle to the front door, set it down, and looked back at the safe. Better to open it and get the drugs and money *after* he'd come back for the trunk. No sense taking any chances. He would have to leave the car in the alley, unlocked so he could get the chest into the backseat without delay when he came down. Even in this neighborhood, one of the best in the city, he would not dare leave twenty kilos of pure cocaine and a million dollars cash locked in the trunk. No, once he pulled it out of the safe, it could not leave his sight. Not until he turned the drugs over to DiNardo's man, and then, on his way to the clinic, he would decide how to safeguard the money all night. As he would have to decide where to dump the body.

He was smiling as he left the apartment, wondering how he would spend the million dollars, how much enjoyment, how much pleasure it could bring him. His heart was racing, he was sweating, his palms were sticky, and he felt a nervous tightness in his bowels, but he always felt that way after snorting a lot of cocaine, and so it was not a problem. He would be left alive. He would be a rich man. All he had to do now was keep cool for a couple of more days, maybe not even that. Maybe he should be wise and not take a chance, just simply dispose of the body and take off with the money *and* the cocaine, not even try to cover his tracks. Yes, that might be better. Ortiz, the muscle-bound pig, might well beat him to death for simply being the last person to know his sister was alive and well and carrying a million dollars cash. Yes, maybe he was, with all this cautious planning, making a big mistake. Another thing to think about *after* he got the body out of the apartment. Something to think about indeed.

In the garage, he hurried to his car, a busy man, running late, no time to talk with the serviceman who also was a security guard, who spent his eight hours watching the cars, getting paid extremely well to guard them, in fact. He got behind the wheel of his precious Cadillac, which had been paid off three months back, now his free and clear, the wages of sin, proving crime does indeed pay, even at the lowest levels. He drove carefully to the gate, and while the guard hit the switch that would open the corrugated steel door to Clark Street, he allowed himself a smile. He was on the verge of becoming an extremely rich man, with enough cocaine to last him the rest of his life. Fuck Ortiz, fuck DiNardo. He'd take it all and go away, now, tonight, before he changed his mind. When he got back to the apartment he would collect the few things that mattered to him, put them in the trunk with the drugs and the cash, and be off. Fuck them all. He'd show *them* who was a loser.

Musing, smiling, thinking that he had it made, he turned off from Clark onto Chestnut, rolling slowly the half block to the alley, where he would leave the car next to the service entrance, and he did not notice the big blue Buick that pulled up next to him, not until the Buick's driver honked the horn, and Chacona pulled the wheel back hard to the left, missing the turnoff into the alley, seeing the man in the Buick curse at him, wishing he had the time to stop and get out of the car and kick his big ugly ass for him. He would have to go all the way around the block now to enter the alley. Waste precious time. DiNardo's men would be there in fifteen or twenty minutes. Shit. He hit his turn signal and speeded up, pulled in front of the Buick and fought the impulse to slam on the brakes. He had no time to play around, because in his haste he'd left his home unlocked.

Fabe was standing across the street, looking directly up at the thirtieth-floor window, watching for the doctor's car to come around the corner so he could signal Doral to make his move.

He'd had a false alarm earlier when a black-on-black Coupe DeVille had turned the corner and he'd been certain that it was the doctor. But he had hesitated until the car was even with him and he could see the driver's face. Then he thanked God he'd waited because it was not the doctor driving the car and as it passed, Fabe clocked the license plates and those weren't right either. Jeez, if he'd signaled Doral over the wrong car . . .

Not wanting to think about it. Doral would make his move and get the door open and—Fabe forced himself to stop thinking about it. All his life he'd been blessed—or cursed—with an active imagination, and it came upon him and did its work at the strangest times.

He waved away a wino wearing about ten layers of clothes

who had approached from North Clark Street and stood in front of him, a filth-encrusted hand held out. Sores were suppurating on the palm. "Get the fuck out of here," Fabe said, disgusted. "Get lost," he told the man, and sadly, hanging his head, the wino shuffled away.

Fabe wondered where the good doctor was. He'd been clocking him steadily for six weeks now. He knew that every Monday from six to midnight Chacona donated his time at the free clinic in Uptown, taking care of the gays and the hookers, the flotsam of the city, in one of its worst sections. Doral was in the alley, barely in Fabe's line of sight, waiting for a signal from Fabe. Then he'd slip right into the service door, using the key Fabe had cut from a wax impression he'd taken, and hold the door for Fabe. Then up the fire steps, one floor at a time, to thirty flights up. Chacona's apartment was the first door on the right from the fire stairs. Fabe knew he could be inside with the alarm deactivated and the safe exposed maybe two minutes after they reached the thirtieth floor.

He was standing in a brick recess of an apartment building at 719 West Chestnut, looking at the entrance of the doctor's building, the doorman over there shivering in the cold, wrapping his arms around himself as he walked in tight circles in front of his station. Poor stiff, Fabe thought.

Across the alley stood an entire block of Victorian mansions that had been cut up into condos. A "Rubloff Assoc." sign hung over the bay window of an obviously empty apartment, advertising a five-story apartment with a fireplace on each floor, hardwood floors, three baths, five bedrooms. The nearest one was white stone, with wide marble steps leading to the vestibule door. Four mailboxes were in sight behind the well-lighted door. A blond woman, youngish, in Marshall Field camouflage carrying a box of groceries from Jewel's, walked up the steps as he watched, leaving white plumes as she breathed heavily through her mouth. She held the box against her knee and rang one of the buzzers. "It's *me!*" she sang into the speaker. The door immediately clicked, and she grabbed the knob and lugged the box in, letting the door shut behind her.

Jesus, Fabe thought. No wonder the Cabrini Green gang-bangers were burglarizing these joints, raping these rich matrons in their homes and taking all their jewelry. It's me, and you open the door, after paying maybe a million bucks for a piece of a hundred-year-old mansion in the heart of the North Side.

There it was! A black-on-black Coupe DeVille turned the corner with a squeal of rubber, and a blue Buick nearly cut it off, and Fabe held his breath, needing an accident now like he needed another nose. But it was all right, the Buick pulled over almost at the mouth of the alley, and Chacona raced by, pissed off, from the look of him, racing around the corner and disappearing. Fabe nodded to Doral, rubbing the top of his navy watch cap roughly, sweating in the freezing cold under his black Levi's and dark-blue peacoat, which was covering his tools under his left arm. Then Fabe walked across the street into the alley, knowing from all his watching that the serviceman who stood inside the door all day went home at four-thirty, knowing they were in, that it was a go, that none of the thousands of little things that could blow a score would happen this time. He felt his heart hammering in his chest. He opened and closed his fists, breathing in gasps, passing one of the three stolen getaway cars that were parked in the area, ready now, feeling *good,* grinning in the five-o'clock darkness of the city, the vapor lights of the alley shot out by the roving gangs of punks, going forth to do his business.

Doral held the door open for him and they locked it the second Fabe was through. They stopped and listened at the fire door, coolly, for a full ten seconds. Nothing. Opening it, they began the long run up, knowing that this was where the conditioning came in, all the long hours of running and training and working out. Silently, on black-sneakered feet, they raced up the stairs and reached the thirtieth floor less than five minutes after entering the building.

Fabe and Doral were sweating, their breathing raggedy and harsh as they rounded the last steps and stood soundlessly at the fire-stair door, listening. Nothing. Fabe reached into the pocket of his coat and removed a dental mirror, inched the door open and scanned both ends of the corridor, the door not open a half inch; he would be able to close it in a second if he saw anything he didn't like. For instance, a tenant or security guard. Nothing.

Into the hall then, Doral walking casually, coolly, as if he belonged, Fabe hating this part most of all, knowing that the next couple minutes were the most dangerous of the night. The walls and ceilings of the apartment were concrete, fireproof and soundproof. They could have a party while he worked on the safe and nobody would hear them. He stepped to the door and hunkered down to check the locks, then jumped back as if they were red-hot. He turned and Doral followed him back to the fire door, out into the stairwell.

"Doral, there're two Dopler alarms on that door, three locks. Meechaim locks, numbered and registered keys." Trying to do all the talking, anticipate any questions, because Doral, for all his badass cool, would be hardly able to talk by now. His mind registered the fact that Doral was standing there listening to him with his chin in his hand, his other arm across his body holding his elbow, like at a boring dinner party or something, at his boss's house. Fabe wondered if the guy was going to get a bad case of ulcers, someday, from being able to hold so much of himself inside. He'd have to make his case so a simple nod of the head would be Doral's option. He continued, hurriedly, urgently, watching Doral looking so cool and in control that he had to fight down the faintest bubble of resentment.

"Doral, neither alarm is turned *on*, and neither lock is engaged. The fucking house is *open*, wide open. Either the fucking guy, he feels so safe in this secure building that he feels no need to lock the place, or he's coming back, maybe expecting someone. We go in or what?"

"Maybe someone's already inside," Doral said. He was slurring his words so terribly that Fabe had to concentrate fully to make them out. He asked Doral if they should call it off, and Doral just smiled.

Back out into the hall, after checking again with the mirror. To the door, reaching out now with a hand that had never felt so unsteady, so insecure about trying someone's doorknob. In a rush Fabe was in, throwing the door wide, pulling his hat down over his eyes, peering around, then going to work, doing his part, his magic act. If there were twenty guys in here with machine guns, it was Doral's problem. His was to locate and beat the box.

On his knees next to the picture now, inspecting the frame, seeing the wire, the first one, the easy one. Laying his tools down before him, gently placing the Wolf DB I Soundenhancer on the ground softly carpeted between his legs. Taking deep, slow breaths, trying to put Doral out of his mind, trying not to think about him soundlessly searching the house, after locking the door, unless he—*stop it*! He had to beat a triple here, had no time for anything else. Triple alarm just on the *picture*. What the hell would be on the *safe*?

But it encouraged him, all the alarms. All the security meant that there was indeed something of extreme value in the safe. Doctors always had tons of money that they had to hide from the IRS. Money that could not be banked or invested, money that they did not want taxed. Which was why more than one professional thief turned to doctors to bankroll their operations. The thief would guarantee the doctor ten percent of the score, and would put the doctor's money to work for him. Getting him a better return, if the score was successful, than any investment plan would. Then, of course, the doctor would have even *more* money to hide and somehow find a way to wash, but that was not Fabe's problem at the moment.

He was taking a two-foot-long piece of copper wire from his pocket, about to bypass the electrical system hooked into the alarm, when he heard the door open behind him.

Doral had been walking around, searching the house, making sure it was empty, finding no one, knowing full well that at thirty stories above ground level it would be ridiculous even to think about finding another way out. But it was a habit left from his childhood days: get in, make sure you were alone, then find a second way out, a safety valve, an escape route. Fabe thought that was an admission of defeat. A good thief, Fabe believed, did not need an escape route, because no one would ever know he'd even been there until the home owner returned, if the guy did his job right. Standing there, in the living room, watching Fabe work, he was vaguely troubled by the cedar chest sitting there right by the front door. Funny place to leave a chest, right there where you could break your leg on it, you weren't careful.

Doral strolled over to the door and leaned against the jamb, staring down at the crate. A puzzled smile crossed his face, no big thing, just a casual wondering was all it was. He bent over and flicked the hasp, and the top of the chest popped up an inch. Hmmm. Must be full of something. He lifted the top and had to stifle a cry.

It was obscenely positioned, the woman's body. The head was bent way over onto the chest, broke for sure, god*damn*! Legs busted, too, bent over the chest, the feet flopping pornographically at her shoulders, heels facing him, toes pointing down. Stuffed right in there. Her thing was jet-black, musta had one hell of a lot of fun before he'd killed her, the good doctor. The cocksucker.

Doral flipped the lid down silently, knowing now that Fabe's second guess back in the stairwell had been right, the guy was coming right back, probably bringing the car around back for some reason. Like, the guy didn't want to horse around, playing with his keys trying to turn off alarms or unlock doors in the state of mind he was in, he might turn one of the alarms loose, bring in the law right away, put himself in deep shit. So he'd left the alarms off, and the door unlocked. Doral smiled, thinking of the good time he was going to have with this rapist bastard who killed young chicks after fucking them. He turned to the door and silently unlocked it. He stepped to the side, and waited.

Dr. Chacona finally made it around to the other side of the block and entered the alley too quickly, sideswiping a garbage can on his way in, cursing, wondering how much damage he'd done to his fender, then laughed outright, thinking, soon I will buy a new Cadillac for each day of the week. He pulled the car over to the far side of the alley at the service entrance to his building, put on his flashers, reached down and hit the switch to bring the front seat all the way forward. There. He was certain he could manage to get the trunk into the back.

He was laughing when he turned the key in the service door, smiling only when he locked it behind him, and was frowning in concentration when he turned the round key in the hole next to the service elevator. Why had he not brought down some rock to suck on? Damn. Well, soon. It would be soon. The elevator whooshed to a stop on his floor, and he hit the Door Open button, turned his key in the inner lock so it would stay open, and hurried from the elevator, down the hall and to the door of his apartment. He flung it open and stooped to pick up the chest, noticing out of the corner of his eye a great big guy getting up off the floor by his safe. He started, squealed in fright, then Doral had him by the throat, throwing him against the far wall of the apartment, following him all the way there, and had his throat in his hands, banging the doctor's head against the wall before Chacona could get enough of his wits about him to scream.

"Dey's a daid guhrl in da crate."

Fabe was looking in shock at Doral, standing there holding the Puerto Rican doctor like a rag doll in one big hand, the doctor's eyes wide with terror, his tongue hanging out, Doral squeezing a little bit to make it awfully hard for the man to breathe.

This was not the time to argue with Doral. He'd checked it out, known there was a body in the trunk, yet hadn't told him about it, hadn't given him the option to abort the score and get the fuck out of there. He hadn't heard a key in the lock either, so Doral had unlocked the door, knowing the doctor was coming back. Doral would obviously now be thinking that they'd have to kill the doctor, as he had seen both their faces. He hadn't even told him so he could pull his mask down over his eyes. Bastard. But he'd square that up with him later. For now, all Fabe was thinking about was the law.

By Illinois statute, burglary, or breaking and entering, B&E, was a class-X felony. First time out, if you got caught, you might, if you were lucky, serve two years of the mandatory six-year sentence. Home invasion, on the other hand, where the people were home and you strong-armed them or held them against their will, or if they came back home while you were inside, would draw you, mandatory, fifteen. First time out. Neither he nor Doral were first offenders. They'd get life without parole. And murder while in the commission of a home invasion would draw you an automatic trip to the chair. Capital offense. Find you guilty, fry you. And this was to be their last score.

"You tell Roland—" the doctor managed to croak, before wheezing, fighting desperately for breath. Doral looked faintly interested and released his grip slightly, still holding the man up on his toes, though, ready to cut off his air if he tried to scream.

The doctor looked relieved and took in two deep breaths, then said, "Thank you," to Doral, who nodded back as if he'd just handed the man a dinner napkin or something, standing there blandly looking at his catch, not acting as if he knew that they were looking at life in prison or death row. They were home invaders. No longer just a couple of high-class thieves. Fabe felt soiled.

"You can tell the man there was no need for any of this, none whatsoever. I was just about to bring him the stuff." He looked terrified and outraged at the same time. He stared at Doral with hatred, but his voice was soft and had a pleading quality to it as he said, "Release your grip, please, and I'll save your friend the trouble of breaking into the safe." Doral let go, smiling slightly, looking away from Fabe, not wanting to meet his eyes just yet.

The doctor walked to the safe, in quick, jerky movements.

"Remember you got a dead body to explain if you hit the wires," Fabe said.

"The body is my concern," the doctor said, although Fabe knew he'd hit home, had brought the man up short when he mentioned the body. The man most likely had not understood Doral. He watched as the doctor hit the dial, after pulling the picture away from the wall. Shit. A coded alarm. He would have been here most of the night trying to figure it out.

The alarm was tied directly into the safe's combination.

Only hitting the random numbers correctly would safely discon-
nect it. Even with the sound enhancer, a ten-thousand-dollar
piece of equipment, which would, once set onto the safe, mag-
nify the sound of the spinning dial a thousand times, allowing
Fabe to know exactly which numbers were needed to fall into
place to open the safe, he would have needed most of the night
to try and beat the alarm. It was the most expensive and current
piece of technology available. Whatever was in the safe would
really be something.

Obviously, this man thought they were someone else,
maybe his bookie or someone, someone to whom he owed
money. He thought they were muscle, come to take what was
their boss's. So, fine. He could think what he liked. Damned if
Fabe would tell him they were there to rip him off. They'd take
it, get the hell out, and let the guy worry about it later. But no,
that wouldn't work either. He'd seen them both, and no wishful
thinking on his part would change that. Doral would want to kill
him. And maybe, Fabe rationalized, the man deserved whatever
Doral had in store for him. After all, he'd obviously killed a
girl, and the doctor had backed up by telling him the body was
none of his business.

Now the doctor swung the door wide, and Fabe grabbed
him by the shoulder and firmly pulled him away from it. Everybody had a piece inside their safe, in case a thief came in and
forced them to open it. And the doctor was no exception. A
Smith & Wesson .357 Magnum lay atop a briefcase, which was
balanced atop a flight bag with TWA stamped on it. Nothing
else. No legal papers, no cash, no jewelry boxes. God*damm*it!

He threw the briefcase in Doral's direction, not trusting
himself yet to look him in the eye, and grabbed the flight bag's
straps, surprised at its weight. Had to be forty, fifty pounds in
the canvas bag.

Suddenly his heart sank and he knew, without doubt, what

was in the bag. The bag would have to have been specially constructed to manage the extra weight, a regular flight bag would not handle fifty pounds; it would rip right off from the straps. And the only people creative enough to come up with a normal-looking flight bag and had the wherewithal to have one made were, naturally, druggies. His heart sinking, he opened the bag.

There, atop the many bags of white powder, was a smaller bag, maybe a pound in it, most of it still rocks, uncut. The doctor made a noise in his chest, a pleading, whining sound, and Fabe understood. This was his personal stuff, maybe his payment for being a go-between. He knew damn well that this man was no big-time druggie. They wouldn't be caught dead with this much dope or cash. Never. There would be three or four layers between the top men and a guy like poor little old Dr. Chacona. Fabe's mind snapped back to something the man had said. Tell Roland something. And also, the doctor had not seemed too damned surprised to see them. As if he were, as if he were—

Expecting them.

Jesus Christ.

"Hey," he heard Doral say. He turned and saw the beaming smile on the big black face, saw Doral holding the open briefcase out to him as if it were a peace offering, saw the hundred-dollar bills, bundled, stacked tightly into the briefcase.

"We gotta get outta here," he said to Doral, knowing that the big dumb bastard had not made the connection yet, did not know that somebody would be coming for the dope or the money or both. He winced a little when he realized that by saying the words he was signing Chacona's death warrant, but he didn't feel too bad. The man was, after all, a murderer, and a drug dealer. "Leave the dope," he said.

"Shee-it," Doral said.

Fabe spun on him. "Leave the fucking dope!" he shouted.

Doral did not think this worth responding to. He turned to the doctor, and Fabe knew that he was making a definite, controlled effort to control his speech.

"Whose shit is this?"

"Pardon me?" the doctor said.

"Who's goddamn dope is this here?" Fabe said, ignoring his beef with Doral for the moment, knowing what Doral needed to know and why, wanting only to get it done and get the fuck *out*.

The doctor smiled. "I do not know," he said, his face very sad. And Fabe knew he was starting to make the connection with what he'd just shouted at Doral, wondering why, if they'd come for the dope, he was yelling at him to leave it.

"I just want to know whose it is," Fabe said, trying to keep the doctor's mind occupied, busy, watching him chew his lips, knowing well that the man was a full-blown junkie, eating a piece of rock even now as he strove for dignity and courtesy to two guys whom he'd found busting into his safe.

"Your friend and you will be finding out very soon, I think." And he knew, suddenly, that he'd just made a big, big mistake, and instinctively looked at Doral, knowing somehow that any physical trouble would come from the shorter, skinny one, and Doral was on him, hitting him on the top of his head hard with his fist, dropping him, dragging him by the armpits over to the crate. Fabe picked up the briefcase, dropped the flight bag, and when Doral had the man in position over the crate, Fabe threw him the doctor's gun.

Doral put the barrel into the man's mouth and without hesitation pulled the trigger, standing way, way back, letting the body jump back and fall against the wall. He knelt beside the body and stuck the gun in the doctor's hand, then let it fall limp, then kicked the gun a few feet away. Perfect.

When the body fell, Fabe had moved, toward the door, the briefcase in his hands, then remembered the open safe. He spun to close it, set the dial, relock it, and saw Doral hefting the flight bag over his shoulder, staring at Fabe with calm, serene eyes.

"Leave it," he said again, knowing that Doral wouldn't, that they also did not have time to battle about it. It would take maybe an hour to whip this bastard, and even then, maybe he'd lose. He turned and locked the safe, hot shame climbing up his spine, feeling as if he'd turned over and shown Doral his ass.

"Shee-it," Doral said again, and threw the bag over his arm, knowing he'd won but not wanting to rub it in, thinking he'd set things straight between them once they got back to the house. He waited at the door for Fabe to walk through first, not wanting him behind him, no, uh-uh. Not just yet.

Fabe hit the steps and began jogging slowly down, while Doral, in a burst of inspiration, went to the elevator and stepped inside, turned the key, watched the doors slide shut. He hit the ground floor button and descended, the bag under his arm feeling good, like a million. At the bottom floor he stepped out, removed the key, twisted it in the outside hole and shut off the elevator. He stood carelessly, his ankles crossed, waiting for Fabe, hoping he'd get just a little smile out of him, smiling himself at what he knew Fabe would see, his big tall skinny black ass leaning against the serviceman's desk, looking a little bored, tired of waiting. Maybe he'd even look at his watch when Fabe came through the door, say something cute, get a laugh. Break the ice.

No such luck.

Fabe came through the door and did not even look at him. His jaws tight, clearly pissed, he burst through the service door clutching the briefcase full of money, looking as if he would kill Doral as soon as the opportunity presented itself.

5 Nobody goes out at night expecting to get busted. Even the most pessimistic and fatalistic thief believes he will get away with one more score, one more time at the old trade. The prisons are filled with them.

By the same token, no mobster goes out and believes in his heart that he will get murdered. Take, for example, what happened to one Ken Eto. He *knew* he was in trouble, knew he'd angered certain people to whom he was a gnat crawling up an elephant's ass, never knowing that the elephant would swish him right off with his tail the second he sensed or felt his presence. And yet old Chinaman Eto got right into the car with a couple of stone killers, thinking they were taking him to a meet where everything would get straightened out. What got straightened out was: the Chinaman, he caught a few bullets in the head, and miraculously escaped and lived to tell tall and long tales to the Justice Department, under the wonderful Witness Protection Program, which rewards lifelong career criminals for ratting out, finking on the very people who had made them rich and comfortable. And the two guys who had bungled the hit wound up in a trunk themselves, having left their houses that day thinking they, too, were going to straighten everything out. No, none of the mob wise guys ever thought they would get killed, and yet O'Hare Airport filled each year with smelly Cadillacs and Lincolns, the parking lots there being the new burial grounds for dying elephants.

A good, smart crook, he always expects the unexpected, and Roland DiNardo was a good, smart crook. He had to be, because he was taking chances that would make Dr. Chacona's sexual fling with Lucille Ortiz look like a Mickey Mouse risk in comparison.

Roland DiNardo was a made mobster for the Chicago Outfit, and he was selling dope on the side.

Not just a couple of kilos here and there, trying to make a couple of bucks to put the kids through school. Uh-uh. Roland was bringing in forty to eighty kilos a week, pure. Stuff nobody had stepped on yet. He paid fifty grand a kilo and turned it over on the street for ten times that. How, he wondered in his rare moments of introspection, could the guys upstairs be dumb enough to think that it could be passed by?

Roland had fought with his boss, Angelo "Tombstone" Paterro, about the hands-off drug traffic within the mob's circles. About the automatic death penalty imposed upon those found dealing from within the family. And Tombstone had told him, "Do what you want, but don't let me know about it." Tombstone needed Roland for the time being to hold together the gambling business on the South Side, where Roland had good connections, but he was ready, willing, and able to sell him out in a hot New York second if things started getting tough.

Roland himself took Tombstone's words to be a green light, not a yellow one, an okay for him to do what was forbidden to others. Because he was special. The same way Ken "the Chinaman" Eto thought he was special. And so he had begun the first serious mob undertaking into drug trafficking in the city of Chicago, but all on the qt, of course. Even with Tombstone's approval, there was no sense in making waves and letting other guys in on the gravy train.

No, Roland figured that you had to be prepared for everything and anything. But he was not prepared to get a phone call from the two hard cases he had sent out to put the fear of God and Roland DiNardo into the second-rate two-bit junkie-ass doctor he'd found to be one of his middlemen. This phone call informed him that there was a phalanx of lawmen surrounding the good doctor's building: nobody in, nobody out. He'd told the man who'd called, "Grease some of the cops, see what the fuck's going on," and the guy had told him, "I only got a few bucks on me," whining-like, the jackoff; and Roland had told him, "Hey, grease the guy and I'll pay you back soon as you get back," and the asshole, he'd made Roland promise to pay him tonight, before he'd do it. It was what he deserved, using brainless tough guys from the streets instead of made guys or his own soldiers. But when you were breaking mob rules, you couldn't let any mob people in on it. Some of these guys, Jesus Christ, you'd think they were old broads the way they gossiped and went on and on about each other after a couple of snorts.

Now the two guys, big beefy suckers they were, hung around the poolroom Roland owned and did a lot of his business out of, trying to suck up to him, get on the payroll, the dumb asses. They were standing in front of Roland, who was sitting behind his desk, giving them the Stare, not saying anything yet, letting them get scared. Which wasn't working. They were looking around the room, at least they had sense to know that they were looking at more money here in the den than they would put together in their entire *lives*, at least they had that much sense. Roland smiled, inside, not letting the humor enter his eyes or manifest itself on his lips. Let them think I'm pissed at them. Maybe it'll make me feel better. But they didn't open their mouths, they just kept gaping around the room at the leather chairs and the good booze behind the bar, at the library shelves of leather-bound books and at the fireplace that was blazing away, big enough to stick either one of those guys into and burn 'em up, if he had a mind to. And he was coming close to it with these two jackoffs.

"Hey," he said, and they both zeroed in on him, looking at him as if they'd just noticed he was in the room, for God's sake. "So what the fuck happened?"

"The guy you sent us out to see, the guy with the stuff, he killed himself, boss, but here's the *good* part." And the dummy smiled, he actually fucking *smiled*, as if there was something *amusing* here, a million dollars cash and a million worth of coke, no, actually ten million worth of coke, you wanted to get right down to it. Roland had had enough of this palooka.

"I'm not your boss," he said menacingly, and got very, very pissed off when the guy just kind of looked puzzled, not understanding what Roland was saying. "You said 'boss' to me. I ain't your boss," he told him, and now the light was dawning, the big guy was seeing it now, getting a little scared in the eyes. Good.

The man had thick, rich, wavy red hair, bright red. Ugly hair, to match his face. Tiny blue eyes shone brightly from inside puffy scarred skin. There were boils all over his face, and to hide them the geek had grown a beard, but it didn't work because the hair did not grow out of the boils, only spurted out in light red tufts around the boils, bringing them more attention. His teeth were almost green, and his lips were cracked and bloody. In spite of the arctic temperatures outside, he wore a red, short-sleeve Ban-Lon shirt under a leather jacket, which he'd immediately removed upon entering the room, so his muscles would bulge impressively. His partner was the same height and approximate weight, but had beautiful black hair hanging luxuriously to his shoulders. His complexion was olivey and clear, and Roland wondered if they were queer for each other. They acted stupid enough to be degenerates. The black-haired man, Elmo, was dressed much the same as his partner, Lloyd. Only Elmo was smart enough to know he was stupid, and kept his mouth shut most of the time.

Lloyd was just now understanding that the doctor's suicide was costing Roland DiNardo a lot of money, pain, and grief, and so decided to play it straight.

"I'm sorry, Mr. DiNardo, I didn't mean nothin'. I did what you tole me, Mr. DiNardo, and I greased some of the fuzz around the buildin', cost me two hunnert and fitty dollars," he said, his eyes filling with greed, and Roland knew that if the stiff had paid out fifty bucks it was a big night, the greedy, silly son of a *bitch*. Fuck him. Let him sweat a little while. Ignore him. Act like you didn't hear him. Lloyd's face fell, but he recovered quickly, and started talking again.

"Turns out, now get this, Mr. DiNardo, this freak, this doctor fella with the shit, he had a dead bitch up there, with all the bones in her body busted, leastwise, that's what the copper tole me. Said she was stuck in a *trunk*, bent and twisted in there, every single bone in her body busted to shit."

Roland DiNardo was starting to get it now, starting to put it together. He stared at Lloyd, who gazed back blankly, then switched his stare to Elmo, who looked away quickly. Good, at least the pretty one knew better than to try and shake him down.

"Lloyd," he said, "this is very, very important. Two questions. Now don't try and bullshit me about this—" And he held his hand up, cutting off Lloyd as he was about to defend his honesty. "Was the broad sexually molested?"

Lloyd said, "Oh yeah, the guy fucked her. She was naked, anyways, so you'd figure he fucked her, right?" And he stood there waiting for the second question.

Roland said, "Did the copper tell you what, er, *race* the woman was?"

Lloyd said, "Definitely a Mexican, no doubt about it. You could tell she was a Mex, 'cause the copper, he was trying to talk like a big shot, you know how they are, 'perpetrator' instead of 'suspect,' you know? Well, he said she was Hispanic, so you know when they say that that they really mean Mexican. That's just the way they talk."

Roland DiNardo had checked these two boys out before giving them any kind of responsibility, and he knew that both Lloyd and Elmo had done time. Otherwise he wouldn't have trusted them as far as he could throw them. Elmo, in particular, he'd done a full six years in Pontiac when he could have walked in two, but he wouldn't give the prosecutors or the state's Attorney's Office the name of his accomplices, who'd gotten away during the excitement when the cops came and put the jiggers on a Sunday night liquor-store robbery. Lloyd he knew less about, but disliked him immensely and would not have cared if he had stood up, done a life term rather than roll over. He was trying to rip Roland DiNardo off, and nobody got away with that. Looking at them both standing there, Lloyd staring at him with a big dumb expression on his face, trying to act like he had nothing in the world to hide and nothing to be ashamed of, Elmo looking off, appearing extremely uncomfortable, hating what was happening, but trying to get through it for his partner's sake, Roland began to form a plan in his mind. But he couldn't give anyone a hint just yet of what it was about, and so he stood up, reached into his pocket, and pulled out a wad of hundred-dollar bills. He peeled off three, threw them on the desk, and nodded to Lloyd.

Roland said, "That's for the copper you paid off." He added two more bills to the pile and said, "That's for your night's work." Lloyd grabbed at the money hungrily. Roland smiled inwardly, hoping the punk had sense enough to spend it quickly. He peeled off two more bills and walked around the desk, personally handed them to Elmo.

He said, "This's for tonight's work," and got a surprise, a pleasant one, and he figured maybe this kid was more than he appeared to be.

Elmo folded the money in half and handed it back. "I didn't do nothin' to earn this, Mr. DiNardo," he said.

Roland took the folded bills, winked at Elmo and stuffed them in the pocket of Elmo's shirt. He said, "Take it, kid, and you can call me Roland." He assured them that he would be using them in the near future and ushered them out of there, past the two guys at the door who owed him their loyalty but who knew nothing about his drug business, or, at least, claimed not to, which was good enough for Roland.

Thinking, worrying, upset, Roland went back into his den and poured a good stiff Scotch, three fingers neat, and sat back behind the desk, putting it together.

He'd told the two runners that they were to go to the doctor's apartment and pick up a small shipment of stuff; they did not know how much. If there'd been any stuff left in the apartment, the copper Lloyd had greased would have mentioned it. Or else the stuff was still in the safe Roland had paid to have installed in the wall. Maybe. In that case he'd have to have somebody check it out, somebody he could trust not to rip him off, and who also could keep his mouth shut. That would be a real bitch, he knew, as most thieves held the Outfit in contempt and had nothing to do with Outfit guys if they could help it.

One thing at a time, he thought. First things first. He sighed. He couldn't put it off any longer. If he did not call Francisco Ortiz now, Ortiz would call *him*, and then it would look as if he were trying to rip Ortiz off. Which was coming, but not yet. In the future. Soon. This bit of bad business might well put that off for a while, though. Roland had found Dr. Chacona. Ortiz had told him only that the middleman had to be a Puerto Rican, that was all. And if Chacona had killed the Ortiz girl and was planning on making a run with the money *and* the dope, it would look to Ortiz as if perhaps Roland was in on the scam, and had somehow fucked up. Maybe by picking a weak link in the doctor, who had been filled with remorse after killing the girl and had then committed suicide, or by killing the girl and the doctor and taking the money and the dope himself. There was no way of knowing what the Puerto Rican would think, as they were more paranoid than your average Sicilian, who had, in Roland's mind, owned the market on paranoia until he'd met Ortiz. But one thing was for sure: he had to call Ortiz, now. Had to be the one to tell him about his sister. Or else it would look as if he were in on it, one way or another.

After he made the call, then, he could worry about getting a thief with a closed mouth to go on in and check out the safe for him. But he had to take every step one at a time.

He picked up the phone, dialed 1, then the area code for San Juan, Puerto Rico. He dialed the seven-digit number that would ring only in Ortiz's private office, in the back of his palatial home which, Roland knew, was overrun by about eight or nine little beaner kids Ortiz claimed as his own, legitimate or otherwise; he was as big on family loyalty as the Sicilians, Roland had to give him that. As the phone began to ring he wondered how Ortiz would take the news of his sister's death, as big as he was on family.

And he wondered if the guy, being such a jerk about it, would insist on an eye for an eye.

6 "When I was eleven, there was this chick lived next door to us, she was thirteen and putting out to all the big guys. She decided one time to give me a piece of pussy, and I jumped at it. What it was, see, we lived with my grandmother, and she was a Baptist from the old South; I mean, radical about it. If the baby'd cry at night, like all babies do, she'd stand over the damn crib, perform an exorcism. She was goofy about it, used to beat my head in at least three times a week, just to knock the evil thoughts she knew I'd be having at that age right out of my head. I hated that old bitch.

"What happened was, I was fucking this bitch, I can't even to this day remember her name, on the roof of our apartment house, and I remember the stars shining and a full moon and thinking I was in love. I had never, *ever* done anything that good before, never could remember anything I ever did or thought being free of pain. *Some* kind of pain. Very low self-esteem, even at that age, what with the old man gone and my momma dumping us off on *her* momma, taking off on us, stopping in from time to time to say hey. And the old lady, her beatings didn't make me feel very good about myself.

"So, that night, I didn't even get a *nut*, man, when, I'm looking down at this chick and her eyes all of a sudden go wild, and I'm thinking to myself, she's coming, I made her come! But it wasn't that at all, uh-uh, what she was doing, she was looking up at my grandmother, standing over us, in shock, and then I felt this terrible, *terrible* pain across by bare ass, never felt nothing like that before either, two firsts in one night, and I was rolling off the girl, screaming like a banshee, and the girl, she takes off like a bat outta hell, grabs her clothes on the run and leaves me to take the heat alone.

"What the old bitch'd done, she'd cut me. She'd taken a razor to my ass and to this day, I got the scars. You musta noticed em, one time or another, well, that's how they got there.

"I stopped rolling when I hit the door to the stairs, and I was about to take off down 'em, fuck the clothes, fuck the old lady, fuck having a place to stay, I was hurt, I felt the blood running down my legs, I seen the old lady with the razor and a crazy, nutso gleam in her eye, and I was ready to take off, make my own way at eleven.

"But she got to me first, she did. Beat me half to death, and I mean beat my *ass,* man, and I was almost out, my eyes swelled shut, crying like a little baby, thinking maybe I'd never want to fuck again, when she did it.

"She sat me up against the door, and she slapped me till my eyes cleared up and she knew I was paying attention. She took my cock in her hand and she squeezed it, *hard,* then grabbed the balls and started squeezing them too. I started screaming, wondering how anything could hurt that much, and with her free hand she pushed my head down onto my chest, so I could see what she was doing, and she picks up the razor again and she puts it right on the base of my cock, starts to cut, and I see the blood, feel the pain, and I'm out, man, knocked me out.

"I come to, I'm in my room, my dick bandaged, hurting like hell, and I feel patches on my ass. She'd doctored me up, and then she comes in, like she been sitting outside the door, waiting to hear me moan. She comes and sits by the side of the bed, smiling real tender-like, and her right hand is rubbin my head, her left below her hip, outta my sight. I smile back at her, feeling ashamed for ever even *thinking* about fucking, but clean now that she'd punished me.

"She says, 'You been a bad boy, haven't you?' and I say, 'Yes, Granny,' and she says, 'You ain't never gonna do that again, are you, son?' and I say, 'No, Granny, I'm sorry, I'll never do it again, *never!*' And the smile goes right off her face and this sort of crazy look comes over her, and she grabs my hair in her right hand and bangs my head against the headboard, hard, and the left hand comes up and there's the razor, glinting in the moonlight coming in through the window, and she hisses at me, 'I'll cut it right off, next time, clean off,' and she's up, making a slashing motion at my cock, and I jump back, cowering. And she leaves the room.

"I'm fifteen, already running a gang, the badass of the neighborhood, man, the top dog, and they all know I shot Billy Green when I was only thirteen, that I didn't take no shit from nobody, cops included, and I been away to St. Charles already one time and looking at another fall for burglary. And this chick, she hits on me, and before my dick can get hard I'm on the ground, feeling the pain of the razor on my cock, knowing it's coming off this time, no fucking around, it's gone for sure, and the chick, she's outta there, screaming, and the rest of the gang hears the story. I'm a wacko, for sure now, can't even fuck, but nobody says anything to me to my face.

"I'm eighteen, I got more arrests than I got years, ain't seen nor heard of Granny since I left home at thirteen. The first time, *adult*, was sent away, I get busted for murder, and I did it, plain and simple. Did four others they never even knew it was me. Enjoyed every one, too. See, I had this philosophy. I never fucked with anyone, ever. Never played bad. Went out of my way to avoid trouble, except for stealing, what I mean is, humbugging trouble, fighting. So, when somebody *did* fuck with me, I had every right to blow his ass away and not feel guilty about it.

"Thing was, since that night when I was eleven, I could never even think about fucking, girl or boy, without falling on my knees in pain, my head on fire, like there's a buzz saw in there, my dick actually *feeling* the razor down there, sawing away. So what do I got to live for anyway? Everyone I knew was either a thief, like me, or a pimp or a con man or a killer or a pool hustler, *some*thing that wasn't straight, wasn't right in the world we was supposed to be living in.

"I was filled with hate, and didn't give a fuck. Not about anything.

"Then, they put you in my cell. All I did, ever, before then, was work out. Keep my mouth shut to the white man, naturally, never talked to a honkie before, even the ones I celled with. Shaved my head, spent some time with the brothers in the yard, but figured out right quick *they* were full of shit, too. Just needed a channel for their hate, and took it out on The Man, tried to blame the white man for all their problems, talking about social disadvantages and terrible hardship. Shit, I was gonna say once, 'Anyone ever put a razor to your cock, motherfucker?' That'd teach 'em about hardship.

"When them guys, they came into the cell to rape you? I had to go to war with them, *had* to. You were this big white dude, didn't say nothing, never bothered nobody, minded your own business. Respected me and my space, never tried to suck up to me or be a pal or anything. Hell, I couldn't help but like you. You were the first sucker I'd ever met, in the joint or out, who didn't have a hustle. Didn't have a reason for every word and act, some reason that was, for God knows what was gonna put them over. You never tried to lie or bullshit, or fuck me or get me to fuck you. Did your own time, went your own way.

"And I'll tell you something else, broham. I was feeling strange things inside, things I couldn't ever remember feeling, thinking things I could never remember thinking before. I didn't want to fuck you. Not like that. But I was having daydreams, you and me, on the outside, drinking cold beer in the summer, laughing at the beach, stuff like that. And more than once, I thought about killing you, because I knew it could never be that way between us, you wouldn't want nothing to do with a fucking badass nigger like me, and I got so mad, so wound up inside behind that, I seriously thought about killing you. Killing didn't matter to me.

"But when I threw that asshole over the railing, I felt something, something *bad*, knew it was *wrong*, man, somehow. Before, it was only: don't get caught, don't get pinched for it. I had somehow gotten a conscience in there. That, more than anything, kept me from throwing the other motherfucker offa there.

"Couple of weeks later, when we started talking, then working out together, I don't think you'll remember this, but I spent a lot of time smiling. I never smiled before. Bad for the image. But for the first time, I had a friend. Wanted a friend. Can you dig that?

"And that's why I threw in with you on the outside. You were my friend. Even though you were the one learned about locks and boxes, you ain't never been there, inside, stealing, and I didn't want to see you back inside. Okay, at first, it was

83

for the money. But now, Fabe, I got more than I could ever spend. Always want more, sure, but shit, I don't need fifteen years, either, over a wad of money couldn't buy one of my cars.

"When I saw the dope, Fabe, I said to myself, Doral, this is it. The one you been waiting on all your life. There was all that green cash there, all that money. That's yours, and I'll give you another hundred grand for your share of the dope. That's fair. I'll make a lot more money, granted, but I'm taking all the risks, too."

They were sitting in Doral's first-floor living room, Fabe in a leather rocker, his shoes off, dressed in his own clothes now, his feet on a matching hassock that faced the roaring fire Doral had built while Fabe was changing. He had a bottle of Haig & Haig Pinch in his right hand, a smoldering cigarette in his left. From time to time he would bring the bottle to his lips, take a short swig, then lower it, then take a deep drag from the smoke, then another, getting the taste out of his mouth. When Doral had finally begun talking, he'd continued staring into the fire for a while, lost in the blue and orange flames as the oak logs burned, enjoying the hissing and popping, mesmerized. But he'd looked up at the soft urgency in Doral's voice, at the incredible candor Doral was expressing. And he'd shifted his gaze to Doral, losing himself in what he was hearing, imagining a little kid getting a razor put to his dick. Jesus.

Fabe did not read books constantly, like Doral did, but he was smart enough to know what was going on here. Doral had known how he'd felt, what he was experiencing. And so Doral had rolled over and shown Fabe his own ass, had told him things that had left Doral emotionally stunted, insane in a way. Had given Fabe a way to put Doral's shit on the street, to ruin him in the eyes of the few people Doral respected, the men he did his straight business with, given Fabe a way to steal his self-respect and dignity.

In other words, he was trusting Fabe with his life.

But he was saying something else.

Fabe knew exactly what Doral was talking about, figured out the transference of affection as soon as he heard Doral talk about it. Fabe, to Doral, was straight. An ex-cop, something Doral, somehow, on some level, had always wanted to be. He'd wanted to earn respect from someone on the outside, someone that wasn't a thief or a pimp or a hustler. Someone who, even though he was in prison, represented to Doral the straight world. And so he'd stood up for Fabe, and Fabe wondered if Doral knew that if he hadn't thrown in with someone, soon, that he would have eventually gone insane. Thinking about it, he guessed Doral did. The pain had got too great. He *needed* somebody. He couldn't hack it alone.

But Doral was also saying he wasn't about to give up the dope. He'd gone along out of loyalty for a couple of years now, just because Fabe was his one true friend. Risked life and limb and freedom itself strictly out of friendship. He now had finally hit upon a multimillion-dollar score, and was not about to give it up. He'd put the ball squarely in Fabe's court. Now it was up to him.

"I don't want any part of the dope, Doral. I'll take the money, you take the dope." He was feeling better now, not taking it so personal, seeing Doral's point of view much more clearly now that he had had time to calm down, have a few drinks, relax a little bit. Outside of Jimmy Capone, Doral was really about the only guy in the world he trusted. And he had resented, just a little bit, the fact that he'd done all the work, set it all up, done all the watching, all the ground laying, and had always, every time, split the take right down the middle with Doral. He'd done this because they were partners, fifty-fifty, but still, goddammit, the first time they'd been in any real shit on a score, Doral had gone ahead and taken matters into his own hands, done what he wanted, without even consulting the guy who'd done all the work. Well, fuck it. It was the last one. It was all over. They'd robbed enough, and now someone had died. Fabe had never killed anyone before, and yet it had seemed natural to throw the gun to Doral, knowing full well what Doral would do with it. He'd killed the man as much as if he'd pulled the trigger himself. No bullshitting his way out of this one. On the last score, too. Shit. But it was done, and all the hard feelings in the world wouldn't take it away. He'd get drunk tonight, good and drunk, and worry about it tomorrow, when he was counting out all of his money. A million bucks could change a lot of feelings. Buy a lot of face back. And besides, Doral had told him things no one else in the whole wide world knew, just to make it up to him. That was worth something, having a friend who cared that much about you.

Fabe said, "Doral?"

Doral said, "Hmm?" Looking away from the fire, a calm, serene look on his face, all the jungle boogie-woogie out of his voice now, speaking with cultivated tones, low and quiet, a benefit of being a heavy reader.

"My grandmother, she caught me jerking off when I was twelve."

Doral had never known Fabe to be a bullshitter, a one-upman, someone who, if you'd have told him you were on a desert island, stranded for a month, would try and top you by having been stranded on one for a year, and so he leaned a little bit closer, sitting on the sofa, looking right into Fabe's eyes.

Doral said, "What'd she do?"

Fabe said, "She dragged me out onto the porch, and there were maybe a million of her old dago cronies out there, shooting the shit, dressed in black, like crows, and she shouts out to them, she goes, 'My Fabrizzio, he'sa joiking off! God forgive him!' and all the crows, they start clucking their tongues and staring at me, warning me that I'll go blind and waste away and die if I didn't stop.''

Doral was chuckling now, deep in his throat. "For real," he said, his voice going way down on the last word, disbelief finding its way in.

"No shit," Fabe said. "I decided I'd just do it till the palms of my hands got hairy."

Doral said, "Or till you needed glasses." And they were laughing softly now, not giving it much, comfortable with each other, glad that the rift was patched.

Doral said, "Who's dope you think it was?"

Fabe did not know, nor did he venture a guess. To Doral, he said, "You just be careful, huh? Selling it?"

Doral said, "I'll cover my ass, Fabe-babe, you can count on *that*. I know some dudes, over in Indiana Harbor, they'd sell their mommas for some scag or some coke. I'll drop it on them, slow and sure, in little bitty, stepped-on pieces. They'll love it." He grinned, a big one, relaxed; acting, as always, as if he didn't have a care in the world, as if he had spent the evening reading in his living room, before the fire, and had been pleasantly surprised when his old friend Fabe had dropped by unexpectedly instead of being out ripping off twenty kilos of cocaine and a million dollars cash, not to mention murdering a guy in the midst of a home invasion.

"Anyways, I get into the shit, I always got you to get me out of it, right?"

"Doral, Jimmy Capone even gets an idea about this, I'm pinched, and so are you."

Doral smiled now, a serene, easy smile, as if thinking about a fondly remembered lover. He very easily laid his hand over his crotch.

"Jimmy Capone can pinch this," Doral said.

Fabe waited a couple of beats, letting Doral enjoy his customary joke, before saying, "You'll wait six months before you sell it."

Doral said, "Maybe even a year," staring into the fire. "Don't worry about it."

7 The thing was, he couldn't get drunk, no matter how much he drank. They'd decided to take it easy, as if nothing much had happened, knowing if they took to their homes, hid out, someone would notice it when the heat was on. And the heat, they both knew, would soon be on. No one gave up a million cash and twenty kilos of cocaine without a battle. Hell, some of the big-time dealers, the Colombians and Cubans from the boat lift, would kill not only a guy they thought was cheating them but his entire family, and anyone in the city with the same last name, for God's sake, as a warning to others. But Fabe wasn't worried about Doral, he had enough money to lie very low with the dope until the time came to move it. And he wasn't worried about himself. He could, he knew, take good enough care of himself. He wasn't even worried about whoever owned the dope and the cash. If they were in that business, they deserved to lose it. As a matter of fact, Fabe wasn't even too worried about Jimmy Capone, although he did feel vaguely guilty; he'd promised Jimmy no dope scores, years ago.

What Fabe was worried about, and the reason why he was pouring Scotch down his throat like there was no tomorrow, with absolutely no effect at all, was the fact that he had never killed anyone before. He could talk trash to Doral, and he could even rationalize a little of it away to himself, bullshitting himself, playing a game, which he was losing, saying, Hey, the guy was a drug dealer, *and* a killer. Shit. He had it coming. But he knew, as he told this to himself, that it was jive bullshit, nothing more. He'd killed the guy, he and Doral. Cold-blooded murder. He'd been a cop for seven years and had never even pulled his gun, and now, on what was to be the very last score of his life, he'd killed a guy.

He remembered the guy clearly now, as he sat in Bunny's Hutch on Rush Street, which he always told her should have been called the Thieves' Den, it would have been more apt. He stared around at the crowd of thieves and grifters; hustlers and small-time pimps trying to fit in, be part of the crowd, but the regulars, who made their money from their own skill and wits, would cut them off, shut them out, and the pimps would leave, resentful, angry, and would probably go out and whip their ladies behind it.

Class joint, that was for certain.

Chandeliers instead of track lighting, which was the current thing. Candles at the tables, small round tables for two or four, far enough away from each other so that conversation could be intimate and private; no dance floor, the guys who hung around Bunny's Hutch sure weren't the type to cut a rug, tough guys don't dance, and all that. Real leather chairs, white, that were cleaned every day, two ten-by-five pool tables in the back, perfectly balanced each week by one of the hustlers who hung around, and who changed the felt a couple of times a year. Most nights, a couple grand would change hands across one of those tables, two or three times a year a big game happened, some out-of-towner gunning for the Kid or Mickey Two Ball, who got his name because he'd shoot the two ball all day long for practice, taking it out after he shot it in, setting it up and doing it again. One night Fabe had seen a game last until dawn, when he left; and it was still in progress that night when he'd stopped in for a quick chat with Bunny before going home. Something like fifty-three grand went into Stash "the Banker" Sansliki's pocket that night, and the kid had gone home, back to Iowa or wherever, broke, dejected, probably wondering where he'd gone wrong.

The bar was comfortable, intimate, the same white leather fringing the bottom edge of the bar and padding the stylish three-legged brass stools. Full tonight, early as it was. The *Monday Night Football* game was just starting, Frank Gifford talking about "the Big Tight End" again, as if any tight ends were tiny little guys who got free and yelled yoo-hoo, or something. Bets were being made on the Giants, mostly by guys who'd either lived there at one time or been in prison with some of the New York wise guys. They were playing their division rivals, the Philadelphia Eagles, who'd had a couple of rough years after Buddy Ryan left the Bears and took over as head coach, but who were on the winning track now, heading into the play-offs, already cinching a berth, with home-field advantage.

Fabe was trying to take it all in, take his mind off things, but he kept seeing a little Hispanic guy, his hands up in the air, his throat held in one of Doral's slender, powerful hands, the guy trying so hard to please, to do what these two guys wanted, thinking they were emissaries of someone else, until the moment he realized he'd fucked up big time—

"You okay, honey?" Bunny Capaletti said, leaning over the bar, touching Fabe's forearm softly, her face a mask of concern and compassion.

"'Mfine," Fabe said, wondering why he was slurring his words, his head was crystal-clear, he didn't feel the least bit drunk.

"Well, you don't look fine," Bunny said, rubbing his arm, conspirators now, ignoring the crowd around them. "You've smoked one cigarette after another since you've been here, and had three-four straight Pinches already. What's the matter?''

"Nothin'.''

Bunny's face screwed up now into an I'm-sorry look, showing a little guilt, a little shame. Bunny said, "I didn't mean to run out on you last night, honey, honest; it's just, you were so *rough*, I mean, I'm still sore. You *hurt* me. When you finally fell asleep, I thought, screw him, and got out of there. I'm sorry, honey.''

Fabe wondered, not for the first time, how any human being who had seen as much and done as much and been through as much as Bunny could be so shallow, so superficial. Thinking that he was hurt and upset and getting drunk because she had left before he woke up. He took a good look at her now, at that phony actress face, playing Jane Fonda looking at Jon Voight or somebody, and wondered how in the name of God he could think she was the woman for him.

Pretty, though, no doubt about that.

Shoulder-length blond hair, dyed, Fabe knew, but soft. Thirty years old, at least that's what she admitted to. Tight, firm body, maybe five-four or -five. Big rack. Soft brown eyes, with a little too many lines at the corners, from frowning, though, not from laughing.

Or from pouting. Bunny was good at pouting.

Fabe said to Bunny, "It's okay. Sorry I was rough.''

She patted his arm and immediately brightened, another point for her, as if love was a game of tennis. Shallow.

Bunny said, beaming, "'Sokay, hon,'' then lowered her voice, gave Fabe a knowing, loving look, and said, "But lay off the sauce, huh? Or you won't make it till closing time. I'm gonna get *mine* tonight.'' And she was gone, bouncing away, the tight white pocketless French jeans she was stuffed into jiggling in the ass as she put on a show for him and all the other men lined up against the bar watching. Prick-teasing little shallow bitch.

Married to Carmi Capaletti for four or five years, loving it, playing the gun moll to the hilt, enjoying the hell out of being mysterious and part of the in crowd, as if Carmi was ever anything more than a mid-level punk in Tommy Campo's crew who turned himself into the Witness Protection Program as soon as he'd learned that he was facing an indictment under the RICO act. And sang his lungs out. Bunny swore that she hated him, but she took every dime he had, and one time Fabe had sneaked a look at her phone bill and seen a string of collect calls she'd taken from a phone number in Newport, Rhode Island, which was where Carmi was reported to be hiding out in a federal safe house.

She'd taken to Fabe right away, and he wondered how long it would take her to tire of him. He'd seen her dump one guy, a con man, like a hot potato as soon as she got a look at Fabe. It was a matter of ego with him, pride, that he dump her first, before she latched on to some stud and dropped him, made him look bad. But a first-rate piece of ass, boy, Bunny was. And that had kept him around longer than he'd planned on staying. That and the fact that she was right there, he didn't have to go looking. He needed *some*body, for God's sake.

He called over one of her barmaids, who, thank God, didn't have to run around in a bunny outfit anymore, like they used to when Carmi was running the show. Hefner had raised hell when he'd heard about it, and Bunny had told him that Carmi had said, Fuck Hefner; he gave him any shit, he'd whack him out, just like that, like a real Bugsy Siegel or somebody. Playing to her Virginia Hill.

The barmaid brought him another drink, and as he raised it to his lips he saw Bunny out of the corner of his eye talking to one of the pool hustlers at the end of the bar, watching him. It made him feel good. He drained the glass, knowing she was watching, ignoring her now, and ordered another one, his mind on a little Puerto Rican doctor whose worst mistake in life had been greed.

He was over Bunny now, atop her, looking into her eyes, trying to see anything but lust there. Love, maybe? Concern? No, uh-uh, not this time. Nothing but lust, and selfish lust at that; instead of wanting to bring him pleasure, she was self-absorbed, as usual, into herself, moving her hips beneath him in perfect time to his thrusts.

He'd drunk oceans of Pinch, rivers and oceans and great lakes full, and still he was cold stark sober, at least in his mind. He'd taken a cab home and knew he was staggering, knew the cabdriver didn't understand a word he was saying and not only because the guy was Iranian or something. In a way, this was good, because Fabe had asked him if his wife wore veils and had a ruby in her forehead, and then had asked him if he owned a restaurant across the street from his house. The guy had looked worriedly into the rearview mirror and hadn't said anything until Fabe had pulled out his wallet and dropped a twenty on the front seat next to the guy, and had shown the guy his driver's license, which had his address on it. The guy had driven like a bat out of hell across the North Side, all smiles now, he was making something like a fifteen-dollar tip, and he'd even helped Fabe out of the cab and listened to some gibberish about the Black Hole of Calcutta and spitting cobra before he got back into his cab and tooled away thinking, Satan!

Fabe had gone into his apartment, not arming the alarm system Doral had insisted on, knowing Bunny would be dropping by later to Get Hers. Feeling crystal-headed still, totally sober, but knowing he was drunk, he began to wonder if maybe he was an alcoholic. He'd read somewhere in the joint that alcoholics often remain totally sober in their heads, but appeared to the world to be rip-roaring, shit-faced drunk. Christ, was this what was in store for him? No fun anymore, just hangovers and remorse?

He tried to read a book Doral had bugged him to buy, but the words kept slurring around on the page, so he turned on the TV and put in a movie video of the Leonard-Hearns fight, watching it over and over, until he heard the key in the lock and Bunny walked in, feeling no pain herself, and without a word she started to strip, doing a little bump and grind for him, holding the fur coat closed around her and doing a little two-step, then throwing it open, giving him only a shot of her fully clothed body, nothing more. He wondered what she'd do if he turned his attention back to the TV screen. But he didn't, and the show got better as Bunny removed a little more and then the rest, and by that time Fabe wasn't thinking about the so-called fight of the century anymore.

He watched now as she achieved orgasm, her eyes closed, her head rolling from side to side on the pillow, her face flushed and her little white teeth on the bottom biting into her top lip, chewing off lipstick.

"Doctor Bunny gonna make Fabey all okay," she told him, and made him remember Chacona, and he almost lost it. But he buried his face into her, taking his mind off it, ordering himself to for*get* it, and he told her, when she tried to say it again, to shut up.

He pounded into her, trying to hurt her, get some reaction that hadn't been planned and performed by Hollywood a million years before, trying to see the real her, but there wasn't one, there sure wasn't a real Bunny Capaletti, he knew now; she was all glitter and sizzle and no steak, and it wasn't her fault, it was just the way it was.

He gave her a little bit of knee for a while, not wanting just to pull out and roll over, not wanting her to think that he figured her for anything but the best piece of ass in the world, not wanting to tell her just yet that it was over.

He nibbled at her lips, and she breathed vodka onto his face, smiling, pushed him away and got up and went to the bathroom, her tight little ass shaking, putting on the show even now.

When he heard the shower running, he got up and staggered over to her purse, opened it, and took out her key ring. He removed the key to his apartment and the key to the outside door. He threw them in the top drawer of his dresser and got back into bed, his hands behind his head, staring at the ceiling, a cigarette dangling between his lips, trying to make his mind a blank.

The hangover was already beginning, and it was going to be a real pisser, he could tell.

He wondered about the other waitress, the girl across the street from the Iron Horse. Sally. That was it, Sally. Would she maybe want to go out with him, see a movie or something? He'd call her today, if the hangover wasn't too bad.

Bunny came out of the shower and surprised Fabe. She went to her clothes and began to dress.

He said, "Leaving?"

Bunny said, a look of concern on her face, the same studied, practiced-in-the-mirror look she'd shown him earlier in the bar, "I gotta, honey, I got a supplier coming in at seven, gonna give me a better deal on the top-shelf stuff."

Fabe wondered if this was true. He decided he didn't give a shit; was, in fact, a little glad. It was finished. Done with. No sense lying next to her all night, listening to her snoring. Since Joliet, he'd been a *very* light sleeper.

"See you," Fabe said, a little sadly.

Bunny looked at him and for a second the phoniness

dropped off her. He saw the real her, a frightened, scared young kid, not knowing who in the hell she was but knowing for sure what she wanted and how to go about getting it. She said, "You mad at me, honey?" And the mask was back on, she was probably already thinking about the next guy, if she wasn't heading out now to see him.

"No," Fabe said, not cold, not distant, but not friendly either.

"See you," Bunny said, and he knew it then, it was in her voice, too.

Fabe watched her walk, swishing, out of the room, giving him a last shot of what he was dumb enough to give up, her head high, flouncing it, really giving him the whole show.

What a shallow broad, he thought. Then wondered what that made him out to be.

8 Francisco Ortiz and Eldemiro Roga were walking down the ramp on Concourse B, heading into the main terminal, both of them looking around, amazed that any airport anywhere in the world could be so busy so late at night, even a few days before Christmas.

They were getting a few amazed looks themselves.

Francisco Ortiz stood five feet, seven inches tall, and weighed two hundred and six pounds. All of which was solid as chiseled stone. The suit he wore, and the topcoat over it, were designed, tailored, to show off his body. He had lifted hundreds of pounds of weights, thousands of times, over many years, and the result was as close to being grotesque as a man could come without being able to make a buck in a circus. He had fifty-two-inch shoulders, and just loved narrow doorways, so he could turn sideways, a look of impatience on his face, as if he didn't enjoy watching everybody checking him out.

The only things Ortiz did not like about his own appearance were his hair and skin coloring. He was so dark as to be almost a Negro, and the kinky waves on top didn't do much to make people think otherwise. He stayed out of the sun so he wouldn't get any darker.

When he walked, he swaggered, his face set in a perpetual

superior scowl, as if he absolutely hated being among inferior Americans, which wasn't far from the truth. He stepped out lively, with his toes pointed away from him, rolling his hips, twitching his shoulders, his arms hanging loosely, fists balled slightly, knuckles touching the outside edges of his open coat.

Eldemiro Roga would have passed for Zapata, if he'd been alone. Flat black hair hung straight down, almost to his shoulders, with a thick bandito mustache twirling down around the corners of his mouth. As they'd gotten off the plane, he'd lighted a small, twisted, ropy-looking cigar, and the passengers behind him had coughed their way hurriedly past him. He'd ignored them, looking around, trying to find the Italian pig, Roland DiNardo, who had promised to meet them when they landed. His clothing told anyone who looked their way that he was the inferior, the bodyguard, the lackey. His pants were a Picasso nightmare, white, with slanted browed eyes covering them. A ruffled red shirt, Beatle boots with zippers on the sides, an open leather Marquis de Sade ankle-length black coat. His black eyes were covered by aviator glasses with jet-black lenses. He looked suspiciously around them as they strutted slowly up the ramp, his eyes alert, vigilant, while Ortiz looked straight ahead, like a businessman.

Without a word Ortiz turned to his left, into the men's room, and Roga followed quickly, cursing silently, wondering how he was supposed to do his job when the man never told him what he was going to *do*. He followed Ortiz, watched as his boss strutted up to a urinal and busied himself there, looking straight ahead still. Roga stood with his back to Ortiz, ready to move in any direction to defend the man who paid the bills and kept him and his wife in white powder.

He heard a surprised grunt from Ortiz, and turned immediately.

Ortiz was staring at the urinal, shocked, a slight smile now on his thick lips. He began to chuckle.

"What's the matter?" Roga said.

Ortiz looked at him, did a Cagney with his shoulders, having fun, and pointed to the urinal. "Piss," he said.

"What?"

"Take a piss, Roga," Ortiz said, a little angry now, but still having a good time, about to show Roga the wonders of American technology.

Roga shrugged, stepped to the urinal and did as he was told, wondering what the fuck was wrong with the man now, in his ass. He'd been on the rag since he'd picked him up. He finished, put himself away, and as he was stepping away the urinal began to flush automatically, and he stared at it, surprised, and Ortiz began to laugh.

"See there?" Ortiz said. "Sloan Automatic Flushing System," he read, proud of being able to read English. He stepped to the urinal again, stepped away. It flushed. He stared in awe, shaking his head, looking at Roga, who had pissed against the wall of his dirt-floored bedroom for the first fifteen years of his life, and Roga looked as if he had seen a UFO. Slowly, slowly, he stepped toward the urinal, and then slowly moved away, and it flushed, and his face brightened, and he laughed aloud, a little crazily, then he stepped back again, then away, then he said, "How the fuck it do that?" And Ortiz showed him the red deep eye at chest level, like the doors in the big supermarkets, which opened and closed when he came close to them, showing off now that he had figured it out.

And that is how Roland DiNardo found them, Roga in his eyeball pants stepping forward and back in front of the pisser, Ortiz, the muscle-bound jerkoff, watching the urinal, both of them with a look on their faces as if they'd seen the image in Christ in a tortilla or something.

100

"Sorry I'm late," he said to Ortiz, then turned to Roga. "Trying to keep a low profile, huh?"

Ortiz turned to Roland, beaming, and said, "Piss."

"Jesus Christ," Roland was saying, "I go to the fucking C Concourse, where the overseas flights are supposed to land, after driving around for a half an hour in the fucking construction fuckup out here, Christmas travelers running around hugging each other, enough to make you puke, then a little nigger, glasses on, sunglasses, middle of the night, the jerkoff, I says to him, 'Hey, bro, where the hell's the Pan Am Flight 17 coming in at?' and he looks at me like I'm from outer space or something, standing there in his orange security blazer, trying to act like he doesn't work there, and he says to me, 'I ain't your bro, man.' And now I'm pissed off, I says to him, I goes, 'Okay, nigger, where the fuck is the plane coming in, or do I gotta splatter your brains against the fuckin' wall?'" He was pulling the new maroon Lincoln out onto the expressway now, heading for 294 South, which was the way home. He was wondering if he could pull off right here somewhere, in the dark, get the two of them alone outside and blow the shit out of them, get it over with, get them out of the way before they did something stupid and got him in a jackpot.

From the backseat, Roga said, "You got something against sunglasses?" Challenging, a threat in his voice.

"Not if you're like Jim McMahon or somebody, got a problem with your eyes, there, gotta wear 'em all the time." Wondering if he sounded like he was backing down, pissed off because he decided that that was exactly how he'd sounded.

"Hmm." A satisfied grunt from the backseat. A smug I-guess-I-showed-you grunt. He couldn't let that pass.

He looked over his shoulder hurriedly, hoping the beaner could see the flashing in his eyes from behind the glasses, and said, "Yeah, well, why don't you just kiss my ass?"

"That is enough," Ortiz said from beside him, and Roland turned to him.

"And *you*," he said. "I feel for you, I show you the respect of coming to get you so you can mourn your loss, but hey, Frank, I'm here to tell you, I ain't one of your flunkies, you got it? *That's enough*, that don't shut *me* up." He was on a roll now, feeling like the man he knew he was, a big shot, a made member of the Outfit. He squared his shoulders, waiting for an argument from Ortiz, but none came. The only sound he heard was the heavy labored breathing in the backseat. A little while later, approaching a toll booth, he heard the quick, sharp, double snort of the greaser back there putting some cola up his nose, and he thought, in-fucking-credible.

Jimmy Capone had gotten the phone call at home, telling him that a stiff Homicide had turned up had been positively identified as being one Lucille Ortiz. She was the sister of one of the biggest drug suppliers in the Chicagoland area, so the Homicide guy had tried to shoulder the murder off onto the Narcotics guys, since it was obviously a narcotics-related hit. Surprisingly enough, to the Homicide dick, at least, Jimmy took the weight right away.

He didn't think he'd ever see a drug war in the city as big as the last one, when Flukie Stokes got hit in '86, right before Thanksgiving. Stokes was a flamboyant, in-the-public-eye drug dealer who passed himself off as a gambler, a guy who had captured national attention when he'd buried his son in a casket shaped like a Cadillac Seville with thousand-dollar bills stuck between his fingers. When he'd been blasted half a dozen times with a shotgun, all hell had broken loose, and Jimmy thought he'd never live to see the likes of it again.

But Jimmy never thought anyone would be crazy enough to hit the sister of Francisco Ortiz, either, and he wasn't looking forward to the time when Francisco heard about it and came to town.

So he was shocked all to hell when, while sitting in the basement of the Chicago Morgue, waiting for the results of the postmortem on the girl's corpse, Ortiz, his pet cobra Roga, and Roland DiNardo strolled in like they owned the joint, arguing with the security guard at the door, demanding to be allowed to view the body of Lucille Ortiz. Jimmy tappped the elbow of the young Narcotics detective snoozing next to him, Terry "Tatum" O'Neil, and got up, thinking, boy, ain't this the grand prize.

He watched Roland DiNardo's face fall when he saw Jimmy approaching, scared now, no doubt about it, then putting on the tough front, a made guy, a wise guy. A tough guy. A punk. The two Puerto Ricans stared when DiNardo said something under his breath, and the three of them watched Jimmy coming, stony-faced now. Only thing was, DiNardo looked a little green around the gills. Jimmy walked right up to them, right in Ortiz's face, but did not acknowledge him yet. Instead he looked to DiNardo.

"Say there, Roland," Jimmy said, smiling, feeling Tatum right there next to him, "think Tommy Campo'd be interested in who you're chauffeuring around these days?"

DiNardo was playing it tough, trying to ignore him, but not a good-enough actor to keep his face from getting chalky as the blood drained from it.

Jimmy turned his attention to Ortiz, who was staring at him, bouncing on the balls of his feet, up and down, and Jimmy said, "Hey, amigo, that ain't gonna make you no taller," and Ortiz turned deadly ball-bearing eyes on him, and Jimmy said, "Your mule, she caught her lunch, this time. Somebody fucked her and busted her up, real bad. Too fucking bad, huh?"

"You pig!" Ortiz shouted, and Jimmy laughed back, baiting him, wanting Ortiz to hit him so they could roust all three of them, stir up a real hornet's nest, a mob guy busted with a known drug importer, that'd make nice headlines, and maybe put Roland DiNardo in deep shit with his bosses.

Jimmy said, "You don't need to identify the body, we got it okay from her prints, from when she was busted a few years ago, with the couple of joints in her purse, caught her sleeping with the nigger guy out in LA." And he looked down at the security guard sitting at his desk, a Chicago Police officer, moonlighting, big black guy, smiling at them, enjoying it. "Sorry," Jimmy said.

"No, you ain't," the officer said, encouraging Jimmy on with his eyes.

"My sister is not no *mule*," Ortiz said, and Jimmy laughed aloud again.

"My seester iz not no muu-ule," he mimicked. "Course not, I forgot, she's a monkey, like her brother, a black-assed, pink-palmed, dope-smuggling fucking monkey." This last he growled, moving right up into Ortiz's face, nose to nose.

Ortiz balled his fists, breathing in huge, gulping gasps, and Roland DiNardo was grabbing his right arm while his pet cobra, Roga, was pulling on the left, dragging him away from Jimmy Capone, and Jimmy was laughing, feeling O'Neil, all six feet, two inches and a hundred and ninety-five pounds of him, right behind him.

O'Neil spoke up. "Shit, I thought he was gonna make a play for you," loud enough for Ortiz to hear, and Jimmy raised his voice so Ortiz could not miss it.

He said, "*Him*?" incredulously, making fun of Ortiz, getting way, *way* under his skin. "He ain't got the fuckin' balls, the little deformed fuckin' monkey-ass *sissy*. . . ."

While Jimmy Capone explained things to Tatum O'Neil on the way back to Eleventh and State, telling him how sometimes you had to be a little *rough* with them, get them to fuck up . . . and while Fabe was tossing and turning, having nightmares . . . Doral Washington was wide awake, not even feeling anything from the past—what—nearly twenty-four hours since he'd been up.

He was sitting at his mahogany table, staring down into the entire 2.2 pounds of cocaine he'd hidden in his coat while Fabe was off in another world altogether, acting like a little kid. Hell, Doral could have slipped a couple more keys out of there, Fabe wouldn't have noticed a thing. He had the coke lying in a big white pile on the table, like that scene in *Scarface*, with Al Pacino, which was one of his all-time greatest flicks, so he'd split the bag open, see how it felt, be like Tony Montana.

It felt great, was how it felt.

There was just the slightest tremor in Doral's hands, but his eyes were blood-red, shot to hell, and he was tight-jawed, every muscle in his body taut, and when he breathed he took great, deep breaths, filling his body with oxygen. Every now and then, when he exhaled, an involuntary moan would escape.

Now he leaned forward and let his face drop right in the middle of the mountain of white powder, and his tongue snaked out and snatched a bit, going numb immediately, and Doral remembered not to giggle when it happened, or he'd blow a couple of grands' worth of shit all over his carpet, the way he'd done the first time. He snorted good and deep, then threw his head back, his muscles all bunched up, and the coke, it went directly to his brain, no fucking around, this was the best stuff he'd ever tasted, and it took him maybe thirty seconds before he could settle down, sure he wasn't going to die and go straight up to heaven from the greatness of it all.

He was thinking about stereotypes. How much bullshit it was to get a certain thing set in your mind as something, and then to have it shattered right to hell when you came face to face with the real thing.

Take his case, for instance.

A few years back, after he'd bought the house, made his scores with Fabe—who was a trip, a real, live trip—he'd had his first real taste of cocaine, and it had been love at first sight. Or taste, as the case may be. Shit, he'd snorted the white lady, and that'd been it. He no longer cared a whole lot for alcohol, or anything else. A little beer or wine, when he was out, so folks wouldn't take a guess, know he was off on his own little thing; just enough to whet the appetite. It was the lady he loved. And hell, he hadn't started shooting it, or mixing it with heroin for a better high. Yeah, he'd gone ahead and built up a tolerance for it, no doubt about it, he could take maybe three grams on a good day without overdosing. But it was still snorting the stuff that got him off every time. And he hadn't wound up a sniveling junkie, mugging old bitches for their welfare checks so he could snow it up. Uh-uh. It was a stereotype, that's all. Hell, he hadn't lost a thing. Maybe got a little slimmer, but that was admirable. Something to respect. Slim, trim, and mean, like a fucking black panther in the jungle. Fabe never even knew, because Doral had gone to great lengths to hide it from him. If Fabe found out that he was doing two, three grams a day, he'd do something stupid, like try and get him into a rehab center or something for addicts, maybe, or volunteer to stand guard over him while he went cold turkey in the weight room. Some dumb-ass thing. Well, shit, maybe he did get a craving for it from time to time, if he was running low. Maybe he did buy an ounce at a time these days, and miss meetings, lose out on a few things now and again, because he hadn't shown up to take care of business. Maybe he did take a snort or two, deep ones, before he filled his vial each time from the main stash, but what the hell, he'd done fifteen years, hard time down in Joliet, and that sure wasn't a day in the park, now, was it? Didn't he deserve a few of the pleasures he could find now that he was free and loaded with money?

And that was another thing he looked at from time to time when he really wanted to think about it. He needed the scores a hell of a lot more than Fabe knew about. Hell, house like his, the heating bills came to a grand a month, cost him a couple grand just to keep the door open each month, he wanted to eat right.

But Fabe, he wouldn't understand this. He'd figure Doral for a goner, and no matter how much shit he talked about being behind him all the way, Doral knew damn well Fabe'd have someone else in with him the next time out on a score. And who could look after Fabe better than Doral could? No one, that's who.

He could still punch a bag for hours at a time, even longer than before. Sometimes he would stay in bed all day, sleeping around the clock, but he never got a hangover from the lady the way alcohol had done him when he'd played around with it. Shit.

No, Fabe wasn't going to find out.

He thought about taking another good one for luck, but he wasn't one of those who'd argue that you couldn't overdose on cocaine. Uh-uh. He'd seen it. As a matter of fact, he'd had tracers himself, seeing things going by with light tails on them, people walking past, see forty or fifty of them swishing by behind them. Scared the shit out of him too. But he knew how to handle it now. See? He was putting the shit up, wrapping it all up in a garbage bag. The shit left on the table, the couple of grams, there, he'd start the day off with tomorrow.

He had to find a way to get the goddamn hiding place open by his own damn self, which wasn't going to be easy, as carefully as those round iron pieces had to be set down, but he'd find a way. And he could cut each gram up into ten. Sell it for a yard and a half himself, low-level, never sell more than an ounce, bring the heat down on him, put him back in the joint. He had ten million dollars' worth, if he cut it ten times, and even then they'd be flocking to his door. Hell, pure, uncut cocaine? He could cut it fifteen, twenty times, it'd still be better than most of the stuff on the street today, no problem. Say, eight million, not ten. He had to keep a couple of the bags for himself, sort of a lifetime supply. Was eight million enough to last him forever? You know good and goddamn well it would be, babe. More than enough.

And the good thing was, he'd never have to work again, stealing or trying to hustle guys who went to school to learn how to beat you out of your money, ever again.

The only fly in the jar was Fabe. If he knew Doral was turning the stuff over himself already, in little pieces, he'd shit his pants, what with his bro-ham being the Inspector of Narcotics over there at Eleventh and State, Police Headquarters for the entire fucking city. In charge of what, now, maybe fifty guys? Big shot. Well, if he thought about it too much, he'd get a headache. Better to go out to the all-night Walgreen's there on Division and get him the mixings to cut this stuff down a few steps or ten. He'd stay up tonight, weighing and cutting the first kilo, put it out on the street maybe later today, if he got up at all.

Grinding his teeth and not noticing it, moving in jerky starts, uncoordinated but thinking he was cool, Doral picked up one of the pistols he had taken out of the hiding place and had left on the table since. A .44 hogleg, aha. Fabe had taken a Smith & Wesson .38 and an Italian .380. Doral thought it was a Beretta but could not be sure. Maybe it was Berlinetta. One of them. The Smith he was sure of, a Police Chief Special, with the two-inch barrel, or was it four? Fuck it. He had the forty-four, with the kidskin holster. Take care of anything that came along. Wouldn't need no ankle holster for this one, like Fabe took for the .380. Just in case. 'Cause you never knew.

He strapped the pistol on to his right side, hitched it up

until it felt right, and went for a quick left-handed draw. Perfect. He shoved it back where it belonged, feeling it shake a little bit as he shoved it in. Hands shaking a little bit, but hell, it was almost dawn, now, and he'd gotten up with the dawn the day before. Twenty-four hours without sleep make anyone a little jumpy. And besides, this shit was grade-A number-one stuff. Five times stronger than what he was used to paying top dollar for.

He threw on his jacket, set the alarms, left the house and headed for his car, thinking how much fun it was to be a rich man. And if Fabe-babe gave him any shit about the dope, he'd just figure out a goddamn lie to tell him. Hell, he'd fallen hook, line, and sinker for the jive-ass fairy-tale soap-opera bullshit he'd laid on him earlier that night, hadn't he? Jesus, he was a nice guy, but dumb! It was a good thing, though, that Fabe didn't read a lot of books the way Doral did, or he might have figured out that it was bullshit. Hell, if he'd had a razor laid to his nuts as a little kid, would he be what he was today? Hell, no. He'd be some psycho, scared of his own shadow, probably married to some bitch old enough to be his momma, remind him of his old granny. With a straight job in some steel mill, sitting back wringing his hands while Reagan busted his union.

No, the fact was, in prison, it was the only way to stay sane, forget all about fucking. Not even jerk off, just let it die. And since he'd been out he'd had his share of girls, but he found hookers more to his liking than anything else, because they didn't demand anything. And since he'd fallen in love with the white lady, why, his sex drive had gone way, way down.

Doral figured it was worth it.

9 At noon Tuesday Fabe was sitting with his head in his hands at his kitchen table, waiting for the coffee to brew. In his right hand, between two fingers, a cigarette jerked shakily back and forth. He pulled on it from time to time, feeling his throat constrict and swallowing rapidly when he did so to fight off the vomit. He hadn't worked up the nerve yet to brush his teeth or to walk out onto the patio for his morning fresh air. The entire apartment stank of stale Scotch and tobacco.

Taking another drag, he noticed a slight wheeze in his breathing, not quite sounding like a railroad train, but working up to it, it wouldn't be long. He ran his left hand through his hair, felt the stubble on his face, and moaned. He'd eaten nothing since breakfast yesterday. Smoked a couple of packs of Pall Malls last night, put away maybe a fifth, fifth and a half of Haig & Haig Pinch. No wonder he felt like shit.

He heard the percolator quieting down, so he got up and poured himself a cup of strong black coffee, couldn't handle it, and went back for cream and sugar. Years ago, he'd worked his way through the morning after by pouring down spaghetti and ice-cold beer for breakfast. He'd given that up when he saw half a dozen cops that he admired slowly sink from the booze. And decided to tough it out when it came.

"Fuck . . ." he said.

It didn't help matters that he hadn't slept for shit, getting up every couple of hours to bounce around until he found the fridge, poured down a couple of cold Pepsis and staggered back to bed. The nightmares had been what had really done him in, though.

Doral driving, he in the passenger seat, down Chestnut, LaSalle straight ahead, leaving the score, the dead doctor, the chick in the trunk, millions in dope in the trunk, looking straight ahead at the Moody Bible Institute, across the six lanes of LaSalle, Doral making a quick right, down a block to Delaware, all this happening in super slo-mo, as Frank Gifford says. Barely moving his head, he turned to stare accusingly at Doral, the prick, who could have told him about it, could have given the option to him, at least, to get the hell out, but didn't. Delaware and Clark, Washington Street Park directly across the street now, concrete park, with chessboards built, poured right onto the walkway, cement benches, never disappear. Homosexuals hanging out, used to call it Homo Hill when they were kids. Look straight up, there's the Hancock Building rising up, guarding the fags. Doral turned right and they were passing the score, Fabe automatically scrunching down on the seat, as if anybody would be looking for them already. Doral grunting almost silently, or did Fabe imagine it?

Dumping the hot car, getting back into the clean car, driving back to Doral's, Doral going into the trunk for the goodies, but in the *dream* Fabe saw the top of the doctor's head back there, in the flight bag, a grisly souvenir for Doral, who was going to mount it or shrink it or eat it, Fabe couldn't figure it out from the dream, but when Doral opened the flight bag and took out the head and playfully tossed it to Fabe, he woke up every time.

111

Nothing made you look at your own life, Fabe was learning, like taking someone else's.

Get your mind off it. Get it out of your head. Think about something else.

Yeah, like Jimmy putting two and two together. Wouldn't *that* be grand.

It wasn't that cops were so smart, but that most crooks were stupid. Almost as if they *wanted* to get caught.

When Fabe and Jimmy Capone were working the Organized Crime Squad, Jesus, had he learned that the easy way. Go into any so-called mob hangout late at night, after the Scotch had been flowing awhile, seeing these so-called men of respect listening to Sinatra records with tears in their eyes, singing "Che La Luna" along with the jukebox. Hell, anyone with a big nose, a pinstripe suit, and wavy hair could have a few pops, listen to all the stories he wanted. Guys like him and Jimmy. As long as they knew the words to "Topolino, the Little Italian Mouse," they were in. Mob guys were big on Louis Prima and Sinatra. Buy a round, Jesus, hear all about how Michael "Web Toes" Persicana got whacked out, dumped in the lake.

But Jimmy, he was a smart one. Smarter than Fabe, that's for sure, who got caught with his hand in the cookie jar. Funny how things turned out sometimes.

Goddammit, get it outta your *head*!

Think about Bunny. That's it. Bunny. Lying in bed, under you, eyes squinched shut, tight, biting her top lip, looking funny that way, screaming, "Jesus, oh, God, dear God!" and not knowing if she was coming or praying. Mind always working, that one. Fine ass and nice tits, good in the sack. Thing was, Fabe needed more than that.

Tits and ass. It rang a bell. What had he heard, recently, about tits and ass? Jimmy, that's who'd said it, and it wasn't

112

like Jimmy to talk like that, unless he was kidding around, trying to get under your skin.

Like the time they were walking into the pizza place and Jimmy had held the door open for some monster of a chick in a tank top, no bra, her boobs jumping around in there like a couple of wrecking balls, ass the size of a dairy cow, short black hair cut in a man's style. "I don't need a man holding the door open for me," she'd said, snooty, a wiseass, as if men were beneath her. Jimmy'd said, straight face, looking up without a pause, "I only was doing it on accounta you're so fucking ugly," and—

He'd said it about the waitress, that's who.

Sally, her name was.

Fabe finished his coffee and got another, smoking one Pall Mall after another, trying to get back to normal. Maybe a run. That might do it. Then again, a run might well kill him, the way he felt. Give him a stroke or something. Heart attack. Maybe a big breakfast, eggs, bacon, ham, a little hot sauce to get things stirring around right. Talk to Sally, kid around with her a little, maybe get her to open up, go out with him, get his mind off the home invasion—

The murder . . .

—Have a few laughs, that's what he needed. A few laughs.

Hop in the shower, maybe brush his teeth for an hour or so, gargle a bottle or two of Scope, shave, he might look halfway presentable. Forget about the guns, too. That was Doral's idea. He didn't want to mess with them, get himself a few years in a federal joint if he got caught with one. Uh-uh. Leave them at home. Well, maybe take the ankle gun, the .380. You never knew when you might need that.

He took two showers, shaving and brushing his teeth between them. He brushed his teeth again after the second shower, still smelling sour whiskey, running water for a hot bath, looking into the steamed-up mirror, thankful that he couldn't see his eyes. It wasn't like in the movies, that's one thing for sure. Doral had pulled the trigger and the next thing you knew all kinds of liquids were spilling down the hallway wall, and the doctor, he didn't have much above his shoulders anymore. He'd avoided looking, had sidled by on the way out, trying not to look, but he'd seen it. Boy, had he seen it.

"Get your goddamn mind off of it," he shouted at himself, fighting the urge to put his fist into the mirror, the wall, some goddamn thing. Toothpaste and spittle dripped off the mirror as he looked at it now, distorting an image of himself. He was seeing himself with Crest dripping down his face, through the clearing steam. He gargled, and got into the tub, wishing he could cry like everybody else.

Soaking, thinking of Doral, wondering how much of the sob story Doral had laid on him was true. He'd told Jimmy Capone, just yesterday, that he only trusted one guy from prison. And that was true, he *did* trust Doral. If he ever got himself into a bind, into something really bad, Doral would be there, he knew. But he also knew that you did not spend fifteen straight years behind bars, and maybe twenty all together, out of forty years—half your life—behind bars, without learning that it was safer to lie than to tell the truth. Without deciding that every time you opened your mouth, you'd try and tell a lie. Better than facing up to the facts of life.

Hell, no convict was truthful, or they wouldn't be cons. One way or another, they all bullshitted, even if it was only themselves. Blaming the guy who busted them for their having to do time. How many times had Fabe heard some crazed convict hollering about what he was going to do to the officer who'd arrested him, or the judge who'd convicted him, or the prosecuting attorney—somebody, had to kill somebody, because they couldn't take the rap, they hadn't done anything wrong. They figured the only mistake they'd made was getting busted.

Fabe got out of the tub, not caring whether Doral had lied. The good thing was, Doral had said something, done something to try and patch the rift. That was what counted. Not how he'd done it. Bunny gone, out of his life. Rationalizing maybe his best friend's lies. All of a sudden, Fabe was feeling very, very alone.

He dressed in new tight jeans, loose enough to fit the gun around the ankle, though, without a bulge. Air Jordan shoes, two pairs of cotton socks to compensate for the cold. A woolen fleece sweatshirt, gray, with a hood. A brown leather bomber jacket with a heavy lining. Before leaving the house he clipped the .38 to his belt, on the inside, between his jeans and his underwear, making sure the safety was on. No sense in taking chances, right? Doral would not have insisted on his taking them if there wasn't a good chance he might need them. Maybe Doral wasn't being totally honest about other things, too. Maybe he was lying about his non-interest in the drug trade. Maybe, somehow, he'd known all along that the doctor was a mule, and what they'd find in the apartment. Maybe Doral even knew who they had stolen the stuff from, how vicious a guy they were dealing with. No matter, the pistols made him feel foolish anyway, like he was a kid again, playing James Bond in the alleys. Only this time, when you pulled a trigger on the bad guy, there wouldn't be any arguments about whether you'd hit him. Goldfinger wouldn't get up, dust himself off, and bitch about always having to play the bad guy. He saw Dr. Chacona's head come apart. Christ.

Fabe locked the door and set his alarm, and got the hell out of there before thinking about it all made him crazy.

• • •

She wasn't there. Gone already, worked six to two Monday through Saturday. Off Sunday. He learned this from the hostess, Katarina. She and her husband, Valentin, had worked their way over from Germany after the war and built their dream all by themselves, with their own two hands. Fabe envied them today.

He walked north on Clark, thinking about calling her but not ready to go home and try just yet, a little afraid to go into his own home, feeling safer on the street, kidding himself that he just wanted to breathe in some icy air, get rid of the hangover, but knowing better.

Morrie the newsguy was watching him approach, his wise eyes trained on him, sizing him up, no pigeon on his thumb today, eating corn out of his palm, but a flock of them were on the sidewalk next to the newsstand, picking at the goodies Morrie had thrown there for them.

"Fabe!" he said as Fabe came up to him and stopped, leaning against the stand with his left shoulder, relaxing, ready to shoot the shit.

"What's to it, Morrie?"

"Coupla guys stopped by earlier, asked if I'd seen you today, knew where you lived."

"Coupla guys? You know 'em?"

"Not from around here, I know that. One redheaded guy, pizza face, got a scraggly beard, best part about it the bebop little tuft of hair under his bottom lip, the only place it didn't look like shit. The other guy's black-haired, long, combed nice. Coupla fairies, I think, but big, tall, muscular guys, looked like they just come around from the gym."

White guys. Fabe was expecting blacks, Puerto Ricans, maybe Colombians. What did a couple of white guys want with him?

116

"Didn't say nothing?"

"Naw," Morrie said, giving Fabe the look, knowing better than to ask anything but trying to pick up what was wrong from the way Fabe was standing, the look on his face. "Just asked about you, like they was old buddies, wanted to get together with you for a couple of beers. Didn't leave no message. I told 'em you'd probably be by for your magazines today or tomorrow."

And Fabe looked around, seeing an old Buick rounding the corner, a red-haired guy driving, probably been hanging around since Morrie told them he'd be here today or tomorrow, wondering if he should take off, thinking, why? Who the fuck are they? Cautioning himself not to get paranoid.

"Here they come again," Morrie said. "They been driving around the block for a while, eyeing me up."

The redhead was trying to find a place to park, and Fabe could easily walk away now, just keep going down Clark, fuck 'em, but he was curious now, wondering who they were and what they wanted. If they were looking for trouble, they wouldn't have let Morrie see their faces. Would have found out where he lived, come there. This also told him that they were not pros. Anybody seeking to do business with him would know how to find him or Doral. Hell, they were easy to find.

Finally the redhead hit the brakes, and the black-haired guy hopped out of the car. This set up a chorus of horns behind him, but the guy driving ignored it, waiting until his buddy had crossed the street and was approaching Fabe, then taking off with a squeal of tires.

"Falletti?" the dark guy asked, smiling. Not looking for trouble, or trying like hell to convince Fabe he wasn't.

"Want something?" Fabe said.

"Man wants to talk to you."

"Lotsa men, they want to talk to me. I'm not big on talking."

The big guy smiled. "This guy, I think you'll want to talk to him."

Fabe decided he wasn't going to get a lot of answers out of this brilliant conversationalist, so he started jiving him. "You taking me for a ride?" he said, smiling, trying to get under the guy's skin and seeing him flush, the tough guy not knowing how to act in front of somebody he couldn't intimidate. He saw the guy in the Buick coming up now on this side of the street, must have gone only down to the alley and made a turnaround, pulling the Buick to the curb in front of the newsstand; Morrie eyeing the plate number, remembering it in case he needed it. The redhead got out of the car, flashers on, an impatient look on his face.

"Hey, Elmo, come on, we ain't got all day, huh?"

"Guy don't wanna come," Elmo said.

Lloyd said, "Well, for Christ's goddamn sake," and was walking around the car now, coming over, no-nonsense, opening his jacket so Fabe could see the pistol stuck in there, in the waistband.

"Buddy, Mr. DiNardo wants to see you, *now*." His hand was inside his jacket, resting on the pistol butt, and Fabe knew it was now or never, belt him one while he was still walking up, thinking he was in charge, then the other one, before the first guy picked himself up off the ground. He let it pass. No sense making a scene.

"Roland DiNardo?" he said, trying to look a little afraid, showing them some respect now. "Why didn't you say so?" Without another word he opened the back door of the car, watching the redheaded geek give the Prince Valiant guy a look, showing him how it was done, then head around to the driver's side, swaggering. Asshole.

118

Fabe winked at Morrie as the car pulled away, thinking about sticking his tongue out, then deciding against it. It would throw off his act, get him out of character. For something to do, he said, "So you guys work for Roland DiNardo, huh?" and saw the zit-faced geek square his shoulders. Damned if the guy didn't sit up a little taller. But neither one of them answered him.

"The security guy, he's scared shitless," Tatum said.

"It figures," Jimmy Capone said. "Got a murder in his building, the tenants, they're already paying twice as much as all the condo buildings around them that have never had a murder in them. They got to have something to say, somebody to blame. Never figure maybe the doctor there, he had it coming."

He turned to the other two detectives in the room, Vincent Dodd and Martin Christovic. "Hear anything from the stakeout?"

Dodd answered for both of them. "Johnson and Parnell are watching the Holiday Inn on Michigan. Neither one of the beaners showed their face all day. Bielak and Olaf are over at DiNardo's, seen a couple of guys go in this morning, late, and come right back out, ten, fifteen minutes later. You get any sleep?"

Jimmy said, "A little." He turned to Tatum. "How about you?"

"A little. Jesus, kids get up early though, you know? Even on Christmas vacation. Think they'd sleep in, try and get it while they can. School days, you gotta blow 'em outta bed with a hand grenade. Weekends and vacations, they get up with the birds."

"Roga and this big shot, Ortiz, they're probably in mourning, not shaving, making arrangements to ship the girl back home." He sat back and thought about it, knowing there were six or seven ways in and out of the Holiday Inn, deciding the stakeout there was a mistake. "Call them in, Johnson and Parnell. They're spinning their wheels."

They were in the Narcotics Division squad room at the Central Police Headquarters at Eleventh and State, a newer building with modern, cream-colored walls instead of the institutional green-colored, paint-peeling, filthy walls they were used to from the precincts. Half a dozen desks were scattered around the room, Jimmy's the farthest from the door. It was the only sign of his status among the men, but they all knew who the boss was.

The men were arrayed around his desk, Dodd standing, Christovic sitting straight in a wooden back chair with a crocheted cushion his wife had created for him, filled with feathers. O'Neil was lounging, drinking hot black coffee from the percolator on the table in the corner. A couple of dozen rolls from Dunkin' Donuts were next to the coffeepot, unopened. He'd brought them in after twelve noon. A bad time for sweets around the squad room. Jimmy swallowed the rest of his cream-and-sugared coffee, waking up, trying to think of what he should do now, what moves to make. He was bound and determined not to allow Ortiz to leave the city without pinching him. He couldn't let that happen. But what had he done, so far, really?

His sister had been brutally murdered, maybe raped. He'd busted Ortiz's balls for him last night at the Coroner's Office, the morgue, baited him, and now he wondered if that had been such a smart move. He should just have brought Ortiz in for questioning. Which was what he'd have Johnson and Parnell do, as soon as they reported back in, warmed up a little, had some coffee and doughnuts.

Crime-scene boys had found nothing at all. No sign of tampering, break-in, no telltale little marks around the doorjamb or any of the locks. But, shit, a guy blows his own head off with a heavy-duty piece like that, how likely is it that the piece'd fall within a foot of his hand? Not likely. Piece like that, he'd seen it wind up clean in another room. And if the guy, this doctor, Chacona, was planning to do himself in, why the hell did he stuff the broad's body in the trunk like that? Hell, she'd over-dosed, they had the report on that. And if the doctor was so overcome by grief that he had decided to do himself in, why the *hell* didn't he do it *before* he stuffed her in a trunk? Doing that seemed to Jimmy as if he'd had a plan of action.

Maybe Ortiz had come in and learned, nuh-uh-uh, quit grabbing at straws, Ortiz hadn't landed at O'Hare until almost eight hours after the first unit had responded to a shots-fired call at the address. He couldn't have offed the doctor.

All right. It had to be only one of two things. Either the doctor had decided to get rid of the body, going all the way so far as to have his car parked at the service entrance, then had decided that there was no place to run, no place to hide, and so thinking, killed himself with a powerful handgun, holding it sideways with his left hand and blowing his head off, and the gun then dropping inches away, which was un-fucking-likely. Or someone had come upon him while he was about to dispose of the—

Wait a minute here, just one goddamn minute.

Jimmy pulled the personal-effects envelope to him, his mind shut in now, not hearing the talking the other guys were doing, focusing only on the long brown envelope in front of him now, in his hands, turning it over, spilling it all out in front of him on the desk. Watch, wallet, $317.16 in his pockets, and—there it was—the keyring. Uh-huh, just as he'd thought. He grabbed the reports, every one of them, including the crime-scene photos, the hallway and fire-stair shots, and studied them carefully. He looked up.

"We got there, last night—hey, *Tatum*, listen up!" O'Neil, getting another cup of coffee, turned quickly at the inspector's voice and came back to the desk. "We got there, yesterday, anybody say anything at all about the elevator, being open, or even on the floor?" He knew the answer already but wanted to hear somebody validate his thought.

O'Neil looked away for a little while, focusing on how the place had looked the night before, then shook his head. "Uh-uh. The security guy, he said everything was normal, and I remember asking him specifically about the elevator, account of I couldn't figure out how the beaner was planning to get the chest down thirty stories."

Jimmy frowned. "Then the murder-suicide's out. Ain't no elevator key on this ring, wasn't in his possession, and even a spaced-out junkie wouldn't think about carrying that thing down all those stairs, uh-uh. Somebody came in, broke up the doctor's play. Now all we gotta figure out is who." And he was off again, remembering lunch yesterday, after the playing around was all done, when things got a little serious, Jimmy ready to leave, Fabe smoking one cigarette after the other, nervous, smart enough to know Jimmy knew something was up, telling him, what did he say, "After tonight it's all over," or something like that?

"Jesus Christ," Jimmy Capone angrily spat out. "God-*damm*it!" Hoping he was wrong, hoping he was being stupid, hell, not Fabe, he didn't even carry a *gun*, for Chrissakes, but knowing he couldn't pass it up, he turned to Dodd and Christovic, who were sitting there looking at him as if he were insane. He guessed he might well look as if he were.

"Get over to the Armitage Building," he told them. "Pick up a guy named Fabrizzio Falletti, get his ass in here for questioning." Seeing their looks, the quick, sudden glances they shot each other, all of them except O'Neil, who was staring at him, Jimmy said, "Hey, *now*, huh?"

"Jimmy?" O'Neil said, and Jimmy looked up from his coffee, into which he'd spent the last three minutes staring. "Listen, I just want you to know, I mean, I know how it is, all right? I had a partner once, got into some—"

"Just watch it now," Jimmy said, knowing O'Neil was embarrassed by this in the first place and just trying to make him feel better, but it wasn't any of his business.

"Yeah, you're right, okay," O'Neil said. "I only meant, I know how it is, is all." And he stood up, left the desk, went into the men's, and Jimmy sat there staring at the closed door, thinking, You honestly think you do?

Remembering Fabey, knowing him like a brother, for Chrissakes, growing up with him, watching him get wilder and wilder after his ma died, the old man drinking himself into a grave a few years later when Fabe and he were in Nam, doing their thing for God and Country and Nixon. Sheesh. What a mixup that thing was. Jimmy had seen himself as the only influence over Fabe after his ma died, the only thing that kept him from going over the edge into full-blown criminal activity, not knowing until years later, after Nam, that Fabe had been a mugger, a smash and grabber, long before he'd smartened up and joined the Army with Jimmy. "Why the fuck I wanna be a cop, Jimmy?" And he'd answer, "Lookit, a few years from now, you got twenty in, you'll thank me." And Fabe took the exam mostly for him, as a buddy, doing better than all but three guys out of a class of seven hundred in the Academy. Fabe showed a real feel for police work, making plainclothes three years later, a couple of months before Jimmy had, even.

Jimmy remembered being best man at Fabey's wedding. Godfather to Fabe and Anita's first kid.

Seeing Fabe in anguish, banging his head against the bar, crying like a baby when he found out that his daughter, Tina, little Anita, had cancer, *cancer,* for God's sake, an old man's disease, not a *baby's.* Fabe spent every minute at home with the baby, calling in the best doctors from out East, guys who specialized in this thing little Tina had, hoping for a miracle, going nuts, seeing the kid waste away. And splitting with Anita, getting separated, when she wouldn't let Fabe take the kid to the Philippines to see a faith healer who was supposed to *rub* the cancer right out of your body. Fabe hated Anita after that, not even sitting with her at the wake, not comforting her like he should have. Then after the funeral, not two days later, before Fabey even came back to work, goddammit, there they were, Captain Jacobs, from right next door now, good old Abe Jacobs, the cocksucker, grabbing him out of a bar, throwing Fabe up against the wall, calling him filthy names, saying that a dirty cop, a cop on the take, his kids had no *right* to live, served him right, and Fabey'd smashed him right in the mouth, busted out six teeth, one punch, God bless him. But the other guys, Jacobs's crew from the OPS, the Office of Professional Standards, who made their living hunting down and throwing cops into the can, grabbed Fabe and kicked the shit out of him. And he'd been held without bond because seven witnesses had heard him tell Jacobs, as they dragged him cuffed from the bar, that he'd kill him the second he got bond, the *second,* and that had been it. The old Gang Crime Unit had been disbanded. They'd been watched for years, and all the guys knew it, but Fabe'd been desperate, he'd needed money to pay for all the doctors, all the specialists. . . .

And Jacobs, to this day, was harassing Jimmy, trying to make *him* look bad, playing tough guy whenever he could, and Jimmy telling him, come ahead and check me out, you son of a bitch, just like that, not pulling any punches. He had nothing to fear from the OPS. But God, did they know how to make your life miserable. Checking you out, having dates and times you were in Joliet, visiting a lifelong friend, making smart-ass remarks in the hall about Jimmy's safeman buddy, the guy he goes to football games with all winter, shit like that.

Jimmy-looked at the closed bathroom door, envisioning O'Neil in there, sitting on a stool, his pants up, just letting off steam, making it worse by just not letting it go like he should have. He stared at the door, awe in his eyes, wondering how anyone, especially a cop, could think he knew how it was for anyone else, unless he'd been there himself.

"You know how it *is*, huh?" Jimmy said to the closed door. "Bull*shit* you do."

Fabe sat in the back of the Buick, squirming, knowing that the two tough guys—desperadoes, they probably figured themselves for—were thinking he was scared, what with all his shifting around. What it was, though, the goddamn gun was cutting into his balls.

The gun Elmo held, though, was pointed into his face.

He was wondering what Roland DiNardo wanted with him, and getting a terrible flash, thinking, the mob's into coke now. He fought off that crazy idea, taking it one step at a time. If he was a suspect, these guys, they'd have roughed him up some. Wouldn't have let Morrie get their license number, either. Morrie'd made it obvious, clocking them, hard, making sure he could pick them up out of a lineup. Fabe saw the driver, whom Elmo had called Lloyd, checking him out in the rearview, chewing gum slowly, a badass, an in-control look in his eyes. Smiling at him, maybe laughing at him.

"Since when does DiNardo use free-lancers?" he asked, trying to put them in their place without pissing them off too much. At least he could let them know he guessed them to be less than gangsters.

"Makes you think that?" Lloyd said, shifting a little so he could see Fabe a little better. Some of the humor had left his eyes.

"Way you're dressed," Fabe said, keeping it light, not pushing it too much. "You ain't wearing pin-striped suits, for one, and no spats. No violin cases. And this car, let's admit, it ain't exactly a new DeVille now, is it? And no garlic, man. The last time I was in a car with some guineas, I smelled garlic on me for two fucking *days*." There. That should do it.

Surprisingly, Elmo laughed. Not a hearty, full-out gut-buster, but enough to let Fabe know he'd got a kick out of him.

"Hey," Lloyd said, "I'm an Italian, so knock off that shit."

"Yeah, where you from, the North? Maybe Ireland or someplace, northern Italy? With that red hair, yeah, you gotta be from the Northland." Elmo was cracking up now, looking at Lloyd.

"What's your name, O'Donnelly-inino or something?" And Fabe was laughing like hell now, enjoying himself. Elmo, in the front seat, turned to him, the gun held loosely, his eyes tearing, turned away to look at Lloyd and there it was, the perfect opening; at least let DiNardo know he wasn't playing with a fool. And he plucked the gun out of Elmo's hand. He saw the laughter die in Elmo's eyes, and God, did he look scared, so Fabe said, "Calm down, Elmo, Jesus, the way you were laughing, I was afraid you were gonna accidentally blast me."

Lloyd was moving his hand toward his coat, and Fabe tapped him lightly on the right ear with the pistol he'd taken from Elmo.

"Both hands on the wheel, *paisan*," he said, and looked at Elmo, to see how he'd appreciated the little dig, but Elmo was

126

staring through the windshield, looking ready to break into tears. . . .

"You shouldn't a done that," Lloyd said, pissed. "Mr. DiNardo ain't gonna like that one bit."

"Real slow like, you take the pistol outta your pants, there, and hand the thing to me by the barrel," Fabe said, and cocked Elmo's pistol and put it right in the middle of Lloyd's neck, in case he got any ideas. He took the second pistol and sat back, feeling better now, more comfortable. The hell with these two cowboys, although, he had to admit, he liked Elmo a little. Kid had a sense of humor, at least. He said to Lloyd, "You know, now that I think about it, Lloyd?" And the kid looked back, his eyes blazing in the mirror, his face red, looking like he was having a stroke. "All of a sudden, Lloyd, your side of the car, it's starting to smell like pussy."

And then it happened, and Fabe was surprised again.

Elmo smiled.

And the smile grew even broader when, at DiNardo's comfortable home on North Astor Street, Fabe drew Elmo aside and handed him both pistols. "No sense getting the man mad at you, huh?" he said to the kid, who was grinning, saying, "Thanks, hey, Jesus Christ, thanks," and Fabe told him, "Don't give Pizza Face his until I'm gone though, okay?" and Elmo saying, again, "Thanks, Jesus, thanks a lot," and not realizing that they had forgotten to pat Fabe down.

Fabe knew from way back, since he'd been held in the Cook County Jail without bond, that to show weakness was to die. This philosophy had been strengthened in Joliet, where the stronger preyed on the merely strong, and the weak were turned out to trick for cigarettes. He'd seen a kid one time, seventeen years old, in for stealing about a hundred cars, get turned into a bitch his first night in, no testing, no checking him out. No, the cellmate, he'd simply knocked the shit out of the kid, young skinny white kid, and made him tie his prison shirt around his young scrawny chest, like a Jamaican woman, or something, and he put makeup on him, told him he had to grow his hair, and started selling him, after teaching him, personally, the right and painless way to suck a dick. The kid, he'd tried for protective custody, asked for a transfer, and the captain, he'd told him, he wouldn't even tell the warden about it. Not when the kid looked like he was enjoying it so much. And the kid, he'd hanged himself one night, the night screw had found him when he wasn't in his cell after supper count, looked in the shower, and there the kid was, hanging, black tongue and all.

No, Fabe knew about showing fear. Show a con your ass, and he'd take him some. It was as simple as that.

And so he showed Roland DiNardo respect, which was customary with Outfit guys who could make a phone call and have you whacked out, but he showed him no fear, either. He played him like an equal, there in his den with his leather books and his blazing fireplace, middle of the afternoon, sitting there giving Fabe the eye, trying to scare him.

"Hey, Roland," Fabe said, "we gonna talk about something, or you just have these guys here pick me up so you could stare at me all afternoon?" Smiling a little, letting him know he was just shitting him, but didn't appreciate being plucked off the street like a pimp.

"Siddown," Roland told him. Fabe shrugged, looked around, then seemed to notice the big wingback chair directly in front of the desk, across from DiNardo. He sat down and crossed his legs, reached into his shirt and pulled out a cigarette, just one, and his lighter. He lit it with steady hands, thinking, Good, thank God, and put the lighter back. He wanted DiNardo to get used to seeing him using his hands, going into his jacket. He thought about reaching into his inner jacket

128

pocket for his comb, zipped into the bomber's lining, then decided that would be pushing it too much.

"Nice place you got here," Fabe said, trying to get the ball rolling.

"You been here before," DiNardo said.

"Yeah, but that time, I had other things on my mind, couldn't check out the decor, you know? Too many guys with guns, wondering should they kill me or not."

"Lloyd, get Mr. Falletti a drink," DiNardo said, and Fabe sat back and relaxed, at ease for the first time. Roland DiNardo wasn't smart enough to play Sicilian with you, get you relaxed, give you a drink, then blow you away. Roland DiNardo, he was mad, would just stick you into the big fireplace over there, watch you burn to death. Might even eat you.

"Scotch," he said to Lloyd. "Haig & Haig Pinch, if you got it." And Lloyd almost stopped on his way to the bar, almost, he was so pissed, but not that pissed, remembering the incident in the car, knowing that if he pushed it too far, this guy might tell the boss about it. He kept going, made the drink, and brought it to Fabe. Fabe took a sip, a small one, his pinky extended, playing the guinea for DiNardo's sake. He spit the whiskey back into the glass, turned to Lloyd, an angry look on his face, his eyes sparkling.

"Jesus, Lloyd, what are you trying to do, get me drunk?" He held the glass out and looked away. The king to the servant. "Put a little more water in here, Jesus," and he held it out, for a long time, before it was taken from his hand, and it was then that Roland DiNardo laughed.

Elmo joined in, enjoying Lloyd's humiliation, seeing the back of Lloyd's neck redden up, and Fabe remembered how the hair on the back of Lloyd's neck had stood straight up when he placed the pistol against it. He knew he'd already pushed the guy as far as he ever had to; if the guy had any balls, they'd be tussling on the carpet right now.

Instead of that, Lloyd slammed the drink down on the bar and stalked out of the room, not daring to mutter under his breath in DiNardo's presence but thinking some pretty dirty things, Fabe guessed.

DiNardo said, "Elmo?" And Elmo was right there, picking up the drink, adding a splash of water, bringing it over and presenting it to Fabe, and Fabe took it, sipped it, and made an O with his thumb and forefinger.

"Perfect," he said.

"Go calm down Lloyd, Elmo," DiNardo said, and Elmo was gone, out the door, and it was just Fabe and DiNardo now, getting down to it.

10 Dale Bielak was sitting in the unmarked Plymouth, cold and angry, knowing it would do no good to beef about it in front of John Olaf. Olaf was a born-again Christian and accepted everything as being God's will for him. He never complained, not even sitting in a green junker of a car with the engine, and therefore the heat, shut off, on a stakeout waiting for God-knew-what to happen. Bielak knew that if he did say something about his ass being half frozen off, Olaf would simply look at him with his maddening, serene smile, then talk some nonsense about having lessons to learn. So Bielak kept his mouth shut, at least for a while. Until the two big monsters whom they'd seen leaving earlier drove up with Fabrizzio Falletti. Then he had to say something.

"One of us got to get to a phone. Report this in. You *do* know who that is, don't you?" And Olaf had surprised the hell out of him, turning to Bielak as if he were nuts.

"You care to call the inspector, Dale, and tell him his best friend is having a sit-down with this mobster? Put it in the report, and we'll naturally tell them if they call in. Our job is to sit here and watch who comes and goes, not to look for trouble."

They watched, halfway down the street, slouched down in

131

their seats, as Fabe handed Elmo two pistols, smiling and joking with him, as if they were old buddies. "Hey," Bielak said, concerned now, "we got a convicted felon in possession of a firearm."

"Listen, Bielak, why don't you go arrest him, try and get him a couple of years in a federal prison, maybe blow the whole thing. I don't know the reason we're here, I don't know what the inspector wants, but if we're here, it means drugs. And I don't think anyone will be happy with us blowing our cover, making a rinky-dink firearms arrest." He was silent again, watching.

Lloyd came out of the house from the side entrance, the same way they'd been in and out all day. He kicked at the tires of his Buick a couple of times, obviously angry. "You make that guy?" Bielak said.

"The only ones I'm sure of, so far today, are Roga and Ortiz, and of course Falletti."

"Wonder what the beaners want?"

"*That's* obvious. The question is, what do these dopers want with Falletti?"

"You think he's in on it?" Dale Bielak was warming up to it now, enjoying the conversation. Olaf was finally acting like a cop instead of a Sunday-morning television preacher. "You think DiNardo's taking a chance, getting whacked out, to push drugs, and Falletti's in on it?"

"Time will tell."

They watched Elmo come out of the side entrance now, come up to Lloyd and talk to him with a lot of hand waving and obvious pleading, watched him take a pistol out of his coat pocket and hand it to Lloyd.

"Jesus Christ," Bielak said. "All the guns changing hands here, the feds would have a field day with it." It seemed like Olaf was finally opening up, being a regular guy.

132

John Olaf turned to Bielak. "Could you," he said, "kindly refrain from taking the Lord's name in vain?"

And his stock dropped once again with Bielak.

Lloyd had been feeling hurt, rejected, confused, generally *pissed*. All this time, he'd been the one in charge, the leader of the two-man team, the one who made all the moves, did all the talking, the sucking up, the one who'd caught the eye of Roland DiNardo, who everybody knew was a big-time mafioso. And suddenly, out of a clear blue sky, that ass-kisser Elmo was the fair-haired boy to DiNardo. It was Elmo DiNardo had called that morning, not Lloyd, and that really whacked him out. All of a sudden, Elmo was coming to him, telling him that Mr. DiNardo had wanted them this morning. What had happened? For one thing, the big wimp had kissed DiNardo's ass last night. "I didn't do nothin' to deserve the money, Mister Big Shot Mobster DiNardo," he'd whined, instead of grabbing the money like he was supposed to. If it wasn't for him, Lloyd, Elmo would still be hustling pool, selling a little dope on the side, getting his ass busted again, instead of being in the employ of a big-time wise guy. And how does he pay him back? He stabs him in the back. Lloyd wondered if Elmo had told DiNardo about Lloyd only paying the cop twenty-five dollars last night. It would be just like him, doing something like that.

Lloyd walked out of the side entrance of the house, seething with resentment. And another thing. Since when do they have to come in the side door, like the help? Didn't DiNardo want his bodyguards to see them? Was he ashamed of them? Then into the house, late that morning, not even a hello or a cup of coffee, just an order. "Go pick up Fabe Falletti," as if they were supposed to know who the hell this character was.

Lloyd kicked out at the tires of his Buick, thinking about Fabe. Not only had he gotten the drop on them in the car, taken their pieces, he'd made Lloyd look like a kid in there, prick, ordering him around, talking down to him. Well, Lloyd was sure looking forward to meeting with Falletti again, alone, without Elmo around to mess things up for them.

And speaking of his black-haired pretty-boy ass-kisser sidekick, here he came now. . . .

Elmo knew that everyone thought he and Lloyd were tight, brohams, asshole buddies, and that irked him. They'd known each other in the joint, helped each other out of a couple of tight jams inside, even had shared an apartment for a while when Elmo had first gotten out and was broke. What the world didn't know was that Elmo hated Lloyd's guts.

Lloyd hung around AA meetings, and Narcotics Anonymous Meetings, and Parents Without Partners meetings, he'd even been to a couple of Emotions Anonymous meetings. Lloyd would look for the sickest, shakiest alcoholic or drug addict or single mother or emotional wreck, a woman who was fighting to hang in there, struggling to get by, and there Lloyd'd be, with his big muscular macho act. "I'll take care of you, darling, let me help you." And before you knew it, Lloyd had another lady on the street, making him a few bucks.

And when they freaked, when they crashed and burned and wound up in a detox or a psycho ward, Lloyd would drop them and move on to fresh stuff. Lloyd had once offered Elmo a shot at a young shaky kid fresh out of a rehab center, whom Lloyd had bullshitted into falling in love with him, and that had been it; Elmo had split, disgusted, getting his own place and not even giving Lloyd the number for a while, avoiding him for a month or so. But then again, Lloyd was a lot smarter than Elmo was, and Elmo had trouble surviving without Lloyd helping him out, getting him scores set up, throwing him a few bucks just for being his friend. And Elmo had to admit, this thing with Di-Nardo was a plus, a real star on the old report card.

What Lloyd didn't know was that Roland had told Elmo to kill Lloyd.

He'd offended Roland's honor the previous night by lying to him, outsmarting himself for a few dollars when there were obviously thousands to be made here, maybe millions. And so Roland had told Elmo this morning in the study that sometime this afternoon he wanted Lloyd to catch a serious case of lead poisoning.

Elmo knew how to do it, was even looking forward to it. The problem was, Lloyd was smart. He had Lloyd's gun right now, and knew Lloyd would ask for it back. If he gave it back without the bullets in it, then he'd be in deep shit if Lloyd opened it and checked, which he just might do. Lloyd was no dummy. He'd known something was wrong the minute Elmo'd come over and told him Roland had called him instead of Lloyd. He might even be figuring that Elmo was supposed to do something to him. Best to play it straight, until the right moment came.

He watched Lloyd kick the tires of his car, like a little kid throwing a temper tantrum. He smiled, tried to look humble, and said, "Hey, Lloyd, come on, man, what's wrong with you, the guy was only playing around." And now Lloyd was in his glory, he had an audience he didn't have to back his words up with. He could rant and rave, play the badass, and Elmo listened.

"Calm down, man, you looked bad, letting that guy get to you in front of the boss."

"Oh, he's the boss now, huh? He told me last night he wasn't my boss."

"Lloyd, come on. Listen, I know a place, over on the

Lake, these young bitches hang out, no matter what the weather, take their dope. Let's go over there, see what we can get.''

"What about the guy, there, Falletti, or whoever?''

"Hey, let him walk.''

Lloyd said, "You got my piece?'' And Elmo wondered if he'd overplayed it, because Lloyd sure did look suspicious. He handed over the piece and said a silent prayer of thanks when Lloyd broke it open, checked the load.

"Hey,'' Lloyd said, "is that an unmarked squad down there?'' And Elmo turned, looked cautiously at the green car halfway down the block. The engine off, no exhaust fumes, but he could make out a couple of figures in the front seat, hunching down. When he turned back to Lloyd, Lloyd was zipping up his jacket, having put the pistol down his waistband, like always. "Let's get out of here,'' he said.

Five and a half years back, when he'd been six months out of prison and making a good buck for himself with Doral, Fabe had been summoned to the DiNardo mansion. And not for conversation.

DiNardo had been there, but not behind his desk; he'd been standing at the bar, playing the host, serving the drinks to his bosses. Tommy Camponaro, aka Tommy Campo, had been behind the desk, sitting there like God or somebody, watching them all with a look of amused contempt. Angelo "Tombstone'' Paterro had been there, Tommy's underboss, who was also DiNardo's direct superior.

"What you gonna have?'' DiNardo had said, like Fabe would be doing him a favor by having a drink with him.

"Nothing, thanks,'' Fabe had said, trying to act cool, like he spent every day in a room the size of the Hilton lobby, shooting the breeze with three mob guys and six bodyguards.

136

"We've had our eyes on you," DiNardo said.

"I've crossed no lines." And Fabe knew this was true. He had never robbed anyone who had a connection with organized crime. He had even steered away from a couple of potential scores simply because the people had an Italian surname and he was taking no chances.

"No, no, no, listen, Fabe, there's no problem." And Di-Nardo was smiling, showing him what a friend he was. "Listen, Fabe, we admire your work. You got to know, you can't fence anything in this city, from TV sets to hot ice, without our people knowing about it. Your name, and your partner's name, the shine, we've had them for months now. The reason you're here, Fabe, is we wanted to tell you, from now on, you're working for us."

Fabe had fleetingly considered laughing, to show them what he thought of that idea, but it is hard to laugh when you are scared shitless. He took his time, his mind racing to figure a way out, knowing that if he gave them an inch, they'd own him. He had to say no to them in a way that would let them think that their honor had not been damaged. As if you could put honor in the bank or on the table.

"Doesn't Doral get a vote?" he said.

"The spade? Why? You're the brains, he'll do what you tell him."

"Mr. DiNardo—"

"Hey, call me Roland."

"Roland, as far as I'm concerned, I've never been here. This didn't happen. I'm gonna leave now, Roland, and that's the end of it, as far as I'm concerned."

Roland DiNardo colored, and was getting ready to yell something when Tombstone spoke up, in a calm, reasonable manner.

"You don't even want to hear our offer, Fabe?"

137

"No, no, thanks, because, all due respect"—Fabe turned now to Tommy Campo, who hadn't said a word, and nodded his head, and Campo nodded back, like a king acknowledging a subject—"what's mine is mine. I go out of my way to make sure I don't step on any of your people's toes. I stay out of some places I could make ten times what I get in an average night, just because the people there got a connection. I don't want trouble, but what's mine is mine, and if I wanted to work for anybody else, I'd go into security. I've been offered a job with a big security company, but I don't want it." He shut up, hoping his reference to the security outfit would imply that maybe Jimmy Capone had gotten him the job.

He knew he'd hit a nerve, because Tombstone said, "Your old partner, Capone. He come up to see you in the joint like we heard?"

Fabe shrugged. "I've known him a long time. Yeah, he came up."

And he'd been excused. He waited in the foyer by the front door, three of the bodyguards standing there ignoring him. He was another job, that's all. If they were told to kill him, they'd whack him and go eat a big lunch. No reason to get to talking, maybe feel bad about having to kill him. Fabe knew this and did not hold it against them. He'd only hoped that if they killed him, Jimmy and Doral would avenge him.

Twenty minutes, and another guard had come out, told him he could go. He'd gone. And heard nothing since.

Now, sitting in the leather chair, lighting another Pall Mall, he wondered if he should bring up Lloyd and Elmo. No, better to keep his mouth shut, not pry. He still did not want to anger DiNardo. He sipped his drink and waited, getting the stare from DiNardo, thinking, asshole.

"Fabe, I'm calling in a favor."

"What favor's that, Roland?"

"Few years back, you *do* remember, don't you?" And Fabe nodded. "Well, Tombstone, he wanted to waste you, and Tommy Campo was on the fence, thinking about the guys on the force still liked you. I was the deciding vote, told them, as long as your business did not interfere with ours, well, this is still a free society, right? I mean, we are not Communists!" And he laughed, and Fabe knew, right then, that it was all a lie.

DiNardo was playing it too cool, too much the big shot. That had been right out of the movie *The Godfather*, and Fabe decided DiNardo was trying to tell him that he was more powerful than he actually was, as if DiNardo's opinion carried big weight with Tommy Campo. But he kept his mouth shut, didn't even try to thank DiNardo. Let him know he wasn't bullshitting him, but not slapping him in the face with it.

"So, are you ready to do me this accommodation?"

And Fabe couldn't help it, he smiled. "Want me to kiss your ring, too, Roland?"

"You know, Fabe, you are sometimes a funny mother-fucker. This ain't one of those times. Now I'm willing to pay you a grand, for an hour's work. Right now. Just get into a place, look into a safe for me."

Fabe said, "Roland, I got to tell you no, but I must give you my reasons." Two could play that game; he wants to play the Godfather, Fabe'd give him the Godfather. "First, Roland, I make a hell of a lot more than a grand to walk into the *door*. I wouldn't waste my time for a grand. Second, I'm retired. I gave it all up. Got too old. Third, I made my decision years ago, I would stay out of your hair, and Campo, he okayed it, said I didn't have to work for you or die for refusing. Doing that, checking this place out for you, would break that agreement, would be spitting in Don Campo's eye, and I could not do that. Hell, you got plenty of thieves on your payroll, get one of them to do it."

As he spoke, DiNardo got madder and madder, Fabe could tell from his redness. It had crept up from his neck, slowly filled his face, flushed him like a high fever.

"I kill people," DiNardo said, "do you know that? That's what I do. I kill people."

"No, you don't," he said. "You're a pimp, and you got some gambling, juice, maybe a few other things going for you. Remember, Roland, the man himself, Don Campo, gave you the word, leave me alone. For my money, *you* wanted me hit, and Tombstone told you not to." He sat back, putting the glass on the arm of the chair, figuring he'd be needing his hands soon. They were trembling now, and as bad as he wanted one, he did not reach for a cigarette.

"You *prick*," DiNardo said, his voice breaking. "Hey, *punk*, I *whistle*, there'll be guys in here, suck your eyeballs out of your *head*!" He was standing now, leaning on the desk for support, the cords standing out in his neck.

Fabe thought of Doral, and how he always had a certain reply to Fabe's warnings about Jimmy Capone. He lowered his right hand to his crotch and splayed his fingers across it, squeezing slightly.

"Suck *this*," Fabe said.

"Herman! Tino!" DiNardo shouted, and Fabe reached for the .38 nobody had bothered to search him for, because everybody knew thieves never carried guns, thinking, here we go. . . .

Lloyd and Elmo were walking on the sand at the beach at Ninety-ninth and the Lake, and in the distance Lloyd could see the Commonwealth Edison Terminal, out there in the middle of nowhere. Behind him were the Series Terminal, the loading docks, but they were closed for the season now. In the middle of the Lake a tugboat whistled, and Lloyd looked out into the haze but could not see it. "Where's these bitches hang out at, goddammit?" he said, his hand on the gun in his coat pocket, where he'd hidden it when Elmo had looked at the car down the block. He'd then zipped his jacket up, so Elmo would think he'd stuck the gun in his pants, like he usually did. He walked now hunched over, Elmo behind him, knowing that if Elmo was planning on making a move it would not be on the sand, he was at least smart enough to know that he couldn't shoot Lloyd and leave him in the *sand*, he had to be that bright.

"Over by the rocks, right over there," Elmo shouted, and Lloyd looked fifty feet away, where the rocks jutted out into Lake Michigan, going down in steps to the crashing surf. Lloyd was smiling.

He reached the rocks first and looked around, making a big show of it. "Ain't no bitches here," Lloyd said.

Elmo pulled his hands out of his pants pockets, looked around, seeming bewildered. "Shit, I heard they *was* always here." And he moved his hand to his jacket, as if to scratch his belly.

Lloyd pulled his piece out of his coat pocket. "You dumb shit," he said, and shot Elmo twice, both in the chest. He knelt beside the dying body and took the wad of money out of Elmo's jeans. "DiNardo give you this?" he asked.

Elmo was shaking his head, back and forth, blood spurting from the second chest wound, up high. His lips moved soundlessly.

"You ass-kissing, stupid shit," Lloyd said, then shot him again, right in the middle of that clean, well-complected forehead.

Lloyd got to his feet, looking around at the deserted beach. He kicked Elmo over into the lake, then started back to the Buick, steamed, thinking, if he had to go out, if he had a con-

141

tract on his ass, then he was taking a *couple* of these assholes with him.

When DiNardo had shouted, Fabe had pulled the .38 out of his waistband and the holster had come with it, unclipped itself and the thing flew across the room, but Fabe didn't give it a second thought; he backed against the wall and stood there, the gun in both hands, pointing at DiNardo's belly, and Fabe watched DiNardo sink into his chair, his hands out, muttering, "No, uh-uh, you don't wanna do that," and Fabe's eyes were on the door, waiting.

"Call them off," he said, snarling to cover the fact that his hands were shaking. *"Now."*

Roland DiNardo yelled, "Herman, Tino, forget about it, it's okay!" and Fabe sidled to the door, took one hand off the pistol long enough to lock the door, the gun still pointing at DiNardo, shaking crazily now.

"Say it again." And Fabe heard the rumbling in the hall, like a cattle drive heading his way.

"Forget it, fellas, it's under control." And the pounding stopped.

A knock on the door. "You okay, Roland?" a deep whiskey voice said.

"Yes, yes, I'm fine, now goddammit, get back to work." And right away the voice came back, asking again if Roland was okay.

"Get the fuck away from the door, you jerkoff!" DiNardo shouted, and Fabe could hear mumbling, but the sound of footsteps moving away from the door assured him a little.

"That was good, Roland," Fabe said. "That was real good. Now, one more time. I'm walking out of here, and as far as I'm concerned this never happened, this is history. I was never here. You want to do something stupid, don't. Because

142

I'm going to call a couple people, soon as I get out of here, tell them to get ahold of Tommy Campo if anything happens to me, tell him you broke our deal.''

Fabe was sidling to the side-exit door when it was thrown open and Lloyd stormed in with his pistol in his hand and murder in his eyes.

Fabe had to give him credit for balls, that was for sure, because Roland DiNardo, he didn't miss a beat. He looked at Lloyd as if seeing his salvation, and said, to a man with a gun pointed at his *head,* "Hey, terrific, where's Elmo?" And Lloyd, well, his brows just squinched up and his face fell, and Fabe knew Lloyd had done something really stupid.

"Shit!" Lloyd said. "*What* did you say?" And Roland DiNardo turned to the man pointing the pistol at his belly, Fabe, and raised his hands in a helpless gesture.

"I said, where the fuck's Elmo?" And Fabe watched Lloyd's hand fall, begin to shake something terrible, his face a mask of confusion and terror.

As soon as the gun lowered to the point where Fabe knew the bullet would not hit anyone if it *did* go off, he took a swing at Lloyd's head with the barrel of his own gun, hitting him square in the temple, dropping him. He turned to Roland Di-Nardo.

"You owe me one," he said, and made for the door, running as soon as he closed it behind him.

Roland dropped into his chair, shaking. Jesus Christ. Two in one day. He hurried to the door to the rest of the house, unlocked it and threw it open. "Herman, *Ti*no!" he shouted, and was rewarded with the noise of their massive feet pounding the carpet, coming from the kitchen. Jerkoffs. Always eating. They raced into the room, reaching under their armpits. They spotted Lloyd on the floor, just coming around now, groaning, holding his head, trying to sit up.

"You want us to whack him?" Tino asked eagerly. He knew he'd get paid more for a murder than his usual nine hundred a week.

"Just get him outta here, clean him up. I got to talk to him."

Herman and Tino grabbed Lloyd under his arms, upset that they wouldn't be making any extra money today. They dragged him from the room, not gently.

Roland locked the door and went to his bar, poured himself a good shot of Cutty, and downed it. There was an angry, muffled knocking from the far paneled wall. Jesus Christ, he'd almost forgotten about them.

He went to the wall and pushed in on the fourth piece of paneling from the corner, and two sections sprung open on well-oiled hinges.

Francisco Ortiz and Miro Roga stepped out.

Ortiz looked at him with his superior, arrogant look, rocking onto his toes, trying to bounce up to where he could look Roland right in the eye.

But it was Roga who spoke, almost laughing. "Well, you sure told *him*," Roga said. "Had him eating out of the palm of your hand, just like you said."

And then he did laugh. But what worried Roland was, Roga didn't even *try* to hide it, and Francisco Ortiz didn't even crack a smile.

11 Jimmy Capone felt as if he spent half his life talking to lawyers these days. As the commander of forty-two men in a squad that constantly had to be updated on the courts' ever-changing drug rulings, he felt it his duty to be in near daily contact with lawyers who could explain the new decisions and laws of evidence to him in layman's language. And he knew plenty of other lawyers for less savory reasons. At least twice a year, the U.S. Attorney made headlines when his crew grabbed one of Jimmy's men who, like Fabe years back, had succumbed to the temptation of a fast buck. And of course the Office of Professional Standards was forever trying to lay something on one of them. Jimmy had six seven-man teams, working six different sections of a city with three million people. Fighting a losing battle and having to face scrutiny all the time because the public just knew that Narco guys were all on the take; they'd seen the movies and read the books.

Trying to watch his expanding waistline, Jimmy had only had coffee. He paid for the lunch of the Assistant District Attorney, who told him that under no circumstances could they use in court any information that Fabe had given him over an informal lunch. Fabe could have told Jimmy every aspect of the score, and unless Jimmy set it up and busted him at the scene, the next day he could not bring the suspect in and summarily charge him with the crime. Not without warning him of his rights before listening to him. Not without corroborative evidence, witnesses, a wire, tape-recorded evidence, something. On the other hand, there was no law that stopped Jimmy from bringing Fabe in for questioning. At least in the opinion of the ADA. They spoke of Ortiz, too, and as Jimmy was thanking him, the ADA pulled Jimmy aside and confided that he was putting his job on the line, but after fifteen years of friendship he had something he just had to tell Jimmy.

OPS had an undercover operative watching him. No one in the office knew where the guy was, or what his cover was, or who was his control, but it was certain there was a guy on Jimmy. It might even be one of his own men.

"Waste of manpower."

"*I* know that, Jimmy, and *you* know that, but they get off on trying to pop the honest guys even more than the outrageous, obvious guys. Just watch your ass."

Jimmy thanked him and left.

Almost half his life on the force, never took a penny, never took a meal, never even took a free pack of smokes, and they were wasting a full-time undercover operative on him. Jesus.

He had forty-two guys working for him. Guys who had to watch it all, see ten-year-old girls selling their asses for crack, these kids never even saw the color of money, just got their little capsule of crack to smoke. Ten years old! These guys saw babies hooked on dope from birth, took them to the hospital and watched them withdraw, two and three days old. Mothers who had the kids at home, on the kitchen table, so they wouldn't have to go to a hospital, see the faces of the doctors and nurses who had their number, who would take their kids away from them. And the kids the cops took to the hospital were the lucky ones. Fifty or so of them a year were discarded and either killed straight out by their own *parents,* or abandoned naked in a freezing-cold husk of a car in an alley somewhere.

Jimmy could just kill the assholes who said that cocaine was a victimless recreational drug.

And now maybe one of these men was spying on him. Well, that was okay with Jimmy. He had nothing to hide. But he couldn't help the strong resentment. That, he figured, he deserved. Because Narco was the elite, the tightest, toughest group of guys around. You saw it every day, the abuse of children and spouses, the fathers selling their own daughters to their pushers for a half ounce of the lady. There never was a day in Narco where you got to the end of it feeling as if you'd helped. It was all downhill, from the moment you woke up till the time your head hit the pillow; you were in the trenches, fighting a losing battle.

And you got tight with your unit.

And you'd give up the badge, the gun, the great big seven-fifty a week you were making when the guys you popped made more than that an hour, you'd give it all up before you'd rat out a fellow squaddie. If the shit hit the fan, if you learned without doubt that one of your team was dirty, you told Jimmy Capone and he took care of it. You didn't go to OPS or the papers, or the TV guys, screaming about corruption. Because it would hurt the unit, the entire forty-two guys would be tainted. But now one of these forty-two guys, *maybe,* was working against him, trying to bring him down.

Incredible.

It was after five before he got back to Eleventh and State. He'd checked in at two other unit headquarters where investigations were in progress. He coordinated these operations. These were the big-timers he was after here, the guys maybe two layers of insulation under Francisco Ortiz. Guys on the level maybe of the doctor who had got whacked the night before. While doing this, Jimmy checked in by phone with the other three teams, out on the street, making buys, busting the small-timers; making sales, busting the small-timers. The numbers were good, and that made him feel a little better.

But not as good as pinching Francisco Ortiz would make him feel.

He learned that Christovic and Dodd had struck out at Fabe's apartment; Fabe hadn't been back. He ordered O'Neil to get them out of there. Fabey, he'd handle himself. Johnson and Parnell had gone back to the Holiday Inn, and sure enough, Ortiz and Roga were out of the room. Still checked in, but just out. Bielak and Olaf were writing reports, having called in and been relieved at four-thirty.

"Relieved by who?" Jimmy wanted to know.

"By Snead and O'Malley, on nights over at the Fourth," Olaf told him.

"Snead and O'Malley are on undercover in the *park,* for Chrissakes." And Jimmy saw Olaf wince at the reference to Christ, and he silently dared him to open his mouth. Fortunately for Olaf, he didn't.

"Can you get a couple of blues over there, Inspector?" Bielak, now.

"I'll get somebody," Jimmy said, exasperated. "At least finish your surveillance reports before you race home, huh?"

"It's two days before Christmas, sir." Olaf again. It wasn't important enough to reply to.

Jimmy sat down, picked up the phone, deciding to stir up some trouble one way or the other. He looked at the phone, then around the room. If there was a traitor, it would be one of the guys in this room, one of the guys he worked with every day. Probably Olaf. Angry at him, he said goddammit too many times, or some such nonsense. He hung the phone up, got up and left the office, walked past OPS down the hall without even looking in, and got into the elevator and downstairs, out of the building. Right in front of the station was a public phone, but it was too close. He walked three blocks north and two east, got to the phone at the corner of Wabash and Balbo. Took out his book. Dialed a number. An unlisted, private number that would ring in the study of a certain Tommy Campo.

"Yeah?"

"Campo?"

"Who the fuck is this?" The voice was outraged, Tommy obviously pissed because somebody called him on his private personal line and dared to call him by his last name.

"You don't need to know who this is. But I'm telling you right now, DiNardo's pushing coke. I find out it ain't just him on his own, I'm bringing you down, too."

"Hey, who the fuck *is* this?"

"Hey," Jimmy Capone said, "this is your fucking conscience." And he hung up the phone.

That ought to put a fire under them.

He felt good, better than he had since seeing Ortiz with Campo's lieutenant, DiNardo, the night before at the Coroner's Office. And he felt good, really, really good, until he perched himself on the edge of his desk and skimmed through the surveillance reports Bielak and Olaf had made up.

Suddenly, the day had gone bad again.

Fabe had raced from DiNardo's house and into the alley, sticking the gun in the pocket of the bomber jacket, zipping it up there, pumping his arms, blowing out his breath, going for all he was worth. "You owe me." What an idiot thing to say to a goddamn egotistical freak like DiNardo. But he'd had to tell him, hell yeah, get him to thinking. Maybe even believe it, leave Fabe the hell alone. He had enough trouble right now.

He was a lot closer to Doral's place than he was to his own, so he headed there, turning left on West North Avenue. He had a hell of a lot to tell Doral. Like, for instance, they had to burn the dope. It was DiNardo's, no doubt about it. Why the hell else would DiNardo suddenly start using lightweight, hell, flyweight tough guys to do his running for him? Why else would they use the back door? Why else would he let a known thief and renegade, a rogue who paid the mob no allegiance— like himself—into his presence for an hour without a bodyguard? He was dealing. Heavily. Without his boss's approval. Fabe could see ways that this information could be used to his advantage. His and Doral's.

But he'd wait a while. He'd told DiNardo that, in his mind, the meeting was history, hadn't happened. Maybe DiNardo would see it that way, get someone else to check out his safe for him. As if Fabe did not know which safe he wanted busted.

So he'd take his time. If DiNardo made any kind of move at all, he'd pay a visit to Tombstone Paterro. Have a little talk. Straighten things out.

But they had to burn the dope. Or flush it. Or something. Because if they didn't, Roland DiNardo would find out about it. He had maybe a million ways to do it, without his boss's getting wise. And Fabe would never, ever trust anyone who would deal in drugs. So if Doral was planning on turning it over, Fabe did not care if he planned to sell it to his mother, she couldn't be trusted. DiNardo'd have one of his bad-assed cowboys stick a nickel-plated .45 in the guy's mouth, and ease back the hammer, and Doral'd be sold down the river right *now*.

They had to burn it. It was as simple as that. And Fabe wouldn't listen to any "Shee-it" from Doral about it.

He jogged to the gate at Doral's mansion, opened it, went into the foyer and winked at the camera, hit the multi-number access code that deactivated the alarm and popped the door at the same time, and walked into the house.

And found Doral sprawled on his couch, before the now-dead fire, out cold. There was maybe an ounce of coke scattered across the table in the living room.

Fabe backed out of the house, in shock, without disturbing Doral. He didn't think he could talk to him right now. Not without shooting him.

Sally Evans was drying her hair, just back from school, when the phone rang. She let it ring four times, allowed the Code-a-Phone to pick it up. If it was important, she could grab it; if it wasn't—some idiot from the job, wanting a date or something—she'd let it go. She listened to the recorded announcement, heard the voice on the other end starting to speak after the beep, let him talk for a few seconds, trying to put the voice with the face, until he indentified himself, then she was scurrying across the room, picking it up, saying, "Hello? Hello, Fabe, is it? How *are* you, I wasn't expecting your *call*!"

Fabe was in a joint on Rush Street, striving to find some sane companionship. Two beers, and he knew he'd never find it here.

He'd never liked Rush Street. The guys all seemed to be macho idiots these days, sizing the women up as if they were lined up in the meat section of the Jewel. Still a lot of chains and open shirts and white suits. And sissy drinks. And Porsches at the curb, leased. *This* joint had video dates, where the prospective datee's face and figure were flashed on the screen and she'd say a few words, tell you what she liked, what turned her on and off, and you could go to the bartender, get a sheet of paper and a pen, and write the video star a letter, giving her your stats, telling her you turned on at the sight of her, or whatever.

Fabe sniffed the air, wondering what had happened to the smell of beer and nuts in a gin mill. He got a lot of stares from the guys wearing a couple of thousand dollars' worth of stuff, there in his hooded sweatshirt and his jeans, wearing his bomber jacket. They probably thought he was a pusher.

That meant they'd be approaching him soon.

He sipped his draft beer, trying hard to work up some sympathy for the women, not getting himself too worked up for it. They all seemed to be wearing skirts with slits, in December, with low-cut, fashionable silk blouses. Without bras. Christ, their tits must be *freez*ing. They checked out the men over the rims of rock glasses as they sipped from them, looking too set up, too practiced for Fabe's taste. He caught the eye of one of them, and she lowered the glass, gave him an open, inviting stare, licked a drop of wine from her upper lip. Fabe turned away. He didn't like advertisements.

He'd have to leave soon. Even Bunny's Hutch was better than this. At least some of the people there were *real*. And if he didn't find someone sane, someone old-fashioned, maybe, someone who could take his mind away from what was banging around up there, he'd go stark raving insane.

He felt in limbo. Not hot, not cold, nobody after him, yet, but he knew they were looking. The shit would be hitting the fan, and soon. If the heat didn't come from DiNardo's cowboys, and wasn't that a can of worms. He'd insulted the guy, Lloyd, and suddenly he ran out of the joint, then Elmo went after him, and an hour later Lloyd comes back with a pistol pointed at DiNardo's head. Christ, what was going on there? He'd thought, at first, that whoever was coming in was coming for him, but he'd held the gun on the boss, making it a Mexican standoff. Then he'd whacked Lloyd when he got the chance, to keep him from shooting the guy, and bringing the entire Outfit down on them both. It didn't make sense. No, if it wasn't Lloyd and Elmo, then it would be, just might be Jimmy coming after him.

That wasn't out of the question. He'd smoked like a maniac the other day in the restaurant, he was sure of that now, and he'd even said some dumb-ass thing about being retired tomorrow, or something, at the end. Jimmy might put it together, he was smart enough. Fabe had given too much away, his mind on other things, the score, the waitress—

The waitress.

He searched the inside pockets of his jacket, found his address book, was turning it to the S's and suddenly he heard, "Gonna write down my number?" and he looked up, shocked.

It was the girl—woman, now that he saw her close up. Maybe a couple of years younger than he was, about thirty-five or so. But a good-looking head, wearing the Joan Esposito look, the newscaster from Channel 7. This was one of the loveliest women Fabe had ever laid eyes on. Her blue-black hair was down around her shoulders, her eyes just with a hint of makeup, because they were big and round and stunning, black as night. Full, rich red lips. A blue silk blouse tucked into a shiny-fabric skirt, slit all the way up to her hip. Dark hose. Almost comical S and M boots.

Fabe said, smiling at her, "Don't tell me, your name is Toni or Joni or Roni or Suzi, right, with an *i* on the end? And you work out three times a week at Charlie's?"

He had to give her credit, she only slipped a little. She

said, "You Lyle-Alzado types are a real turnoff, you know?" And she turned away, and he called after her, "You ain't Joan Esposito yourself, sweetheart," a little too loudly.

They were watching him now, seeing the black-haired beauty stalking away. On either side of him, for maybe three stools down to his left and right, they had stopped their tribal rites and were checking him.

The black-haired girl sat back on her stool, and her eyes flashed at him, once. But brutally. Then she turned it back on for the bartender, who was standing there, saying, "Is everything okay, Lori?" And Fabe thought, Lori, bingo! And got up and went to the phone, feeling their eyes on his back.

Out of place. He didn't fit in. The story of his life.

He dropped a quarter into the slot, dialed the number he'd written down yesterday. The phone rang. "Hello," she said, and Fabe began to speak, feeling suddenly warm, but it was a recording. Damn, Fabe hated recordings.

But he waited this one out.

"This is Sally Evans, and I'm at class right now, so at the sound of the beep please leave your name and number and I'll get back to you as soon as I can, and thanks for calling." Fabe waited for the beep.

"This is Fabe. You gave me the number at the restaurant yesterday? I was the guy in the next-to-the-last booth carrying on with the big guy—" And he felt suddenly foolish. He was about to hang up and never call again, never eat in the Iron Horse again, either, but she picked up then, a little breathless, as if she'd just walked in the door.

"Hello, Fabe, is it? How *are* you, I wasn't expecting your *call*!"

"Listen," Fabe said, trying to think up something witty to impress her right off. Nothing came.

154

"Your name isn't S-a-l-i, is it, with an *i* at the end?"

"What? Sali? Is that Japanese or something? No, it's S-a-l-l-y, old-fashioned, plain old Sally." She giggled then, and won Fabe's heart. "Are you in a bar?"

"At the moment." If he let her know he'd been there awhile, she'd figure him for a drunk, or a nerd who had to get a few belts in him to call a girl on the phone. "It's the only pay phone around where I was, so I stopped in to call you." There was an awkward silence, and he knew he'd have to fill it. He had to see her tonight or he'd die, and he couldn't blow it now, had to play it straight, couldn't come on like some damn Steve Martin clone or she'd see through it and dump him before it got started.

"Say," Fabe said, "are you free this evening?"

Sally said, "Call me back in five minutes, okay? Will you?"

"Sure," Fabe said, and the phone went dead in his ear.

Strange. He went to the bar, hefted his draft, drained it, waved the bartender away, thinking maybe he should slap the guy, just for looking at him that way. He checked his watch. Two minutes. Two and a half. Three.

Fuck this.

He returned to the booth, dropped in another quarter, dialed the number.

Busy.

Okay, wait right here. Don't go out there, not feeling like this. Insecure, like he was feeling, there was no telling what he'd do. Might start busting the joint up. Last thing he needed, carrying two pistols on him, getting popped in a gin mill just because he'd asked some goof of a broad a couple of questions.

This time she picked up on the second ring. She didn't even give him a chance to say a word.

"Yes, as a matter of fact, I do happen to be free tonight!" Obviously happy, as a matter of fact, to Fabe's ear, she sounded elated. It couldn't have happened at a better time for him. He wondered about something for a second, then decided he was on a roll and he could ask, it couldn't hurt, and it sure as hell could help.

"Sally? Did you break a *date* for me?" he asked, and she said, "I sure did," her voice rising on the last word, making him feel ten feet tall, as if he couldn't lose.

"What's your address?" Fabe asked.

He took a cab to the Armitage Building, in a hurry now because he told her he'd pick her up at seven and it was almost six. Up the stairs, into the apartment, no time to shave, dammit, a quick shower, dress in warm, solid casual clothes, throw on a long dark coat, knee-length, tweed. A nice blocked hat. No jewelry. He didn't want to look like a lounge lizard or anything. Down into the lobby, outside again, into the garage. And Billy Boy the night attendant studying in his cubicle, making it through Roosevelt U. by working here twelve hours a day, sleeping after his last class.

"How's it going, Billy Boy?" Fabe asked, then wondered if he was still hot, because Billy Boy looked up at him as if he were from outer space or something.

"What's the matter, Billy?"

"Mister Falletti, jeez, Philly, on days, he told me the cops were here asking about your car before."

"Billy Boy, did Philly tell you what they wanted?"

"No, sir," Billy Boy said. "Only that they checked to see if your car was here, then they left right after."

Fabe reached into his pocket, pulled out his money and peeled off a twenty. "Merry Christmas, Billy Boy," he said, still on a roll, because if they'd been really interested, they'd have stuck around. Probably about parking tickets, or some such nonsense. He got into the Eldorado and drove over to the door, waited while Billy Boy hit the button, rolled it up, and then pulled out onto Clark Street, heading south.

"Merry Christmas," Billy Boy said, as the car hit the street, feeling guilty about having to do it to such a nice guy, but feeling as if he had no choice. He sighed, put his book down, and reached for the phone.

12 Fabe drove toward Sally's, thinking about another time, another night on fabulous Rush Street, getting his first taste of life in the big city. He was trying to remember, how many years had it been at that point, since he'd been with a woman? Four years in prison, okay, about seven months in County awaiting trial. His time with Anita had been short, a couple of years, but since baby Tina's illness, well, sex became nonexistent, although he had remained faithful. They both had had other things on their minds. Okay, so over five years, at least.

Doral had been worried that Fabe would wind up back on the inside before he got his dick wet, and had tried to set Fabe up, using a hooker who Doral had said was related to him and had helped him get set up after his release from the joint. Fabe had got out two months later, and was insulted by the gesture. After their first successful score he'd gone to Rush Street.

He'd been sitting in a place called December's Mother, six years ago or so, in the early eighties, before the term "yuppie" had been coined. A spectacular blonde had approached him, wide big blue eyes, set well apart, full sensual mouth, she looked a little like that Hemingway woman Fabe had seen in one of the few movies he'd seen in Joliet, where the girl whacked out the guy who'd raped her, then her sister after. Great flick to show in Joliet.

Neither Fabe nor Doral had been into pictures. No *Hustler honeys* were taped to their walls, no Polaroids from home showing women in erotic full-color poses. Neither of them were into that much. They just wanted to do their time and get the hell out. So this was new to Fabe, the feeling of being on the prowl, wondering how it would feel, getting in again after all this time, somewhere in the back of his mind the doubt. Could he still get into it, would it work?

And the Hemingway-looking woman approaching as he sat in his Ultra-Suede jacket with a yellow polo shirt underneath, drinking a Grant's with a little ice, water back.

She was wearing some kind of sheath or frock, light material, and her body jiggled wildly underneath it as she walked, clinging tightly to each curve and protuberance; a shiny thin material under which he could see there was nothing else.

"Hi," she'd said, sliding in, next to him, giving him a little thigh against his hip, nothing much, there in the booth, strangers on the make, sizing each other up.

"So, how you doing?" Fabe said.

She looked at his drink, called out from the booth to a passing waitress, "Another for him, okay, and an Amaretto for me?"

"Rocks, honey?" the waitress hollered.

"Just two," she'd said, and turned back to Fabe. "Too much ice just wrecks the taste."

Fabe didn't think there was much that could wreck the taste of Amaretto, seeing as it already tasted like shit to him, but he didn't want to blow it, he didn't know her yet.

"At least with Scotch," he'd said at last, "good stuff like this, ice melting just makes it better." He was starting to panic a little bit, not knowing how he was doing. They spent some time debating the merits of the strong stuff versus wines, horoscopes, how often they went to bars, what movies they liked, who their favorite stars were.

Fabe was shocked at how easily she said "Fuck" and at her insistence on paying for every other round, and he was amazed that she put the stuff down like water, while he himself was getting a little buzzed. Culture shock crashed down around him when she opened her purse right there on the table and reached for a fresh pack of Eve's cigarettes. She had a toothbrush and a traveler-sized tube of Crest in there. Something silky crushed into a square under the Crest. He caught sight of a strap. A nightgown, a teddy. Oh, Lord.

Now that he knew he was in, it came a little easier for him.

With Anita it had been a year of dating and messing around, setting the wedding date before he scored. Now he was in a world where the women set out to spend the night with someone they'd never seen. And he'd never fallen into the trap a lot of the cops played, fooling around, hitting on anything that wore a skirt, falling into the arms of the cop groupies that hung around the bars they frequented. Hell, Fabe never even went *into* one of those places. His home was his refuge, his wife his friend. But it hadn't been enough. Not strong enough, at least not to handle the pressure when the baby got sick. Maybe if they'd been together longer, maybe if he hadn't been a cop, had a more stable job, had been home more, maybe they could have gotten through it.

"Why so somber suddenly?" she asked.

And Fabe knew he couldn't tell her, knew he'd be biting off more than he could chew. She'd start the mothering, the "Poor baby" stuff, if he said a word about Anita or the baby. And he'd somehow be cheapening the child's memory if he told this woman with the traveling overnight kit about her. So he'd smiled at her, said something about Italians being moody, and that had been it, that had set her off, going on and on about Pacino and Stallone and De Niro and who was his favorite actor?

"David Janssen," Fabe told her, and she'd said, "Who?" as if he'd said Elmo Lincoln or something.

"David Janssen. Played the fugitive, Richard Kimble, searching for the one-armed guy?" And she'd thought he was kidding, laughed it off, and told him how witty he was.

Getting down to it now, the hour getting late, she'd looked him dead in the eye, serious, as serious as she was capable of being, establishing a "relationship." She'd asked him, "What're *you* searching for, honey?"

At the Holiday Inn he remembered some pleasure, some fun, some action, but he hadn't given it more than maybe half; it was a farce, really, a game to her. She'd moaned and turned it on, trying to be the best piece he'd ever had, and he'd gone about it like a machine, getting it, one part of his mind disgusted with himself.

Six years later, he couldn't remember her name as he drove down Canal, looking for a one-way westbound street that would take him to Jefferson, and Sally, with a *y*, thank God.

There had been a few women since that first time, but nothing important, nothing that gave him that urge he'd felt while dating Anita, the desire to sweep her into his arms and hold her forever, bury his head in her hair. He felt the gun in his right topcoat pocket and the tightness of the ankle holster strapped to his left leg and thought that maybe it had something to do with his life-style.

Christmas was coming around, and everything went to hell.

Jimmy Capone was at his desk, in the chair, drinking another cup of coffee, wondering if maybe all the ADAs and the OPS guys were right. Maybe there shouldn't be any elite corps of cops. He smiled, thinking, the Cops Corps. Join up, and see nothing but shit the rest of your life. Get paranoid, get old before your time, lose your hair, and make peanuts while everybody around you figures you're on the take because you work out of Narcotics Section.

All the other detectives, all the other dicks in the city had to fight and scratch and trade with the non-Christians for Christmas off. Not the Narcotics guys, though. To them, it was a paid holiday, as if they were construction workers or something. Oh, some of the undercover guys, the deep cover workers, would put in a few hours, calling some of their connections from the warmth of their hearths and homes, wishing them happy holidays, setting them up, but that was pretty much it. Because the crooks, traditionally, at least the crooks they were after, did not work on Christmas.

And so it had somehow gotten to be a tradition around the Narco squad to take Christmas off, and, for most of them, Christmas Eve.

And Jimmy had not changed things, eight, nine years back, when he'd taken over. He figured his guys worked all the extra hours during the other 364 days of the year, overtime without pay on scheduled days off, holidays, weekends, kids' birthdays, anniversaries, First Communion, graduations. Let them have Christmas at home. Feel like normal human beings for a change. There was a major net being dropped New Year's Eve, thirty names in a blanket indictment, under wraps, and every one of the guys would be busting their chops a week from now, going into dope houses in parts of the city where a white face was cause for major suspicion and a white man with an orange jacket with "Police" written on the back was considered a target. Let them rest the next couple of days. The hell with it.

162

But it was only the twenty-third, and they should have been more alert today, was all.

Bielak and Olaf should have known that Johnson and Parnell were on stakeout over at the Holiday Inn, trying to get a line on Roga and Ortiz. They should have *known*. They were on the same *team*. And they didn't even call in and report it. Olaf, he expected it from. For all his posturing and holier-than-thou bullshit, Olaf was a lazy slob, trying to get through eight hours so he could run to church and speak in tongues or something. But Bielak was a good cop. Should have known better. Jimmy would have to give Olaf a lot of thought, maybe transfer him into the Officer Friendly program or something, where he would fit in and not be such a pain in the ass to regular working cops.

And Fabe being escorted in, laughing and joking with a couple of slobs nobody had ever seen before, passing guns around, that was unforgivable. They should have called him, at the very least. Jimmy knew if he called them both in right now, what they'd tell him. It was a judgment call. They had no business out there, and could not use the car mike to talk about unauthorized stakeouts, or some reporter or crook would hear about it, and the next thing you knew, a guy like DiNardo, he'd have F. Lee Bailey in court, suing the department over the callous violation of his civil rights. And on North Astor Street, it wasn't like there was a 7-Eleven on the corner or a gas station every block. This was the high-rent district. Why break up the team to have one guy search out a telephone? What if something big happened? He could hear the arguments, and knew damn well that the PBA Union guys would back Bielack and Olaf up to the hilt, but that still didn't make it good police work, Goddammit.

He had half a mind to call Olaf in tomorrow and work him on Christmas Eve. Olaf would probably resign, sue him *and* the department, religious persecution or something, his job keeping him away from handling snakes or being baptized again, some garbage like that.

To Jimmy, Christmas was just another day. He had a meaningful relationship, a seven-year-long relationship, with a thirty-three-year-old divorcée who had no desire to marry again. And they went to dinner often, they spent the night together three times a week, took their vacations at the same time. Sometimes she accompanied him on his frequent out-of-town trips, the seminars that were part of his increasingly administrative duties these days. Teaching kids how to Just Say No. *When* she could get away from her duties as a legal secretary for Jacobs, Weinberg, Associates. But she spent Thanksgiving and Christmas with her aging parents in Omaha, Nebraska. Thank God. Jimmy wasn't much for handing out gifts, playing the game society had invented. Madison Avenue garbage. So he could concentrate, this Christmas, on Fabe.

Who, one way or the other, was in deep shit.

Either Fabey was working for Roland DiNardo, which would, two days ago, have been in the impossible category, or else he and his jailhouse roommate had walked in on Chacona thinking he was gone, and found him with a stiffening Lucille Ortiz, and had proceeded to rob and kill him.

On the one hand, Jimmy knew about Fabe's lifelong hatred of the mob. They both considered the gangs beneath them, ignorant, useless slobs who had to have an army of idiots behind them to be effective, to instill fear. But, on the other hand, it didn't seem, from the Olaf-Bielak surveillance, as if he'd been dragged into DiNardo's house kicking and screaming. Laughing and joking, giving the black-haired muscleman a couple of pistols. That's the way the report read.

Would Fabe dare get into drugs? After all they'd been through together, with Fabe knowing that Jimmy would move the earth to bust druggies, would he play around like this?

Had he fallen so low?

Lucille Ortiz was a mule, Jimmy knew this. Ortiz used family on the first three or four levels of his operation, people he could count on to keep their mouths shut and wait for bail money if they got popped. From that point on, things got a little fuzzy. Chacona was a Puerto Rican, that was certain, but Jimmy knew that although Chacona had to know who the big guy was, any Puerto Rican from over there in the last fifteen years or so would have to know about Ortiz, who did not exactly live a reclusive life-style at home. So Chacona knew; but had he ever met the man? Jimmy doubted it. On that level, Ortiz would want the middleman to know who he was, sure, put the fear of God into him. But he would want that knowledge to be purely speculation, so it couldn't come back to haunt him in an American courtroom.

So how did Fabe come to be in the same house with Ortiz and Roga, if they weren't doing business together? And if they weren't, why was Fabe allowed to leave? Especially if he'd seen Lucille's nude, shattered body?

Jimmy Capone had baited Ortiz last night, sure. On purpose. But he was under no illusions about Ortiz. Ortiz was a killer, worse than any whacked-out Indians from Colombia, the guys they were starting to see in Chicago now. Guys who took out entire families just to get a fella's attention. At least with those guys, the wild Indians, it was all from the cuff, shoot first, then find out if the guy deserved it. They were short-sighted, thinking they could hide behind American laws to make themselves rich. They'd learn. But Ortiz was far worse, because he was wily, guileful, thoughtful. And he was already rich. He would order a murder on the phone, having his morning juice, and send the money out after he ate, and it would be taken care of for him, the heat never reaching him. He was established, a

165

role model back home. Someone the kids in the barrios and tenements could look up to. A success. Almost untouchable.

Almost.

Jimmy had touched him, yesterday, had got under his skin. Had seen his swarthy face turn darker with blood when he insulted the man's dead sister. Good. Maybe, he wouldn't leave the city without trying for revenge. Jimmy would give almost anything to get Ortiz down in Joliet, without a manicurist or bodyguards or maids or servants or women or his personal barber to shave him every morning. Because he knew he'd lose him within a year, lose him to the feds, which would really be a gain for all of them. Because Ortiz would roll over and sell them all out, his entire line, from the growers in South America to his lowest-level pusher, just out of the desire for freedom. Otherwise, it was a straight fifteen years in Joliet, rather than two or three years in a safehouse somewhere, singing, then freedom. Or at least the illusion of freedom.

He'd give almost anything to get Ortiz. Even his best friend.

And it had to be Fabe. They'd found a safe behind a picture of a bullfighter in Chacona's apartment, with three alarms on it. A heavy-duty, high-class item. It took their people most of the night to get into it. Just to find it empty. People like Chacona did not spend thousands of dollars for personal safes to keep the family jewels in. It had been installed for him. By either DiNardo or Ortiz. Or their people. And Lucille had been found in a cedar trunk, her body broken to fit. Without a penny in her purse. Or a gram of cocaine. It was not possible that she was just carrying on an affair with a lowlife like Chacona. Impossible. He'd either raped her and then had doubts about it and killed her in a drug frenzy, or they'd had sex and she'd overdosed. Or somebody else had raped and killed her and tried to pin it on Chacona, and taken the dope, money, or both. Because it stood to reason that if Lucille was in town, she would be carrying either dope or money. One or the other. And they'd found neither. So somebody had it. Chacona's car had been empty.

So where the hell was the product, or the cash?

He'd get no answers here, sitting on his ass trying to outthink guys who were treacherous from birth. Even a Sicilian like him could not stoop to their mind-sets. He needed answers, and when in doubt, work it out.

Probably he couldn't bring Ortiz in and grill him, as the ADA had suggested. The papers and DiNardo's people would have a field day with that, what with poor Ortiz's sister dead not twenty-four hours. He'd throw up his hands, saying, "What drogs, señor, what mooney? Why in the name of the Holy Mother are the *policía* harassing a jonest beesneesman for?" And he'd be cut loose, get an injunction filed, put them all in their places. Jimmy had done what he could about DiNardo. If he was a breaking the code, Tommy Campo would take care of him.

But there wasn't a damn thing stopping Jimmy from confronting his old friend, Fabrizzio Falletti, and finding out what the hell was going on.

Jimmy left the office and turned off the lights for the night. Eight o'clock and the squad room was closed down. Lord. He passed the Major Crime Unit headquarters office, looked in, and God, there had to be ten guys in there, hustling. OPS right next door, the same, the headhunters coming and going, bustling around. He could see his hated enemy, Abe Jacobs, whose brother his girlfriend worked for in the legal office, waving his arms around, lecturing a bunch of clean-cut-looking guys, probably on how best to snooker a fellow cop into a confession, get him to sell out his best friends, his partner, his mother, probably. Jacobs looked up as Jimmy passed, as if whoever was walking past the hall was intruding in his home, or something, and their eyes locked. Jacobs's eyes narrowed, and Jimmy thought, as he passed the doorway and headed for the elevator, that the man was beginning to smile.

He thought of Fabe again as the elevator was descending, of Fabe's hatred of elevators, his almost *fear* of them. Walked nine floors up to his own apartment building, rather than get on an elevator.

What a shame. What a dirty, filthy, crying shame. Fabe, in somehow, with drugs.

His mood darkened further as he passed the front desk. There was an extremely overweight black woman crying to the duty officer that they had nowhere to stay, no place to go, tomorrow was Christmas Eve, could he help them? She had eight frightened children winding around her legs, hanging on to her, dressed in rags.

Jimmy left the building, not wanting to think about it.

13 "I have got to go in to Police Headquarters, Homicide Section, at eight o'clock in the morning on the twenty-sixth. I have convinced them that I am in mourning and that the holidays are extremely important to me, as I have many children. I will be going home for the Christmas holiday."

"You'll *what*?" DiNardo's shout came over the receiver distorted.

Francisco Ortiz laughed into the phone. "Do not be afraid, amigo," he said, enjoying the implication of cowardice. "I am booking a flight, it will be paid for, and a cousin of mine from Indiana Harbor will be on the plane, going home to my house for the days. He will come back on the twelve-fifteen A.M. flight that night, the morning early of the twenty-sixth. That will cover *me*. You better get something to cover yourself for tonight or tomorrow night, my friend, because without your help any, I have found the man who stole our goods."

DiNardo would be sitting on the floor now, Ortiz guessed, shaken by the insult in the idea that a stranger to this country had learned what all of his powerful friends could not. Ortiz waited, hearing the sharp intake of breath on the other end, DiNardo having a heart attack maybe. Finally DiNardo spoke. Ortiz smiled at Roga and winked.

"Who?" DiNardo asked.

"I will tell you later, so that this thing does not get fucked up like this afternoon's problems at your house. You should have took care of both the thief and the muscleman on the spot, Roland."

"You don't tell me my business, I won't tell you yours," DiNardo said, walking into Ortiz's trap.

"But is not my business your business?" Ortiz said, and hung up the phone.

Roland DiNardo sat in his study at his desk, staring at the book-lined walls, trying to control himself. He'd lost enough face today already. No more. After a long while, when he felt good enough to speak to Lloyd, he summoned Tino and Herman and told them to get his ass in there, *now*.

Tino and Herman had locked Lloyd in the basement. The windows were thick-block privacy glass, unbreakable. The only door out was heavily secured. There were a bathroom and a small refrigerator and stove, pots and pans under the shelf. All the comforts of home. As good as a federal prison, at least. But when they went to get him, they were both surprised that he hadn't used any of the comforts at his disposal. Lloyd was still sitting as he'd sat when they left him down there. The blood washed off, the shirt changed, sitting there on a cot holding his head in his hands.

"Hey," Tino said, but Lloyd did not look up.

"Yo," Herman said, pissed. If he had to go down the stairs to get this goof, he'd slap him a couple of times, let him know what he thought of free-lance muscle. "Hey, asshole," Herman said loudly, and Lloyd looked up. "C'mon, the man wants you."

"Let me get this straight, Lloyd," Roland DiNardo said calmly, but with wonder in his voice. "You thought I paid

Elmo to whack you *out*? The fuck's the matter with you? I wanted you dead, you think I'd have your buddy do it?"

Lloyd was almost whimpering now, which made Roland feel pretty damn good. It reminded him of one of the last scenes in *The Godfather*, when Michael had his no-good rotten brother-in-law Carlo pinned down in his house, telling him he had to answer for Santino, and all of the color drained from Carlo's face, and he'd copped, then Michael had wasted him. He felt like that now, looking at this pathetic tough guy sniffling in the chair across from him. He'd had Herman get the kid a glass of whiskey, like in the movie.

"I—I thought that was the way you people did it," Lloyd stammered.

"My people, what you mean, my *people*? You mean Sicilians? You saying, Lloyd, that you think Sicilians would need to use a guy's best friend to whack him out?"

"No, uh-uh, really, I didn't mean that, no, sir."

Roland let it drop, but he was wondering about the wad of money he'd given Elmo. If Lloyd'd had it, then it would never be seen again, because after Roland had Herman and Tino whack him, they'd take it.

"So, thinking I paid Elmo to kill you, you kill him first, is that it? Then you come back here looking for revenge?"

Lloyd nodded dumbly.

He knows this is it, Roland figured. He knows damn well all I have to do is raise a finger and he's history. Roland looked at him, came around the desk and took the glass of whiskey from his hand. He put it on the desk. He stared at Lloyd until Lloyd dropped his eyes, shivering now, he was so afraid. Good.

"I forgive you," Roland said.

Lloyd looked up, terror in his eyes. "No shit, Mr. Di-Nardo?"

Roland said, "Hey, I said I forgive you, okay? I felt like

it, I'd stuff you inna fire over there. You're a punk to me, nothing else. I say I forgive you, I forgive you."

Lloyd made Roland DiNardo feel ten feet tall then. He grabbed DiNardo's hand and kissed the big diamond ring on his little finger, saying over and over again, "Thank you," until Roland pulled his hand away and patted Lloyd's cheek. He nodded at him so he'd leave.

As Lloyd went out through the side door, counting his blessing, wondering how he could ever have been so dumb as to jump to the conclusion that Roland was planning to have him whacked out, hurrying to the Buick without even looking to see if the cops were still down the block, Tino and Herman were staring at Roland DiNardo, waiting for him to look up from his desk.

When he did, looking surprised to see them still there, Tino said, "Should we whack him out, or what?" And Roland saw the greed in his eyes.

"You want us to go after him, do the job?" Herman said.

"He got one more thing he gotta do," Roland DiNardo said, "then he's all yours." And he waved his hand and they left.

The word had been out all day: Anybody found dealing who had never been dealing before was to be followed. You were to find out who he was and report to any of the Ortiz family of East Chicago, Indiana. Out of that headquarters, and in their Indiana Harbor, Indiana, offices, the Ortiz family controlled ninety-five percent of the cocaine business in the Cook and Lake counties area.

There were cousins and uncles, relatives and friends of these uncles and cousins, nieces and nephews, who hid their product in the diapers of their children when they drove it across the border into Illinois. Lately, however, there had been some dissension. Someone, on a very high level, was obviously displeased with their work. Because all of a sudden their business had dwindled to a trickle of what it had been. The trickle still paid the bills and kept the big dealers in the family in secondhand Eldorados and Lincolns, but it was nothing next to what it used to be. And the Ortiz family, they were willing to do whatever it took to make amends to the Man, Francisco, who everyone knew owned a mansion out on his very own island, where his family could visit if they did very well and made him happy. A place with enough extra rooms that Francisco could easily make it into a hotel and make very much money. But he did not. He kept the extra rooms ready for his children's friends, for his extra women, and for the members of the family in the United States who pleased him greatly. The problem was, no one had pleased him in quite some time.

No one in the family had been to the island in so long, they thought that perhaps Francisco had sold it. But phone calls made there always got through. How were they to know that Francisco had made a deal with the American Mafia, and had been using Roland DiNardo for his distributor? This effectively cut out the middleman. Francisco shipped the cocaine over, it was given to a courier of DiNardo's choosing, he turned over the cash, and that was that. The few dollars his family lost on cutting and selling was a small price to pay, when you consider that he no longer had to pay outsiders who did the cutting, nor spend time worrying about the constant legal fees and rip-offs that occurred when uneducated, gringo-ized *puertorriqueños* made a couple of bucks and wanted more.

No, after he had made his deal with Roland DiNardo, Francisco had allowed the other end of his American business to suffer. He could, if he could get the product, keep it flowing smoothly, but why? Was not a million dollars a week in profit enough for any one man? Tax-free net income? Yes, more than enough. He would send them a little something every month, to keep them earning a decent living, but the days of the big buck for them was over. They would have to learn English now, if something wasn't done, and take jobs.

So when Miro Roga came to town, telling them that a vacation in the homeland was free for anyone who gave them the right name, the name of the man who had ripped off one of Francisco's lieutenants in Chicago and had probably killed his sister Lucille, they went to work. Miro had told them, "No one kills this animal. He is Francisco's. He is to be found, but not touched, *comprendéis*?" And the word had spread quickly, from Ortiz to Ortiz, then down through the family-by-marriage people, who were not strictly Ortizes but who had a stake in the business. After the weeping and obligatory threats and curses and vows to revenge Lucille Ortiz, whom very few of them had ever even met, they went to work.

There was a North Side nigger faggot, the pusher told his supplier, at least, he had to be a faggot to live in a mansion alone like he did, and the supplier told him to shut the fuck up and get on with it, and the pusher had told him, "Look, bruh, I ain't one of your PR toadies, so don't tell *me* to shut the fuck up or I'll get my shit elsewhere."

The supplier, a white upper-middle-class store owner who passed the cocaine on to the street-level pushers after cutting it four times to ensure himself an immense profit, apologized. He needed people like this, even if he wanted nothing to do with them socially.

Well, it turned out, this nigger had been buying from him for a couple of years, great big vast quantities of coke, and suddenly, out of a clear blue sky, he calls at five-thirty in the morning, wasted, telling the pusher that he had an ounce to turn over, right now, with many more to come. The pusher had gone and bought it at a great price, and here it was, right in his pocket.

The supplier had thanked him, told him he was going to have an extra merry Christmas, and had called his distributor.

The distributor was a white doctor married to a Puerto Rican girl whose father was related by marriage to Francisco Ortiz's sister-in-law. He took the call in his paneled office after shooing out the child he was examining for the Asian flu. They laughed a little about the quality of people they had to deal with, with the distributor thinking, yeah, assholes like *you,* then they got down to business. The doctor thanked the store owner, hung up, and told his nurse to hold the next patient for about five minutes. He picked up the phone and called his father-in-law, who had set him up in a business that brought him in almost as much as his thriving practice, and got him all the good coke he needed.

The father-in-law called Hector Ortiz, a second cousin to Francisco, and told him the news. "What is the nigger's name?" Hector asked.

The doctor's father-in-law said, "Doral Washington," and that is how Miro Roga learned the name of the man who had ripped Francisco off and who had probably raped Lucille, then given her an OD.

Sitting in the Holiday Inn double room on Michigan Avenue, Francisco Ortiz told Roga, "Send Hector down to my house for a couple of days, alone. Make the plane reservation in my name. I want him back Christmas night, late. Tell him after New Year, when I return home, his family will come with me, spend a month."

"They will enjoy that," Roga said.

When he'd learned the flight schedules and Hector had

been called and told what flight to take out that evening and when to return, Francisco Ortiz had called DiNardo to rub it in. And to learn whether DiNardo was afraid. If he was, that would prove to Francisco that he was in on the murder of Lucille, and he would have to pay. DiNardo's reaction had told Ortiz that DiNardo was not involved in it, as much as anything like this could be proved, anyway. So now he had to go over and talk to DiNardo face to face, because he had to avenge his sister. Had to kill this nigger who had killed his sister and stolen his product and his money. He needed DiNardo along to guarantee the clout he might need if he got arrested avenging Lucille.

Loyalty was a wonderful thing, but it did not mean so much when you are serving life for murder. So he would cover his ass. Get DiNardo's powerful protection. Then get his product and his money back, and the whole thing would be over.

Francisco Ortiz held no hard feelings toward the policeman who had cursed him at the morgue. Of course, if it had not been for Miro and DiNardo, he would have beaten the man to death. But he did not hold grudges. He had been shot three times, back when he was making his name. He had been held in a deserted Wisconsin cottage in the middle of February, his clothing had been taken, and he had been cut slowly from his groin to his toes by men trying to take over what he had put together from the ground up. Men who had wanted his people's names, so they could make them an offer after they killed Francisco, put them to work for themselves. Stupids. And when two of these men were sleeping and one was watching Francisco shiver on the wooden floor of the cottage, freezing to death, waiting for morning when they would give him one more chance to talk before killing him, Francisco had moaned loudly, his finally free hands concealed behind him, his wrists cut to hell from playing with the bond for two days, his arms under him, on his back, twisting and pinching the fibers of the ropes until finally they snapped. The guard had said, *Qué*? and had come closer, seeing no threat in the dying man on the floor, the beaner, as they called him constantly. Francisco had moaned and had spoken a name, and the man had stepped right up to him, got down on his knees and had put his ear to Francisco's lips, and Francisco had grabbed his throat then and snapped his neck back, breaking it with weak hands. He'd taken the man's pistol and had gone into the bedrooms, waking both men up and taking their blankets to cover himself with. He'd made them kiss each other in their private places before shooting them in their stomachs. After something like that, an insult from a policeman in Chicago was less than nothing.

So he had no honor to defend with the policeman, no face to save, no revenge to extract. His business here was first to seek revenge for his sister's death, and then to get his money. The product was DiNardo's problem. He had sent it in with that stupid cow sister of his, Lucille. She was in DiNardo's mule's house when she'd finally managed to get herself killed. So the product had been delivered. No one could doubt that. And so Francisco believed he had a million dollars coming. If not from this Washington guy, then from DiNardo. He would not leave this city without his million dollars, of that he was sure.

He would wait until after the time when Hector's flight was gone, and then he would go to DiNardo and explain the facts of life to this ignorant person. Washington had to pay for Lucille. As stupid as she was, she was still family. Close family. Their mother would never allow Francisco into her home if he did not bring her the bloody ears of the man who had killed her youngest child, her baby daughter.

Francisco himself was going to kill this Doral Washington only to save face within his community, to spread a warning. To maintain the fear he had instilled all the years of his life into the souls of lesser men. But as far as he was concerned, Lucille had gotten what she deserved, sister or not. It would only have been a matter of time until she was either killed or sent to prison. The woman had no brains, no sense. And Francisco had effectively disowned her from his family when they had caught her in an LA apartment having sex with a black man. This he could not ignore nor forgive. But appearances had to be maintained

And so he would defend the honor of his sister, kill this animal who was selling his dope on the street as if he'd found it somewhere, instead of having taken it from Francisco. Or, rather, from DiNardo. Oh, he would get his money back, one way or the other.

There was no doubt in Francisco's mind, not since he'd heard from Miro that Doral Washington was selling quality cocaine, that he was the man who had stolen the drugs and and the money from Chacona's safe. Naturally, the safe would be empty. DiNardo had been a fool even to think otherwise. The police in America are not stupid, they would have found the safe and opened it. And maybe stolen some of what was inside. But not all of it. They would have left some of it, surely, to stir things up in the press. So he would talk to DiNardo and learn from him what he had to know about Washington. Then the two of them together would go and do what had to be done.

And if this Washington did not have his money, DiNardo would have to come up with it. Or else Francisco would have Miro kill him. They could do their business with someone more reliable. Someone they could trust to get help that would not try and fuck you around.

Francisco settled back, there in his room in the Holiday Inn on Michigan Avenue, wondering where they would spend the night after they snuck out of the place. It would not do to have himself on an airplane heading toward Puerto Rico at the same

178

time some policeman spotted him coming out of the hotel, or the police at DiNardo's house spotted him coming or going.

Francisco believed that he had gotten as far as he had because he was smarter than the people he did business with; he outthought them, much as he would if he played them in a game of chess. And so he had not told DiNardo that the police were watching his house, nor had he asked why. It was not his business. The police already had Francisco and DiNardo connected to one another, the big policeman at the morgue last night had made that clear. So it did not matter to him now if they were watching DiNardo. Nor was it his place to tell DiNardo about it. If DiNardo was dumb enough not to know what was going on around him, it was his own fault. And if he was that dumb, then maybe Francisco would be better off by far doing business with someone else.

He waved at Roga to get him a drink, and put his feet up on the edge of the bed. He wanted to think things through thoroughly before he went off to meet with Roland DiNardo.

The place on Jefferson was much better than Fabe expected. He'd been too long on the North Side. He'd forgotten that it wasn't all slum on the other side of Randolph. Then again, a couple of years ago the south Loop hadn't exactly been a part of town you'd want to raise kids in, either. But the neighbors had gotten together to pressure the city, and with everyone working together they'd cleaned the place up quite a bit. No winos on the corner, for one thing. And although he could see in the distance one of the high-rise public housing buildings, it wasn't as if it was across the street or anything.

Fifth floor, and the place even had a little bit of security; he'd had to buzz and have her ring him in. Of course, the cheap little lock there, he figured, would take him maybe thirty seconds to beat with a bobby pin. But no sense in showing off.

She was waiting on the fifth-floor landing in a pair of jeans and a knee-length rabbit coat, high black boots on her feet. Gloves and a loose watch cap covered her ears, flattening her brown hair some, giving her an almost severe look. A bad sign, waiting for him, not asking him in to warm up or anything. Or have a drink. But she'd broken a date for him. That had to count for something, didn't it?

"You took the *stairs*?" Sally said, looking puzzled, and Fabe had looked at her, smiling a little foolishly, feeling awkward but pleased.

"I got a heater in the car, you know," he told her.

She touched the cap on her head self-consciously, grinning at him. She said, "I'm used to walking most places." And reached out for his arm, wrapped both of hers around it. "You want to walk down, too, or can we take the elevator?"

Fabe walked firmly to the elevator and pressed the "down" button without answering. He did not want her to think he was weird or anything. He was enjoying the warm feel of her hands on his arm, the automatic closeness she'd assumed, none of this backing off and playing games until she thought she knew him. Straightforward. Confident. He still sensed shyness. And yet he didn't feel as if he had to fill the air with words. He could be quiet with her and she wouldn't think he was boring.

"Where'd you like to go?" he asked when they were standing on Jefferson and she'd steered him away from the car, looking up the street, then up into the sky.

"Would you think I'm weird," Sally said, "if I said I'd just like to take a walk, get to know you a little bit?"

Fabe smiled. "You don't want to get in the car, go to Ditka's or McMahon's or someplace, maybe get to see some real-live professional football players?"

She looked confused again and said simply, "Why would I want to do *that*?" And as she said it and her breath fogged the clear black night air between them, Fabe decided he was going to enjoy getting to know this one.

They took Jefferson south to Monroe and from there they hiked to Michigan, walking a couple of miles right there, talking. "What do you do?" she asked and he told her he was retired, was into investments these days, was all, and she said, "At *your* age?" making him feel pretty good about his rapidly approaching fortieth.

"I'm almost forty," he said, and she squeezed his arm playfully.

"I like them older," she said to him, walking next to him as if they were longtime lovers instead of out on their first date. She was holding on to him with both hands around his left arm, closest to the buildings, while he walked on the street side. He'd read somewhere in the joint that the gentleman always walks on the street side.

Somehow it was important to impress her with decent manners.

At Michigan they crossed the street, running in the chilled night to Grant Park, ignoring the honking horns and the shouts of cabbies and bus drivers. They sat down on the first bench they came to. The park was seemingly deserted at this early hour. Fabe was on the right, at the end of the bench, with a good view all around him, and Sally perched next to him, just touching. He felt his body begin to react to her and crossed his legs, toward her, though. He turned his head away a second as he lit a Pall Mall away from the wind, using cupped hands, and he had to pull out of her grip to do so. When he sat back straight she scrunched up against him, as if he could protect her from the cold, and now her arm was almost around his shoulders; her head was resting on his chest.

"If I opened your coat and put my ear right here, I bet I could hear your heartbeat," Sally said.

Fabe said, "If you opened my coat and put your ear there, I might not have a heartbeat left on account of the heart attack I'd have."

She surprised him then, by not taking it further. "Are you a cop, Fabe?" Sally asked, pulling her head away just enough to look up into his face.

"Not anymore," he said, looking down at her, seeing a genuine look of concern. "Why?"

"Then why do you carry a gun?"

Fabe sighed and stood up, helping her to her feet. "To protect my investments."

Crossing Michigan Avenue in a suddenly uncomfortable silence, Fabe said, "Look, if you want, I'll switch it to my other pocket, or you can carry it, you're worried I'm gonna pull it out and scare you with it, or something." She was still holding his arm, that was one thing on the good side of the list, but he was feeling that he'd just lost her.

"I work six mornings a week, Fabe," Sally said, hopping onto the curb, steering him north toward the bright lights on the dead-silent streets. Some cars and cabs cruised Michigan, but they were the only pedestrians in sight. "I go to John Marshall Law School three afternoons and three nights. I won't be a waitress forever; it's not a life goal of mine." And she pulled away just a little bit, looking at him sideways, eyes merry, smiling now, and Fabe thought, terrific. "I graduate in June, you know, and I'll be twenty-six in August. I was born and raised in the city. I live alone, walk to work most mornings unless I'm running late, for the exercise. And to school, too."

She stopped in the middle of the sidewalk on Michigan

Avenue, where they stood as if they were the only two people on the planet. She pulled away from him and stood facing him, and the smile was gone. She looked concerned now, a little hesitant to continue, and so Fabe smiled and nodded at her, give her a little encouragement.

"I'm not sure if I want to be with a guy who isn't a cop and carries a gun, is what I'm saying."

Fabe wasn't used to this kind of woman. "Listen," he said, "this is the first time in my life, since I got out of the Army, that I carry a gun with me, and if you want, we'll take a little walk, I'll throw it out into the middle of the Lake."

"Would you really?"

"Say the word."

Sally surprised him then. She just took his arm again, held it tight, and restarted them northward.

They went a couple of blocks in comfortable silence, Fabe looking at the corny Christmas setups in the windows, closing in on Randolph Street now. After that, he knew, there would be other people, more intruders upon their own little world, and he felt a little sad. He liked it this way.

"You know," Sally said, "I've had my eye on you for a couple of weeks?"

"Come on."

"No, really, you come in there, every Monday and Friday, sit with the big guy who dresses like he makes five dollars an hour in a factory somewhere, and you're always dressed well, always smiling and laughing, goofing around, kidding me and the other girls. I looked at you and I said, 'Sally,' I said to myself, 'that's the kind of guy you want to get to know.' You know, I've been with guys, not often, anymore, jeez, not with my schedule, but sometimes I go out. Met a guy at school, his father's got the big house in Kenilworth, a weekend retreat in Michigan, you could put up half of the city's homeless in it, and these guys, they're just plastic, all phony. They tell me stories about how many country clubs they're in, how well they know Michael Butler, or how they stood in the line at Oak Brook and watched Prince Charles play polo. I'd listen to them order something expensive at Nick Nicholas's fish house, and I'd think, God, is this all that's out there?

"Yesterday, when you and your friend were in the back booth laughing so hard everyone was looking at you, I thought to myself, I thought—" She hesitated. He squeezed her arm with his free hand, then put his hand back into his coat pocket.

"I thought, God, what would it be like to go out with a guy who didn't have to act so together? Who didn't care if he was choosing the right wine? Who knew how to *laugh*. Fabe, these guys, they don't laugh; I mean, they try, they go, 'Ha-ha-ha,' but it's like they're in a comic book and there's a bubble over their heads." She shook herself as if there were a goose on her grave.

Fabe was wondering if he was supposed to be saying something funny, get her to laugh. Then decided not to. That's not what she meant. Try and understand what she was saying. Christ, it had been so long since he'd made the effort.

"Sally," he said at last, deciding to open up some, see how it went. "Listen, I'm having trouble here. Don't get me wrong, okay? I'm not stupid or anything. But look, I'm not used to being with a nice person, you understand? I mean, everyone *I've* been out with lately, the past few years, anyway, knows the score. We've, the both of us, been around the block a few times. All of them, I'll tell you something, if they knew I was carrying, had a gun on me, they'd be pumping me about it, getting off on it, like a gun moll or something. Just do me a favor, okay? Forget about the gun. Let's take it slow and natural, act like nothing was in my pocket, and go with my apology.

I got a good reason to carry this thing for a couple of days, but after that, forget about it. I mean, it's not even *mine*."

"So you think I'm a nice person, Fabe?" Squeezing, letting him know she was kidding around. Telling him, you'd *better* believe it, mister.

"Nicest girl I've been with in a *long* time."

"Is there . . . someone steady?"

"Not anymore." He thought about the date she'd broken earlier. "You?"

"Not until now."

Fabe felt himself suddenly warm. They were past Randolph now, heading into the heart of the city, and there were other people on the street, more with each block they walked.

Sally said, "Tell me about her."

"Who?"

"The one who's not there anymore."

"Why would you want to know about *her*?"

"So I won't make the same mistake she did, and—and lose you."

It was Fabe who stopped this time, in front of the Sun-Times Building, and he took both of her hands in his. People walked by them almost constantly now, out Christmas shopping in the city, dressed to the nines, passing and staring at the tall, good-looking couple smiling at each other, and Fabe smiled for them as much as for Sally, feeling like someone in a perfume commercial.

"Hey," he said, "she never even tried to *find* me."

And Sally smiled really wide. "Was she a gun moll?" They started walking again, holding hands. Fabe felt her warmth even through the gloves.

"She tries to be. Matter of fact, her husband went stoolie, into the Witness Protection Program."

"You're kidding."

"No, I'm not."

Sally said, "That guy, the big guy you have lunch with, *he's* not a crook, is he?"

"*Hell* no."

"Tell me about him!" she said, all enthusiastic like a kid on a field trip or something, and so Fabe told her.

14

Jimmy Capone had assured Billy Boy that his misdemeanor grass bust was a thing of the past, and warned him to ring up in Fabe's apartment the minute he came in. He told Billy Boy that he'd be waiting there for Fabe to come home. Billy Boy was smart enough to keep his mouth shut and not ask questions, for which Jimmy was grateful.

Standing in Fabe's hallway, looking around, he wondered why Fabey even bothered, if he was only going to put in an alarm system any journeyman locksmith could beat with his eyes closed. He picked the Mosler, using a nail file he'd sharpened and twisted to suit his purposes, and as a matter of fact as he picked it he did indeed have his eyes closed. Remembering Fabe's father telling them in the kitchen with the table covered with locks and parts of locks and alen wrenches, "Always *feel* for the tumblers, *fisha* for dem, like if you are a-gonna die if you go too fast. Always take you' time, never rush." And he or Fabe would slowly put one of the angled thin wrenches into the keyhole of the big steel padlocks, twisting, turning, and the old man would go berserk, shouting and hitting them on the top of their heads and screaming "Mamma Mia, stùpido!" at them until they got it right.

Dead all these years and Jimmy still could not think of Mr.

Falletti without smiling and feeling a queer sensation of sadness, mixed with anger. At the small immigrant who was maybe the best thief in his time Chicago had ever known. Could pick a lock or crack a Mosler safe in less than a minute, beat the primitive alarms with alligator clips, disdainfully. He had taught his son and his son's best friend all that he knew.

He unclipped his bypass after he got into the apartment, closed and locked the door, then reset the alarm from the inside. If Fabe came home now, he'd be unprepared for any surprises.

It took Jimmy three and a half hours to search the apartment the right way. He found nothing out of place. Nothing he could pin on Fabe. No evidence of any involvement with drugs or the murder on Clark Street the night before.

Naturally, he'd found some things that interested him, but they had to do with what Fabe was, things of no concern to Inspector Capone.

Like the tightly wound bundle of hundreds hidden in the false wall in the closet. Next to three different Illinois driver's licenses, all with Fabe's picture on them but with different names. Not the kind of thing you'd turn up in your average apartment burglary. But he knew what Fabey was. He'd gotten used to it by now. All major credit cards accepted.

It was close to eleven when he finished, and no one could ever tell he'd even been there.

He should go home, get some rest. He should make a couple of calls, at least, see about the surveillance at the DiNardo house, how it was shaping up.

The hell with it. The watch commander at the First Precinct knew damn well that there were two guys sitting on DiNardo's place, and that two more would be needed in the morning. No big thing, just an average stakeout, gathering intelligence. They couldn't even use anything they saw in court, if it came down to it. Not unless DiNardo freaked, shot a couple of people in his house, and even then the cops would have hell to prove, trying to convince a judge that they just happened to be passing by and heard gunshots.

What Jimmy Capone did was, he plopped down in Fabe's leather armchair and picked up the remote-control box from the end table. He hit the "play" button and saw that Fabey had been watching the Hearns-Leonard fight. He rewound it to the beginning and started to watch it, wondering how late Fabey would be, and, a little later, where the hell he was.

Roland DiNardo was trying mightily to keep a straight face, not to show these beaners that he was about to explode, to go nuts. To kill something. Slowly.

"Doral Washington," Ortiz had said, and Roland had looked at the little muscle-bound freak standing there bobbing up and down, up and down on his toes, Roga behind him still wearing his sunglasses at night inside the house when Roland had only a sixty-watt bulb burning in the desk lamp and the light from the fire to see by, and he'd had to fight the urge to shoot them both right then, blow them the hell away, get these little greaser sons of bitches out of his life once and for all.

But he didn't.

Because he still needed them. And probably more than they needed him.

Francisco was talking now, as if he was on top of things. Roland let him talk, because he had no choice. If Doral Washington had been the one to take the money and the dope, then it stood to reason that Roland had made a gigantic asshole out of himself that very afternoon because everyone knew that Doral Washington was a gofer. He was smart, stand-up, he wasn't a rat, but he was basically a dime a dozen, hired muscle, and the brains behind the outfit, behind their two-man burglary ring, was Fabrizzio Falletti, who had stood across the desk from him this afternoon and held a gun on him. Who'd laughed at him when Roland offered him a grand for ten minutes' work. Who'd known all along that Roland was wasting his time trying to get into the safe because he himself had ripped it off only the day before. That cock*sucker*!

Oh, how he'd pay. How that dirty northern bastard would *pay*, and Roland didn't give two shits anymore if the guy had a deal with Tommy Campo or not.

So he needed the beaners still, because Fabe and his nigger chum had his money and his dope, the sons of *bitches*. And if Roland just killed them, Campo would whack him out for breaking the peace, no doubt about it. But, if it looked like a drug score gone bad, if Fabe and Doral Washington got wasted by this psycho Miro, who would probably cut off their balls and make them eat them before he slit their throats and carved on them for a while, if it could be made to look as if the two of them were killed in a bad drug deal, well . . .

Campo couldn't blame him then, could he? And so he'd use these two animals for that little job.

But the cop, Capone, had seen Roland with Ortiz and Roga last night, over at the morgue. He'd put two and two together real quick, too.

Tommy Campo, or Tombstone, for that matter, his own *padrone*, would kill him in a second if he knew for a fact that he was openly disobeying orders and selling drugs.

The heat was getting too damn hot.

And so, it was logical for Roland to conclude that after they whacked out Falletti and Washington and recovered the drugs and money, Ortiz and Rosa would be suddenly expendable.

Knowing it was almost over for both of their arrogant asses, Roland began to smile at them. It was okay now if this little shrimp freak who probably couldn't wipe his ass because he had so much muscle rocked on his toes and stared down at him. It was okay that his partner, the skinny fuck in the strange clothes all the time attracting attention, looked at him from behind sunglasses at eight o'clock at night. It didn't matter. Roland sat back in his big chair and put his feet up on the desk, tuning the little shit back in.

". . . and so you see I cannot do it all by myself, me and Miro. I need you with me in case we should get in trouble, how you say, *busted.*" And Roland smiled at the way the little beaner said it, "bosted," and nodded his head, agreeing with whatever the guy was saying, keeping it all cool, because this would more than likely be their last night on earth.

Suddenly he was happy as all hell that he had allowed Lloyd to live. It was all falling into place. He had let Lloyd live because he'd planned all along to let Lloyd do the job on these two when the time was right, but he had no idea then that it would be so soon.

It had been a good night, all things considered. Around one she'd said, "My *God,* I've got to work in the morning," and he'd looked at her and she'd looked back as if he were a loony-tune, saying, "Hey, Greek joints, you're lucky to get Christmas *Day* off."

They'd taken a cab back to her place. Fabe felt pleasantly tired but happy. He overtipped the guy, listened to him say something cheerful in a foreign language. In the elevator he said, "Do you think he called me an imperialist asshole or something, just because I don't understand Iranian?" And he'd gotten a laugh, hearty and rich. A laugh he'd been hearing since they'd stopped dead on Michigan in front of the Sun-Times Building and she'd said what she had.

Then into the apartment, no question he'd be coming in, none of this coy gamesmanship, turning to him with a phony

smile and a handshake saying, "Thanks for a wonderful time."
On the sofa, thinking, my, this is a nice joint, fancy shag rug,
some kind of prints on the walls. No TV, but a nice stereo she
was now tuning to something classical. Feeling comfortable and
at ease and not at all surprised when she disappeared into another room, had to be the bedroom, down the hall there. Knowing damn well she'd come out in a nightgown or something.
Fabe sat on the sofa sipping his drink, his hangover forgotten,
remembering her and what they'd done this night.

Walking down Michigan, he'd said, "Did you ever notice
how the better-looking women, they all walk on the *east* side of
Michigan? I'm serious, Sally, take a look." And they'd
watched for a while, counting the pretty women on both sides of
the street, crossing this one off the list, that one going on, not
because she was pretty but because she was wearing a nice fur.

"Maybe it's because they all come from Water Tower
Place, the Ritz-Carlton, the Westin. They're all on the east
side."

"No," Fabe said, "I bet it's because all the really expensive shops are on the east side."

But then Sally was giggling.

"I say something funny?" he said, and she pointed across
the street.

He'd looked, but it had been hard to see any names on
storefronts; his attention was captured by the festive street
lamps, done up like candy canes, holly-wrapped, tinsel and everything. Why hadn't he ever noticed this before?

"Look," Sally had said, and he saw "Cartier's" right
there in script, low-key and classy.

"Kind of blows that theory all to hell, huh, bucko?" Sally
had said, and they'd laughed some, got loose, nothing hysterical
or frantic, but a real laugh, feeling good inside. Sharing something no one else knew about.

192

Telling her about Jimmy, she asking some good hard questions, so many that he'd asked her if she was in journalism school or what and she'd laughed again, saying that the man fascinated her.

Inside Water Tower Place, telling her about Doral and the punk rockers, enjoying the sound of her laughter, now with an outraged edge to it. "He'd really done that?" And Fabe assuring her it was so, telling her that Water Tower Place had a total of 125 stores, shops, and boutiques, 11 restaurants, 2 banks, and 7 movie houses.

"How in God's name do you know all that?" she'd asked and so he decided to impress her further.

"All together these stores take in $583,000 a *day*. Total of $210 million a year." And she'd just looked at him, maybe not really wanting to know why he'd taken the trouble to learn these facts.

He used the seventh-floor men's room, came out and Sally was nowhere in sight. Then a glimpse of her, across the hallway, on one of the public phones. Walking over to her, smiling, feeling better than he had in a while, hearing her say, "I don't care, Marsha, I'm not going to study Christmas; God, can't I take one day off?" then hanging up angrily, turning to him, seeming surprised by his appearance.

Looking up at him shyly, saying, "My studymate. God, she'd have me studying around the clock, seven days a week if I let her." And Fabe smiled inside, wondering if this was the date she'd broken earlier.

Into one of the eleven restaurants, eating well, drinking little, getting to know each other, Fabe wondering if she ever was going to let Jimmy Capone alone. "How'd you meet him?" or "Isn't it a little strange to be almost forty and still have the same best friend you had in grade school?" or "Do you and him do business together?" And Fabe had given her simple answers, feeling a little jealous, wondering if maybe it was Jimmy she was interested in all along. Fabe had been the first one to talk to her, had been all.

But soon she changed her tack, asking about his childhood, reaching up once to push the hair out of his eyes.

"Your eyes are so pretty," she'd said, "you should wear your hair shorter so people can see them."

"Hey, you want me to, I'll shave my head." And she'd laughed again. He was getting a kick out of listening to her laugh.

Now, in her apartment on Jefferson, he heard her moving around in the other room, sounds of her voice, was she singing? Yes, or humming, that was it. He sipped his drink and was just about to get up and look at one of the prints on the wall when her hand touched his left shoulder. He turned.

She was standing there, all five feet eight inches of her, standing behind him in all her glory, wearing a satin, tiny, almost nothing of a slip or nightgown or something, and Fabe could not find his voice. Her legs were long; perfectly proportioned, smooth, well curved. Her breasts were better than they looked under an engineer's uniform, or a coat. Through the satin he could see the large nipples, hard and uptilted. She was looking right at him, not challengingly or aggressively, but shyly, as if this offering was the most important thing in the world to her.

Fabe put his glass down on the end table, looking at her, his eyes taking in every inch of her loveliness, then he reached for her.

In bed, in the back of Fabe's mind, there was the thought: This is the way it's supposed to be. Two mature adults, taking pleasure and enjoyment from each other without any bullshit. She didn't act as if he were the greatest stud she'd ever come across, nor did she act bored. She got into it slowly, shy at first, as they felt each other, played around, turned each other on, no playacting. That's what he liked best. He watched her, on his elbows, and liked what he saw. Her eyes closed, a tiny smile on her lips, her forehead scrunched up a little bit, moving with him slowly, as one. He was smiling down at her when she opened her eyes, and they went from dreamy and placid to almost shocked, then she smiled back, it was all right.

They watched each other until it was over.

Roga and Lloyd both cut themselves going over Doral's iron gate. Roga got it on the leg, slicing right through his pants and into flesh. Lloyd ripped his leather jacket and cursed loud enough for Roga to tell him to shut up, which pissed Lloyd off to no end. But at least it was a job; jeez, his first hit. In the employ of a made member of the Chicago Outfit. If his mother was still alive, Lloyd thought, would she ever be proud.

Even if the two big shots, DiNardo and the other spic who hadn't been introduced to Lloyd, stayed in a car two blocks away—well, they were the bosses. This was handywork. He felt honored. But not to be working with this guy here, no, sir.

As a matter of fact, with the sunglasses this guy had on after midnight, it was a wonder he didn't slit his throat on the fence. Jesus, Lloyd thought, what kind of animal sharpens his fence posts?

Roga crept silently to the front of the house, nodded at something he saw inside, then moved to the back of the house, to the garage, and took up a position in the deep shadows there, standing ramrod-stiff and with his back against the wood. Lloyd watched him take out the walkie-talkie, press the button twice, then heard him talk Puerto Rican into it for a while. The guy finished, put the walkie-talkie back into his coat pocket, and waved frantically for Lloyd to get out of the driveway there and into the shadows.

"We gonna wait outside?" Lloyd said. "In the fucking cold?"

"Hey, the guy ain't home," Roga said, as if he was explaining something to a retard, and Lloyd cursed himself for having shot Elmo. He'd much rather have Elmo there with him now than this dude.

"Why don't we just go in?" Lloyd asked, and the dude, he stared at Lloyd for a while, and Lloyd could almost swear he could see the flash of anger behind the fucking glasses.

"Look, you ever kill anyone before?" Roga said, and got Lloyd's dander up.

"Sure, lots of times." Thinking of just that afternoon, on the rocks at the beach.

"Well, we ain't gonna get the element of surprise," Roga said, "if we go in, bust open his alarm system."

Lloyd, standing there next to him, could smell foul breath as Roga spoke. He felt foolish, as if he suddenly was fifteen years old again, going into St. Charles for the first and last time, not on top of things anymore, the older, wider guys drawing straws to see who would make him their woman.

Resentful, angry, Lloyd said, "Hey, you always wear those goddamn glasses at night, or what?" And the guy turned to him, looked at him hard, but didn't say anything.

Pretty, smart, well-built, a good lover, and now, he was finding out, a cleanliness freak. Five minutes after they were done, Sally was up and out of bed, into the shower. Good. Healthy. Fabe rolled over and stretched. It was good to be retired. Everything would work out. They'd got away clean. Doral was on his own. He could take care of himself. He wasn't Fabe's problem. DiNardo would never find out. They'd covered their asses too well.

It was funny, but he didn't feel too guilty about the dead

man anymore, either. It was something in the back of his mind, pulling him just a little, not too much, though. It would fade, go away. There always was that chance, when you were in the life. Death was always a possibility. The guy had taken his chances, and he'd lost.

Fabe was fumbling through his clothes, looking for his Pall Malls, wondering why in the hell the woman had her phone-answering machine in the bedroom. Then making the connection. *That* was what he had heard before, when he'd thought she'd been singing or humming. He'd heard the steady cadence of her recorded message speaking before her messages came on the speaker. It was an old-fashioned machine. Poor kid, she'd have to listen to every message after hearing her own announcement. Must get boring. Fabe guessed he'd buy her a new one for Christmas. The kind where you never have to listen to your announcement after recording it. And you could check your messages from any Touch-Tone phone in the state. That'd get her attention. Show her he was thoughtful. He smoked a cigarette, looking at the telephone stand, deep in thought.

Sally soaped herself down, feeling alive, awake, on top of the world, but with small nagging doubts. Had she moved too soon? Would Fabe think she was easy now that they'd made love on the first date? The hell with it. If he thought that way, then she had grossly misjudged him, and she could write it off to experience. Either way, he was one remarkable piece of ass.

Sally had almost died when she'd opened her eyes during their lovemaking and had seen him staring down at her face, not with a look of conquest or domination, but rather kindly, almost . . . lovingly. After her initial shock she had just looked back, and that had been a powerful and new thing for her; she'd never just looked at a man before, right in the eyes, trying to get inside of him mentally. It had moved her emotionally as well as erotically. Maybe more so, although that would be hard. She'd found it one of her most erotic experiences, staring into his eyes as they built up together to a crashing, earth-shattering mutual orgasm. Much better than trying something novel like hanging baskets or something, or trapped together with eyes squeezed shut trying only to get off, selfishly, forgetting completely that there was another person there with you.

She turned to face the spray of the shower, smiling, feeling a tingle throughout her body, no longer worrying whether she had blown it or not. Time would tell.

She started a little bit when the shower curtain was drawn back, because she had been lost in thought. And when he stepped in next to her and took the soap from her hands, they smiled at each other again, knowingly.

"God, I've got to get to work," Sally said, and Fabe started from the light sleep, looking around.

"What?"

"It's time for work," she said.

Fabe said, "Take off. It's Christmas Eve."

"You know how hard good jobs are to find? I don't have *time* to look for another job, Fabe. By summer, I'll be able to quit. Till then, it's six days a week, buddy, six till two."

Dressing, both of them tired and yawning, she said, "It's only till noon today anyway. We're splitting shifts, 'cause the place closes at five. And I'm off tomorrow."

Fabe watched her dress, totally unselfconscious now, at ease with him, stepping into her panty hose and pulling on her uniform, turning him on pretty good.

"Sally, why don't you drop me off, take the car; I'll grab a cab over here later and we can do something together for Christmas Eve."

"You don't have a family?"

Fabe said, "Shit, hey, I'm sorry, I didn't even think. You'll want to spend Christmas with your family, right?"

"Well, only the morning. Tell you what. We'll get together this afternoon, you spend the night here, then you can wait for me to come home from my mother's, and we'll spend at least most of Christmas together."

There it was. You spend the night here and that was that. Pretty simple. She sounded sincere, too. As if they were long-term lovers instead of relative strangers. It made him feel good.

Fabe said, "How about I give you a key, leave the alarm off, you come on up after work."

She turned to him, brushing her hair now with long hard strokes. "I'd like that," Sally said.

He left her the car, taking off in the cold biting wind on foot, wanting to clear his head, think things over. She could go back to sleep for an hour if she wanted, now that she had the car. She wouldn't have to walk to work. Had to be there at five-fifteen. Jesus. Start at six. Spend forty-five minutes setting up, getting things ready, without pay. What a way to make a living.

Quarter after four on Christmas Eve morning. Walking around, thinking about people who worked full-time and still carried a full load of credits trying to make it through law school. And he'd spent most of his life sliding by, doing what was easiest, and bullshitting himself that it was what he had to do to get even. Christ.

Bunny's Hutch had a four-o'clock license, but they'd had their Christmas party last night. It was probably still going on. Most nights, they just locked the doors and partied until they felt like going home. Or if there was a serious game of pool going on in the back, the place would have customers around the clock.

Fabe had to think of what in the hell he was going to say to

Doral, and did not want to try and think about it at home. The hangover was gone entirely now. He felt worked up, wired, happy but a little tense. Things were getting heavy all of a sudden. He decided to stop at the Hutch and get himself a drink, maybe apologize to Bunny about the way he'd grabbed the key out of her purse. Let her know it was over, but without any hard feelings getting in the way. Say his farewells to the gang there, make it his last hurrah, get the feel of corruption and the smell of the hustle one more time before he called it quits for good.

God, it was going to be hard, retiring.

A driving beat told him that the place was still jumping. He heard it as he approached the back door, where the pool tables were, coming in through the alley in case a squad car drove by and saw him entering the front way. Bunny paid the local boys off and never had any trouble, but you couldn't slap them in the face with it. He knocked loudly, seven or eight times, and Stash the Banker let him in, greeting him merrily, hitting him on the shoulder. Fabe guessed Stash was having a very hot night.

And he was right. Mickey Two Ball was running the table, playing straight pool, a Camel screwed into the corner of his mouth, squinting past the smoke as he shot. A tall and lanky drink of water with hustler written all over him was standing over by the dozen or so seats, looking ready to break into tears. Two Ball shot, setting himself up perfectly for the break, his cue along the rail on the far side; the seven ball hanging by a thread in the corner. "Hey, Fabey," Mickey said, "come on, bankroll me for a while, Stash is starting to take twenty percent, for God's sake." And he laughed, the winner, doing what he did best in the world, enjoying the hell out of taking the money away from the young kid who was slamming the balls into the rack now, in a hurry, no time for jokes or any other bullshit. Not when he was the loser.

Fabe winked at Mickey, deciding not to say anything smart-ass to the kid. He had enough problems. He walked across the room to the bar, and there was Doral in deep conversation with Bunny, sitting on the last stool at the bar, leaning over and talking intensely. Bunny had her elbows down on the wood, hugging them with her hands. She was wearing a low-cut silk blouse with nothing underneath. Fabe saw Doral staring at her breasts and thought, Grandmother, my ass.

"There he is," Bunny said, and Fabe caught the look that passed between her and Doral.

"My man," Doral said, grinning his million-dollar smile, putting his arm around Fabe's shoulders. "Either you believe in psychic phenomena or you don't. We was just talking about you, and here you are."

"Pinch on the rocks," Fabe said to Bunny, smiling warmly, trying to be friends. Bunny stared at him for a second, hard, then turned around to make his drink.

"On me," Doral said.

"I was out to the house this afternoon, Doral," Fabe said, not trying to hide the implication.

Doral smiled wider still. "Shoulda woke me up, Fabe-babe. We'd have had us some fun." And Fabe looked into his eyes, trying to see if they were stoned on stolen cocaine.

"You dumb enough, try to turn any of it over, Doral?" Trying to talk low, so no one else in the jam-packed, feeling-no-pain crowd of Christmas revelers could hear him. As quiet as he was, his voice sounded as if he were pleading, begging Doral to say "No."

"Just a little bit, Fabe-babe." And Fabe winced, so Doral hurriedly added, "To a brother, man, a bro-ham. I can trust him, don't have a whole lot to do with any Rican dudes."

"You scamming me, Doral? Running a game?" And now Doral looked pained.

"Me? Doral, your number-one bro-ham?" He spread his hand across his chest and Fabe could see the smile in his eyes; Doral was making fun of him. Doral said, "Would *I* do that to *you*?" Every instinct told Fabe: Get out, right now, before you whack this guy in the mouth. He picked up his drink and moved down the bar to an unoccupied chair. Looked around him and knew why the chair was empty.

Leo the Limey was seated to his left, bending the ear of an attractive redhead with a lot of miles on her. Fabe had never liked Leo the Limey, especially because Leo had served time for manslaughter in the minimum security prison at Vandalia and acted like he was James Cagney or something because he'd picked cherries in a joint with no walls or bars for a little more than a year. He'd gotten the cherry assignment because his uncle in England was the head of an organized-crime outfit who called themselves the Merry Marauders and who had strong ties to the Tommy Campo mob.

Bending the girl's ear, Leo was saying, with a strong British accent, "I'd been in the can back home, you see, but there weren't no niggers there. I get slammed up out here, for killing a man with me bare fists, mind you, and all I see is niggers. It's like maybe I'm in the wrong place, the only white guy around. And the myth of the sex thing? It ain't no myth, let me tell you. I never seen a bleeding wanger like those guys carry around, never." He hit the bar with his hand for emphasis, the girl grinning at his ribald remarks. Fabe tried to look away, but couldn't help wondering what a two-bit small-time slob like Leo, who was probably a three-hundred-a-week numbers runner or something, was doing here in the Bunny's Hutch.

"Falletti!" Leo said, looking at Fabe now, as if he'd just noticed him. He excused himself to the redhead, who looked relieved for the break and hurriedly picked up her purse and made for the ladies' room. "Saw your partner down there,"

Leo said, "and was wondering where you were tonight, what with your relationship with the barkeeper and all." And he winked at Fabe lewdly, and for the second time in five minutes Fabe was tempted to strike out violently.

"Don't go away," Leo said, and disappeared into the back room on the fly, staggering some, and Fabe saw Bunny looking at him strangely, worriedly. She turned away and Fabe moved away from the stool and stood against the wall, looking at the action, knowing coming in here was a big mistake; it was over, all of it.

Finish the drink and get out. Clear your head on the walk home, get the stink out of your nostrils. You don't fit in here anymore. Feeling strangely depressed, Fabe decided that he wouldn't even tell Doral he was coming by tomorrow for his money, packing it in for good. The false boards in the floor would pop open just one more time. In a year, Fabe didn't plan to have what it took to lift the damn weights to open it anymore. Lie back, take it easy. Get fat. Retire. Finally.

If he didn't get his goddamned head blown off first due to Doral's stupidity.

He swirled the ice in his glass, swallowed the rest of the Scotch, and as he was walking back to the bar to put his glass down, there was Bunny with a fresh one, still looking at him like she was seeing him in his casket or something.

"Sorry about the way I did you this morning," Fabe said.

Bunny looked at him with burning eyes. "No, you're not," she said, and almost said something else, but didn't.

There was Leo, at his left elbow, saying, "Jesus, I thought you were gone," then switching gears quickly. "I ever tell you about the time I did some boxing? Went eighteen and six before I give it up. Lost twice to Henry Cooper, the European champion."

"That's nice, Leo. I'll see you around, hey?" And Fabe

was dropping a five on the bar for his drink and a tip when Leo grabbed his arm, squeezing a little bit, man-to-man being friendly, telling him without speaking: You aren't going anywhere. Fabe looked at the smiling face with the bloodshot eyes and said, "Let go."

"Sorry, mate, you can't go just yet. We're waiting for somebody." The tough guy now, letting Fabe know who we was.

"Let go, Leo," Fabe said and Leo rocked up on his toes so he could look Fabe in the eye.

"Fabe? Read me lips. We're waiting for someone, okay?" But he let go of Fabe's arm. Fabe looked at Leo standing there ready, his feet planted, his hands balled into fists, his eyes twinkling at the prospect of physical violence, and he wondered what Leo would do if he pulled the .38 and put it under his chin.

"Read your lips?" Fabe said, angry now. "Read your *lips*? Leo, you talk to me like that again, I'll bite your lips off of your goddamn *mouth*." And he saw Doral gliding up behind Leo, standing now directly behind him, whispering something into Leo's ear. Leo relaxed, and a tic started in his right eye.

"Would have been eighteen and seven, you'd have swung at me, Leo," Fabe said, and walked to the end of the bar.

"See?" Doral said, catching up to him. "You need me." And he took his seat, smiling at Fabe, holding the wineglass loosely in his hand now, swirling it, trying to be buddies.

"Hey, Doral, Leo just fingered us to somebody. You up to it, push come to shove?"

"Thought you were leaving."

"Might as well get it over with, find out where we stand."

"I been here all night, Fabe, and nobody fingered me. Seems to me the fingering started when you walked in."

"It's like that, is it?"

"Who walked away from who just now?"

"Why'd you back my play with Leo, then?"

"Shee-it. All I did was tell the man he was gonna get killed if he didn't lighten up. So like Tonto said to the Lone Ranger when they were surrounded by Apaches, 'What you mean *we*, white man?'"

"Someone aces me, you get all the money, is that it?"

Doral put his glass down on the bar, not meeting Fabe's eye. He said, "You're about as close to a real ass-kicking as you're gonna get without taking one, hear?"

Fabe said, "You playing with me, or are you behind me?"

Doral shrugged his broad shoulders and looked at Fabe now. "We been this far, haven't we?" Fabe nodded. "May as well play the hand we're dealt." He gestured to one of the barmaids for a refill on the wine. "Hurt my feelings, is all," Doral said.

"Rocks don't bleed," Fabe told him.

"Don't have a lot of real friends. The one I got, he got no right walking away from me, I'm trying to kid him a little."

"You know what I think, Doral?" Fabe said, serious now, concern in his voice, squinting as he stared at Doral.

"What do you think, Fabe-babe?"

"I think," Fabe said, "your best friend is white and sprinkly powder." Doral didn't answer, and so Fabe added, "It's all the same to you, I don't want any backup."

Doral started, his eyes flashing hurt and anger. "Have it your way," he said, and turned to call out to Bunny. "You coming over after you lock up, like we talked about?" he said, looking at Fabe out of the corner of his eye.

Bunny shot him a worried glance, then looked at Fabe, just met his eyes for a moment, and Fabe could see the unfinished part of what she'd said before.

"Doral," Bunny said, "I'm not gonna get out of here until after daylight."

"No problem, sweetie," Doral said, turning to Fabe to twist the knife a little. "I'll be up. Me and my number-one lady. . . ." and he walked slowly away, putting the bop in his walk, the challenge. You want to fight over your lady, pardner, I'll be out in the street at high noon.

Fabe was trying to think of something to say to Bunny, but he never got the chance, because the Banker and Two Ball and the sad-faced kid and the three other spectators spilled out of the back room. Something was going on that they wanted no part of. Out of the corner of his eye, Fabe saw Leo the Limey coming toward him, bouncing up drunkenly.

"'Ey, wiseass," Leo said, "someone wants to talk to you."

15

Doral had a canary-yellow BMW 635CS tonight, with the license plates reading I B DORAL. He idled it at the curb for a few minutes, wondering if he should go back in, back Fabey up. He snorted a good line from his two-gram vial, licking some of it from the snout. Getting off on the sensation of numbness that set in on his lips, mouth, and tongue.

Fabe had hurt his feelings, simple as that. He was playing a game, being funny, and the man had simply up and walked away from him. His daddy had told him, when Doral was maybe five years old, "Don't never you trust no white motherfucker," and Doral never had, never until he'd met that big strapping white boy in the joint, when Doral had been dying inside from having no one to talk to. All the years since then, what, ten now? Being friends, crime partners. Ripping off folks who only had to call their insurance man in the morning to make everything right. And as soon as the man finds out I got a lady friend made out of white powder, he walks away from me.

Doral did not worry that any harm would come to Fabe, not in Bunny's Hutch with a full house boogying inside. Someone just wanted to tell him something. And seeing as Leo the Limey had ducked in back and then almost got his head busted by Fabe, it was logical that whoever wanted to speak with Fabe was some Outfit guy from the Campo Family. And everybody knew that the Outfit didn't have anything to do with dope. So it couldn't have had anything to do with the score, with the home invasion. With the murder.

Fuck it, Doral thought. Give him a couple of days to calm himself down, then turn up at the apartment. Better yet, wait until Friday, pop in on him when he's having lunch with his policeman buddy. That would be worth a laugh.

Doral put the car in gear and coasted away, making the short jaunt home slowly, sniffing, Barry White blasting from the cassette deck, thinking, if he don't come around, fuck him. Doral didn't need friends now. Life's a bitch, and then you die anyway, so why sweat a white dude he should have figured all wrong from the start. Hell, once a cop, always a cop. The man can't calm down, let his hair down, have some fun, then Doral didn't need him.

He turned the corner leading to his house, hit the button on the opener that would slowly open the iron gates, and whacked his hand on the steering wheel to the Barry White beat, wondering if he'd fucked up by turning over the shit this morning. Hell, he'd had to turn some of it over. He had to find out if he could cut it ten times. And the brother had been overwhelmed with gratitude, the shit had been so good. So now Doral knew. When the time came to turn it all over, he could cut it ten times and make a fortune. Matter of fact, he'd been so elated at the man's response, he'd nearly given the shit away. Man was getting such a deal, he wouldn't turn Doral in knowing that he had plenty more coming at dirt prices, would he?

Doral parked the car in its slot, between the Mercedes and the Caddy, all with plates with his name on them in one form or another. He sniffed deeply, dug a finger into his nose as he got out of the garage and hit the button that would close and lock the garage door. Walking to the front door, he pulled his finger out and stuck it on his top gum, and there it was, sweet numbness again.

He went into the reception hall, winking at himself in the window, making faces at the video camera mounted on top there, enjoying himself, wondering if Bunny really was mad enough at Fabe to give up some pussy. He punched the numbers into the alarm box, taking his time, cold in here but at least no wind, and as soon as the door popped open he heard the sound of the door behind him opening and he spun around, reaching for the .44 hanging at his side, fumbling with the coat, ripping off the buttons, and there was a redheaded guy, ugly as all hell, pointing a .38 right at his head and a dark-skinned dude, maybe a—oh goddamn, maybe a Puerto Rican, and the guy was wearing shades and pointing a mini-Mac subgun right at him. Doral heard the guy say, with a Spanish accent so thick he could barely make him out, "Hey, nigger, we come for our shit."

Doral had been in prison for half of his life. He'd been cut. He'd been shot in the belly twice on the street and left for dead, only to recover and kill the man who'd shot him. He'd read something in prison that was written in the fifteenth century by a samurai warrior. Attitude is not a state of mind. To be truly free, attitude must be a way of life. And so he would die before showing fear, before backing off to dudes with big mouths, or guns. Shit, they were in *his* goddamn house.

And so he looked at Miro Roga and let his hands drop. Smiling arrogantly, falling into barely remembered South Side speech patterns, he said, "Who be that mans behinds them Foster Grants?" and sure enough, the redheaded ugly one with the warts smiled. Divided and conquered, already.

"Fuck you laughing at, pizza face?" Doral said to him, and saw the one with the glasses move quickly, saw it coming and tried to stop it, the redheaded son of a bitch turning beet-red in the face, raising his .38 right up between Doral's eyes, and while the Puerto Rican jumped at the freak, Doral made his own move. . . .

Lloyd had got tired of waiting after maybe fifteen minutes. What made it worse was this jerk here, wearing the glasses, wouldn't talk to him. Lloyd guessed he probably shouldn't have said anything about the shades, piss the guy off for nothing. He'd tried things like, "When you figure the nigger's gonna come home?" He knew that much, the guy was a dinge they had to hit. He'd make his bones on a *muscadat*. It stopped being exciting for him when he started shivering, and the Rican, crouched there loosely against the wall like he was sunning himself on the beach, didn't make things any better for him. He just looked at Lloyd funny. Well, he'd just have to tell Mr. DiNardo that he wasn't going to work with psychopaths like this guy anymore. The hell with that. Wearing sunglasses at night, carrying a machine gun just to whack out one guy, for shit's sake.

Lloyd had checked his watch every ten or fifteen minutes, certain each time that at least an hour had passed. He had tried not to, knowing the weirdo was watching him, but he couldn't help it. He was shivering in the early Christmas Eve cold, his teeth chattering, wishing he'd known that Mr. DiNardo was going to put him on a stakeout so he could have put on warm long underwear. Then he could have had a cool contest with this tortilla eater.

Finally he'd seen headlights and heard the motor hum as the gates wound open, and the beaner was on top of him, dragging him back, holding his mouth shut with one hand, the mini-Mac at Lloyd's ear now, and the beaner whispering, "You fool," not even seeing the big black guy lock the garage or anything. The PR didn't let him up until the guy was almost to his front door, and then he was gesturing with the mini-Mac, giving silent orders, and Lloyd stared at him hard but the beaner

210

ignored him and they began running to the front of the house, into the vestibule, Lloyd overflowing with resentment. The beaner was cool, holding the mini-Mac casual-like, while Lloyd was so tense, so full of hatred that he held the .38 in both hands. He knew they were shaking, but the spade was tearing his coat apart and then Coolbreeze over here was saying something about they came for their shit and the nigger said, like he'd rehearsed it for hours, "Who be that mans behinds them Foster Grants?" And Lloyd gave him a chuckle, letting him know the act was appreciated, and the nigger, the son of a *bitch*, called him pizza face.

Lloyd had been called that throughout grade school. Always, always there had been someone there calling him pizza face, making him want to kill somebody. And then the two years he was in high school, the same thing. In prison, too. No black-ass son of a bitch was gonna get away with it, not after he'd waited out in the shivering cold and taken a lot of silent bullshit from a spic bastard in glasses. So he put the barrel right between the nigger's eyes when he saw out of the corner of his eye the beaner jumping at him. The spade was moving now, reaching into his coat, moving backward, and as the beaner hit his free arm Lloyd saw a long black barrel clearing the spade's coat, it had to be the biggest magnum Lloyd had ever seen, and so he adjusted, moved his arm just a little, and capped the guy, two times, dead in the chest, driving him through the open door, into the house.

Lloyd turned to the beaner and told him, "You almost got us *killed*, motherfucker," and the beaner was looking at him very strangely, all scrunched up, very ugly in the face all of a sudden.

Now the beaner was bending over the nigger, shaking his head, the mini-Mac machine pistol on the tiled floor beside him, shaking his head, telling Lloyd, "You *ass*hole, you dumb son of a *bitch*, Ortiz will have your *nuts* for this," over and over.

Hey, DiNardo had told him he had to whack out a nigger, and that was all. So why say that someone was going to cut his nuts off for doing his job? The guy hadn't said a word for over four hours; now he wouldn't shut up. So Lloyd figured maybe he had something there.

He strolled casually over to where Doral's pistol lay in the reception hall, a big hogleg .44, and he picked it up, made sure the safety was off, and said, "Yo, beanhead," and when the guy looked up he shot him in the head. Lloyd walked back through the door and smashed the video camera. In a hallway equipment closet inside, he found the tape, took it. Now anyone who walked in could see that the spade had shot the PR just as Lloyd had taken him out.

The really hard part was going into the guy's pocket for the radio without getting too much muck on himself. Jeez, the guy was covered with it. As was most of the rest of the room. There wasn't a head there anymore, either, just a stub at the top of the shoulders, in the middle. All stringy and red and blue. Cheerist. Walls covered with it, too. Good thing the beaner had shut the door when they'd come into the entrance hall, out of the vestibule. Now that put two doors between the gunshots and the street. Old-fashioned brick, sturdy house like this, they could probably have a gang war in here and none of the neighbors would hear them. Far apart too, the houses were. No, he was safe. At least from the cops.

He got the radio out of the guy's pocket and was about to hit the switch when he had an idea. He went over to Doral and gave him a quick search, found a wad of hundred-dollar bills in his right front pants pocket, and Lloyd smiled. He made a quick search of the downstairs area, found almost a full kilo of white powder in a kitchen cabinet, inside a large spaghetti pot. He

212

stuck this down his shirt, patted it until it was almost flat against his belly, rezipped his jacket, and went to find the bathroom. He looked in the mirror, didn't see any bulges, went back to the two bodies in the entrance hall. He lifted the radio to his lips and pressed the button as he'd seen the beaner do in the backyard, once, held it, let it go, then started speaking into it, excitedly, trying to get into it, the way a guy on TV would in this kind of situation.

And it had worked like a charm. They'd come in, DiNardo and the short freak of a spic, and Lloyd had almost laughed when the massive dude went down on his knees at the beaner's side, took him right into his arms, headless and all, getting slop all over his cashmere overcoat, sobbing and rocking around like the guy was his brother or something.

Lloyd walked over to the front door and picked up the miraculously unharmed little piece of steel and plastic eyewear and walked over to the dude, winking at Roland DiNardo, thinking this would really put him in with the Outfit, when *this* story got around, and he handed the sunglasses to the guy on the ground, who looked up at him with dying eyes, red-rimmed and tearing, still holding the body in his arms.

"Here," Lloyd said, "he won't be needing these no more."

Francisco Ortiz could not believe his ears. First this son of a whore tells them how this drug-stealing bastard had gotten the drop on Miro, on *Miro,* for God's sake, which just wasn't possible, but then, as he grieved over a man who was more than a brother, worth more than ten *putas* like his sister Lucille, why, the man had come to him with Miro's sunglasses, like a joke. Francisco Ortiz leapt to his feet and grabbed the bastard by his throat, squeezing, driving the man backward into the wall and slamming his head hard against it, squeezing, squeezing, until the man's face was blue and his tongue hung from his mouth like a dead serpent. Then he let him go and allowed his lifeless body to drop to the floor.

"Jesus Christ, oh, Jesus fucking Christ," Roland DiNardo said, over and over, having a very hard time believing what he was seeing. He'd almost said to Ortiz, "Are you fucking crazy?" It had almost slipped out, but seeing the man's eyes blazing as he choked the life out of Lloyd, acting like he was maybe roughhousing with a puppy dog or something, for all the fucking effort it took him, Roland knew that if it had slipped out, he would have been dead.

He watched the guy calm down, Jesus, in stages. First his neck stopped bulging and got back to normal, what there was of a neck on this guy, Christ, then his face got black again, instead of almost gray with anger. Slowly, slowly, Ortiz was getting it back.

When he thought Ortiz was back to near normal, Roland said, "We got to get out of here, *now*." Ortiz turned to look at him as if he were nuts.

"Are you crazy?" Ortiz said, and Roland thought, Christ, it's contagious, we both think the other guy's nuts, and Ortiz said, "I am not leaving without my cocaine and my money."

As they began the search, Roland DiNardo was wondering what the little shit was talking about, *his* cocaine and *his* money. He wasn't feeling anything at all like a Mafia big shot right now.

Angelo "Tombstone" Paterro was leaning casually against the rail of the middle pool table, smoking a cigarette, flicking the ashes, when Fabe came into the back room with Leo the Limey right behind him. When they came into Angelo's view, Leo prodded him on, shoved him one with the flat of his hand,

214

and Fabe thought, here we go, as he turned to flatten him but Angelo put a stop to it right then.

"Leo!" Angelo shouted, shaking his head. "Fucking guy, he thinks he's still in Liverpool, bodyguard for the drummer in the Animals." To Fabe now, shaking his head, an apologetic smile on his lips. "He tell you that one?"

Fabe said, "We never got past getting creamed twice by Henry Cooper."

"That's his favorite one." Angelo turned to Leo. "Go on, what're you waiting for?"

"You don't want me to hang around, Ange?"

"What the fuck *for*?" And Leo turned, dejected, disappointed, back into the bar. There was another bruiser there, Fabe didn't recognize him, and Angelo nodded and the guy was gone, nodding at Fabe, smiling as he went by, no hard feelings, partner. Fabe couldn't help it, he nodded and smiled back.

"Ahh, Fabrizzio," Angelo said, and Fabe loved it, the sound of his voice like his father used to say it, Fah-bleetz-ee-yo. Fabe liked Angelo Paterro, even if they did call him Tombstone.

Angelo was a tall man, slender and aristocratic. He looked more like a downtown banker than a right hand to the Outfit's new head honcho. He was a smooth talker, a real lady-killer. Talked fast, used his hands a lot, his face, to express himself. When Fabe had been called on the carpet that time, he'd never even heard Tommy Campo speak. It had been Angelo, cool, level-headed, reasonable. Fabe knew that Angelo more than anything else was the reason he'd walked out of DiNardo's house that day.

"I never did get a chance to tell you thanks, Angelo," Fabe said. This wasn't a guy you grabbed your crotch at or cracked wise to. When Angelo stopped being reasonable, he earned his nickname.

Angelo waved a hand in the air, gesturing for them to sit down in the spectator's gallery. "Shit, that was a grandstand play by DiNardo. We shouldn't have a problem with a *paisan* making his living outside the law, eh? I mean, what the hell are we now, the government or something?" They settled in, lit cigarettes, crossed their legs. Angelo sighed. His face impassive, showing maybe a subtle hint of humor, if anything.

"Jesus. Drugs. You know, Tommy, he got a seventeen-year-old son, be lucky to make eighteen, he got into drugs when he was fifteen, selling them, using them. He got busted, Christ, can't take the heat, he tells the cops, 'I'm Tommy Campo's son!' and the next thing you know, Tommy's telling me, 'Let him fucking rot,' and we don't go his bond. Let him sit. Let it go to court. *Then* we help him out, after he's scared shitless." Angelo took a deep drag on the Camel, shaking his head, shooting the shit and telling war stories after work.

"We get him off the hook, the old man kicks the shit out of him, you think he'd learn? First week out, he comes home wasted. Here you got a kid with the world before him, handed to him on a silver platter, Harvard, anything he *wants*, the kid, he fucks it all up. Tommy puts him out, now his sixteen-year-old daughter comes crying to him, 'Why you wanna do that to my brother?' raising hell, the old lady on his ass. Ahh, hell.

"DiNardo, he comes to me with this idea to organize drugs here in Chicago, I say to him, 'You fucking *goofy*?' I says, 'The way the old man feels about dope?' And this big shot, he goes, 'Hey, this is business, not personal,' like in a paperback book or something. I tells him, do what you gotta do, just don't let me know about it. See, DiNardo, he's a good guy, knows how to keep the jigs in line, runs the South Side for us like a champion, then when he gets ahead he runs up north here, buys a mansion on Astor Street. The boss himself, the old man, still lives in Escanaba Avenue on the East Side, not six blocks from where he was born.

"Boss gets a call, somebody calls him on his private line, tells him he's gonna take the old man down if he finds out he's dealing drugs, tells him Roland DiNardo is in it up to his ears. Boss tells me, 'Look into it, *now*.'

"There's a guy works for us, not for DiNardo, for *us*, Herman Machechelli, lives in, he's queer for another guy with us, Tino Mastriona. They take care of DiNardo. I gets ahold of Herman, I says, 'Hey, what gives?' and Herman tells me there's a Puerto Rican drug dealer coming around, there's cops on the corner, and Fabrizzio Falletti gets picked up by two muscle guys the little shit DiNardo recruits on his own, has 'em bring Falletti around the side, like him and Tino ain't got eyes." Angelo sighed again, not mad, not angry; more distressed at having been awakened to finish a piece of business that should never have been worth his trouble.

"Fabrizzio, your business, it ain't none of mine. But DiNardo's is. So I gotta ask you: You dealing drugs for him?"

"*Fuck* no." Amazed that Angelo even thought that. "Christ, you know what Jimmy Capone would do to me he ever finds out I'm dealing shit? Not to mention I got a pass once, from Mr. Campo. I ain't looking to face him again."

"Yeah, he is kind of scary, ain't he? Just sits there and looks at you, stares right through you. Hell of a mind, that guy. Could have made a billion in the regular world, he put his mind to it. Like you." And he let it lie there, nothing more to say, looking at Fabe with a benign expression, waiting.

Fabe said, "Angelo, DiNardo had a couple of goons pick me up, asks me to break into a safe for him, place on the North Side. Just go in and take a look. Offers me a grand."

"What'd you tell him?"

"I told him Tommy Campo let me go once and I get the message, don't mix in his business. I told him he gotta have a half a dozen guys on the payroll can break into safes."

"And he said?"

"That was it."

Angelo lit another Camel and blew smoke out of his nostrils, thinking. Fabe had to admit, he liked his style.

Angelo said, "Fabrizzio, I believe you. I say *I* believe you. That don't mean the old man will. I'm gonna give you a choice. Your first option: Go to the old man, tell him what you told me. He believes you, you're out of it. Free. But lemme warn you, he rarely gets a guy on the carpet twice. It ain't worth his time, setting someone straight two times.

"Second option: Roland DiNardo, he put together a few loyalties over on the South Side. He organized them down there, give the jigs more money than they'd ever see in their lives pimping for their sisters or something. They worship the ground he walks on, hardly ever even *steal* from him. That, and a couple of other things I can't talk about, are the reasons it might get a little troublesome we whack DiNardo out. Which brings us to you.

"You go to your friend Capone, set DiNardo up, I can give you the boss's guarantee that no one will come after you, give you any shit. Or else you whack him out, clean. Kill him. You do that, we'll forget all about your being in DiNardo's house yesterday the same time as a couple of big-league Puerto Rican drug dealers, which you failed to mention to me and which the boss will probably take into consideration when he hears your case."

"I didn't see any—"

"Hey, I don't wanna hear about it. They were there. I got two guys seen them come before you got there and seen them leave after you left, running down the alley for some reason."

Angelo stomped on his cigarette butt, got to his feet, and smiled down at Fabe. "Now I'm gonna go back to bed. Too old for this late-night shit. You wanna go tell my driver I'm waiting in the car for him?" Like they were old pals, breaking up the card game on Friday night. And now Angelo called at Fabe's back and Fabe turned, confused, a little afraid.

"Merry Christmas, Fabrizzio," Angelo said, then said, "I don't think I mentioned: you got two days."

16 "You are unbelievable," Jimmy Capone said, sitting in Fabe's rocker with a glass of wine in his hand, his head hanging, shaking it from side to side. He was leaning forward, his elbows on his knees.

Fabe had come in with the dawn, not seeing his car in the Iron Horse's parking lot, smiling, thinking, I bet she went back to bed the minute I left. Up the stairs to his floor, into his apartment, finding Jimmy there asleep in his chair with the TV screen beaming white noise at him.

Fabe woke him up and told him everything.

"Your partner, he's got the dope and the money at his house?"

Fabe nodded.

Jimmy shook his head again. "You are unbe*liev*able."

Fabe was relieved that Jimmy was mad. If he'd gone cold and given him the fish-eyed cop look, he'd have been in trouble. He knew Jimmy was thinking frantically, trying to find a way out of this for them both. Fabe did not want to die, and Jimmy did not want to lose a friend.

"Two days he give you?" Thinking out loud now, not looking at Fabe. "He means today and tomorrow. Christmas night, you don't have the job done, you get whacked out with him." He looked up now, glared at Fabe. "I ought to bust your ass right now."

"Even if you were asshole enough, nothing I told you would stand up. Couldn't use it in court. Didn't advise me of my rights."

"You think that would stop me?"

"You gonna, Jimmy?"

Jimmy said, "Maybe protective custody."

"Bullshit. Then what? In the can, somebody poisons my supper or something. Throws lighter fluid on me while I'm sleeping, drops in a match. Uh-uh. I ain't going to jail."

Jimmy looked at him. "You know, growing up, I always thought I could take you. Now, it's up in the air. You go and do four years, lift the weights every day in the joint, run a couple of miles, get in the best shape of your life. But I got half a mind, anyway, to kick your ass for you."

"Maybe just shoot me, put me out of my misery."

"There's always that."

Fabe crushed out his cigarette, lit another one. "I've got an idea," he said.

They began at 9 A.M., the two of them, and at first it was like old times, with their situations reversed. On the force, with the old Organized Crime Squad, Fabe had been impatient, ready to go, gung ho, while Jimmy had been the stickler for details, never wanting to move until all bets were covered.

Jimmy waited outside in the car while Fabe went into the bank with his black leather satchel, heavy, double-handled and durable. Well used. Damn near a suitcase. It took a few minutes, and Jimmy could picture Fabe in there arguing, "It's my damn safe-deposit box, you better let me at it, Christmas Eve or not!" knowing how hard it was to find banks that allowed access to boxes during all working hours. If they only knew that

Fabe was going to bring out a million bucks, or anyway, nearly a million. Less than five minutes and Fabe was sliding into the passenger seat next to him, saying, "Next stop, the Harris."

"You got more than one box?"

Fabe looked at him. "You think I'd put a million bucks in one place? Christ, what if I had to get away fast, and someone was watching the one bank? You better believe I got more than one bank." Self-righteous, almost arrogant, as if Jimmy didn't know what was going on in the world.

"How many we got to go to, Mr. Paranoia?"

"Ten."

Jimmy said, "You're kidding me. Ten banks between now and noon?"

"We'd be at the second one already if you weren't giving me a bunch of shit."

By eleven o'clock the satchel was bulging a little. By eleven-thirty, Fabe was having a little trouble carrying it back to the car, mainly because his right hand was in the pocket of his overcoat and his neck was making out like a swivel, trying to find a wise guy setting him up.

"Finally?" Jimmy said, after Fabe came back from the tenth bank, looking around, slipping into the car saying, "Hit it!" like he'd robbed the bank instead of having taken out what was his.

"That's it," Fabe said.

"Now listen, when you go, don't be calling anyone, there's gonna be hell to pay, Fabe, I mean, the shit is gonna hit the fan—"

"I know that," Fabe said. "Christ. Like I'm a kid or something." Trying to remain calm inside because they were pulling up at Doral's driveway. This was going to be the hard part.

"Let me go in, talk to him first," Fabe said.

"Uh-uh, forget it. What if he decides to shoot you, call me in like everything's cool? Forget about it, we go in together, get the shit, whether he likes it or not. He gives me any shit, I'm shooting the crazy bastard."

Fabe looked at him. "Hey, this's *Doral,* Jimmy."

"Yeah, a ex-con with twenty years of his life in one joint or another. And while we're out here shooting the shit about what a sterling character he is, he could be looking out the window, loading his rifles." He got out of the car and slammed the door, watched Fabe get out with his satchel.

"You aren't going to leave it?"

"Locked in the *car*?"

"Let's just go."

A minute later, they were looking at the trashed remains of Doral's once meticulously kept mansion. For a lot longer than that, Fabe couldn't allow himself to look at Doral.

Doral saying, "Life's a bitch and then you die, Fabe-babe. Might as well try everything once."

Funny, the things you remember.

The house was gone, entire walls knocked out, all the furniture cut up, carpets torn to pieces. When he finally got it right in his mind that Doral was dead and the house had been searched, he noticed the other two bodies, which was surprising, as one of them had no head and the other one was Lloyd, the muscle boy DiNardo had sent to pick him up. Jesus. Fabe had to turn away, thinking, you never get used to it, trying not to think of Doral anymore, putting him out of his mind until it was all over.

"This changes things a little bit," Jimmy Capone told him and he said, "*Fuck* it does, goddammit, *don't you turn cop on me now*!" And Jimmy told him to calm down, everything would be okay, it was part of the game and they both knew the rules, it happens.

Downstairs then, and thank God, it was torn up, weights overturned, but the machines still stood bolted to the walls, and although maybe half of the carpet had been torn up, the important three-by-one section hadn't.

Fabe was shaking, trying to fight tears. He walked over to the boxing area, the corner where they did their workouts, and stood there touching Doral's satin trunks. Shaking his head.

"Hey," Jimmy said.

"Yeah, I know."

"Let's go, huh?"

Fabe not getting it, saying, "Let's *go*?"

"Fabe, we got a triple homicide here, they got the shit, we blew it; now let's just go and get you the fuck out of town, I'll make an anonymous call, get the Homicide squad out here."

And it dawned on Fabe, got through his fog. Jimmy thought the shit was gone, and in spite of his grief, or maybe because of it, he smiled.

"They didn't get *shit*," Fabe said.

Jimmy was out of shape. No way he could boost six hundred, so Fabe had to do it both times himself, with Jimmy helping only a little, because when they moved the weights off the bench covering the valuable spot of carpeting, Jimmy had strained and grunted and dropped his end. And when Fabe showed him how to position the little pieces of round iron, and took his position on the bench, Jimmy was gasping, as if he'd worked out all damn day, or some goddamn thing. Fabe tried not to say anything. Jimmy could still turn cop on him, bust him.

Rolling off the bench, dripping sweat from having to do it

all himself, he told Jimmy, "You think you can get this other one okay?" Jimmy just looked at him.

Fabe got onto the other bench, tired now, fatigue setting in. It had been a while since he'd slept. Up, the iron round under, and rolling off with a loud sound of relief. Hearing the hiding place pop open.

Jimmy said, "I'll be goddamned."

Fabe stumbled over and saw the bags of cocaine and the tightly bound bundles of money on top of the blue flight bag. More money than Jimmy Capone had ever seen. He'd seen larger amounts of drugs, naturally, but never a million dollars cash before.

Fabe stuffed the money into the suitcase, the drugs into the flight bag. He took the run-away money and stuck it into his left-hand topcoat pocket, knowing better than to offer any of it to Jimmy.

"Let's get the fuck out of here."

Jimmy said, "Don't you think you'd better let me carry the drugs?"

"Why's that?" Fabe said, suspicious.

"You got your own million to carry, on top of that one. I wouldn't want you to strain yourself."

Jimmy coming up in the elevator, Fabe fidgeting, hating the damn thing. Checking out his apartment. "I'll hang around outside until you're ready to take off." Fabe nodding, and Jimmy leaving then, dropping the flight bag with the dope at Fabe's feet.

Fabe went to his wall safe in the back of his bedroom closet, hit the digital readout buttons to open it, got out his forged driver's licenses and his ready cash, his house deed and the title to the Cadillac. They'd made one more stop that morning, at a real estate office. Fabe took the residential real estate contract out of his inner pocket, took all the documents to his desk, and filled them out. He made a phone call and talked to Roland DiNardo for a while. Hung up, dialed another number, heard the familiar sound, in singsong cadence, of her answering machine. He hesitated, but when the beep came, he said, "Sally, I've got a couple of million cash and ten times that worth of coke. Come over around four, I'll be back by then, we'll take off together. Forever. You and me—" and was about to say more when the second beep cut him off. He took a last look around the apartment, left the door unlocked and the alarm off behind him. Fuck it, he didn't care anymore.

Then he stepped back in and locked the door behind him.

There were only nineteen kilos left. And a million dollars to pay for twenty. He removed fifty thousand dollars from his stolen suitcase and put it in his satchel. Flipped the flight bag onto his shoulder, carrying the suitcase in his left hand and his satchel in his right, he walked out of the apartment and headed for the elevator.

The Cadillac was in the lot, finally, across the street. Fabe put his things in the trunk and was already in the car when he changed his mind. He looked at the window of the restaurant. He would be able to see the car if he sat in one of the front booths, or at the counter.

In the restaurant, Sally sat at the counter drinking a cup of coffee, counting her tips. She looked up as he sat down next to her, smiled wide and pretty. "Fabe!" Her face lit up, until she saw the look on his. "What in God's name is wrong?"

"Sally, take a cab home, check your messages." He thought she turned a little white. Hurriedly he added, "I left a call for you. I gotta go. See you at four." He dropped a couple

226

of twenties on the countertop. "For the cab," he said, and was gone.

They'd torn the nigger's house apart, and Roland could not think of the last time he'd done physical labor. Shit, he *hired* guys to do the heavy stuff. But Ortiz, Christ, he was like a man possessed, going from room to room, busting things up, grunting with surprise when he found bags filled with white powder; stopping when he found nine of them, knowing there was nothing left. His chest heaving, his eyes on fire, his muscles bunched up and threatening to pop the sleeves of his shirt—he'd long ago removed his topcoat and suitcoat—he'd looked at Roland with contempt.

"And you wanted to *leave*," he said. He ripped open one of the plastic bags, stuck his finger in, removed a few grains of the powder. He touched them to his tongue. And he screamed.

"This is not my stuff!" Surprised, outraged. Roland thought he might race over to Doral Washington's body and kick it to death all over again. "This is cut! God*damm*it!"

It had taken Roland a while, but he'd managed to get the goddamn guy out of there, and they left as it turned ten o'clock and the chimes started playing a Christmas carol at the church a block down the way.

"We'll go to my place, think things over," Roland had said.

"The thinking is done for now." Cold now, distant. Something on his mind.

"I'll get a crew, we'll send them in there later, tear the place apart."

"With the police right behind you?"

"What police?"

"Oh, come now, it's a holy day in the country. Surely someone somewhere is expecting him someplace, this animal

227

who steals from us. He'll be missed. And besides, if there was anything more there, I would have found it.''

Roland thinking, jerkoff, because he'd searched Lloyd, Doral, and Roga as Ortiz was tearing the upper floors apart, and he had Lloyd's kilo of coke and several thousand dollars inside his coat as they spoke.

''We'll get a crew, go over to his partner's house. The dope's gotta be there. These two guys, they don't trust nobody else; it's just the two of them.''

''Perhaps,'' Ortiz said.

Roland looked at him sideways. ''Whaddya mean by that?''

Ortiz waited. ''I mean,'' he said finally, ''that perhaps you and these guys, you had this little farce all set up for me, huh? And now the partner, this Falletti character, his ass is in the wind, and he kills his friend and takes all the money for himself?''

''You nuts?'' Roland said, taking his eyes off the road, almost taking his hands off the wheel. ''Your man, Roga, shit, he killed Washington. The man wasn't even *home* when they got there.''

''Maybe that was part of your plan, too.''

''Fuck you mean?''

''I mean I hear nothing for hours, then your man comes on the radio and tells us that we better get inside. Roga is already dead, and the nigger. I did not check. They could have been dead for hours. Your man, the one with the bad face, he might have been waiting inside for all that time, eh? On your orders.''

Roland was about to pull the car over and take his chances. Fuck this guy, fuck his muscle, fuck the fact that he'd choked Lloyd to death. But he looked over, amazed at all the bullshit the guy was rattling, and aw shit, he wasn't the only one who'd snuck something out of the house under his topcoat.

Francisco Ortiz pulled the mini-Mac automatic pistol from under his coat and pointed it at Roland. "I think," he said, "that we will go to your house now and you will pay me my money."

It took a couple of hours, but Roland had finally convinced him that you didn't just go to the bank on Christmas Eve, an hour before closing, and drag out a million. Even if you had it in there, which Roland didn't. His dough was tied up, either on the street or in a bank in Jamaica, in several accounts in various amounts, all under false names. But he alone had the numbers. At last they'd compromised. They'd give Falletti a shot. Go there that night, just the two of them, covering each other, looking at their backs together, in it one way or the other. And if Falletti didn't have the money or the dope, Roland would make it good. But Ortiz would have to be reasonable, give him a little time.

"I give you until New Year."

"More than enough time," Roland told him, trying to think of a way to kill this greasy bastard that night, get under his guard. Then fuck Falletti, fuck the money and the dope. He'd made enough. Christ, millions. It was getting way out of hand here. Before long, Tombstone or Campo or somebody would want to know why he was spending all of his time away from his business. And he did not know how far he could trust Tino and Herman. Thinking, shit, in the past few days he'd run across more fags than he had in ten years; Lloyd and Elmo, had to be queer for each other; Tino and Herman, though he'd known about them all along. And didn't mind it. They did such good work, Roland wouldn't have minded if they woke up at dawn and fucked chickens. And now, judging from the Betty Grable act Ortiz had put on at Washington's house when he'd seen his buddy Roga, the two of them, too.

No, what he'd do, he'd get this beaner away from the area, over on the South Side, where he had strong connections, and leave him with the fishes.

They were discussing the best way to try and take Fabe when the phone buzzed softly. Roland reached for it, saying to Ortiz, "If it's your old lady, you here?" but Ortiz just looked at Roland. "Hello?" he said.

"Roland, this is Fabe Falletti." And Roland covered the mouthpiece, signaled for Ortiz to pick up the extension, over by the bookcase, frantically because the jerk, he still wasn't understanding. But then he was getting up, and Roland began to talk loudly and rapidly to mask the click as Ortiz picked up the phone.

"What can I do for you, Falletti?"

"I—I found Doral," Falletti said, and Roland smiled at Ortiz, showing him how easy it was when you were a real power in this town.

"Is that right?"

"And I got something belongs to you."

"Don't say nothing over the phone!" Shit! Lost it a little there.

"Doral got one-twentieth of the package himself. I'm taking one twentieth of the other package, for my time and trouble. The rest I give back to you, but you gotta give me your word; it's over after that."

Just like Falletti to try and rip him off when he knew damn well that Roland had no choice but to settle. But he wouldn't have trusted the guy if he'd offered the whole package. This showed he was on the level. His larceny was still in his heart.

"Hey, we don't blame a guy wanting to go to the well, as long as he doesn't dip his beak too far into it."

But this idiot, this guy said, "What the fuck did you say?"

230

And now Roland got mad. "Just tell me when and where." And he pulled a pad over to him, wrote the instructions down. "I'll be there."

"Come alone, or I'm gone," Falletti said.

"Now hold on, I'm bringing a business associate got a stake in this thing. But that's all, me and one other guy. And Falletti, let me tell you, you play any games this time, there'll be no place to hide for you."

"Me! I'm the one in the shit!"

Roland would have liked it better if the guy had said: "Don DiNardo, you give me too much credit, I am the hunted one," but this was close enough.

"Don't forget it," he said.

"And, Roland?"

"Yeah?"

"I got your word?"

"You got my word."

"Good enough. But in case you can't speak for your associate, let me tell you something. I wrote it all down, every single thing I know since going into the home invasion, and I'm leaving it with someone who'll deliver it to Jimmy Capone, to be opened in the event of my death."

"Smart thinking, Falletti." Thinking, Bastard.

"See you at three." And the line went dead.

Ortiz hung up his phone and came back over, sat down in the leather wingback across from the desk. "So, after tonight, my friend, you and I are quits, eh?"

And Roland felt so damned good, so in charge, so in control that he couldn't help a little dig at this guy who'd done none of the work but who thought he was gonna get a million dollars off Roland DiNardo. What he'd get would be a bullet in the brain.

"Yes, my fren'," Roland said, "after tonight, we are—how you say—queets." But the dumb fuck, he just stared back at Roland blankly.

17

Fabe was sitting on a bench in Lincoln Park, all alone, the place deserted on Christmas Eve. He didn't even see a jogger. Less than a block away was the entrance to the park. From time to time he heard the roar of a polar bear or some other caged beast, thinking, as he listened, do I know how *you* feel. Trapped. He'd have his ass in the wringer if things didn't work exactly as he'd planned. He hugged the flight bag to his chest, the strap around his neck, his left arm on the suitcase. His satchel was locked in the trunk of his Eldorado, the alarm on, the car in sight a block and a half away on the corner of Orleans Avenue and Lincoln Park Parkway.

He saw the Lincoln turn in and park in front of his own car. He took slow, deep breaths. Trying to get it all together, pull this last bit off. Second-to-last bit, really, but the last bit would be personal. This one was strictly business. The business of survival. He watched as the tiny wide one walked over and put a coin in the meter, and he almost laughed. Multimillion dollar crime happening here, and the guy was worried about a fifteen-dollar traffic ticket, wasn't even his own car.

The two crooks, DiNardo and Ortiz, crossed the street, neither one of them taking their eyes off Fabe. An old black wino shuffled into the park now from the zoo entrance, carrying three shopping bags.

Ten feet away now and the greed was in their eyes. They never looked back, did not see the Illinois Bell Telephone repair truck pull to the curb in front of their car, effectively cutting off their escape. The Lincoln was trapped between the van and Fabe's Eldorado.

Looking at Fabe, both of them, like the wolves must look, down the block there at the zoo when the keeper throws them a steak. He checked the angle of the repair van, got up and stepped ten, then fifteen feet away. To the right of the bench, leaving the flight bag and the suitcase there. At the near entrance to the park, a prosperous-looking couple now came in pushing a baby buggy, a covered one, old-fashioned blue with the hood, out enjoying the sun on baby's first Christmas Eve.

They were right there now.

Roland DiNardo said, "It's a wise thing you are doing for yourself today." And Fabe wanted to say, almost desperately wanted to tell him, "You have to answer for Doral," like in *The Godfather*, but it would mess up the plan. He nodded over toward the bench.

"There it is."

DiNardo squinted at the wino shuffling their way. "Christ, is that Johnnie Bratten?" he said, while Ortiz went over and gave the drugs a quick check, riffled the money.

A female jogger with gigantic breasts and long, flowing hair ran toward them now, heading for the lake. She was wearing a bright blue warm-up suit and a headband.

DiNardo walked over to Ortiz, seeing the strap of the mini-Mac as it hung down around the man's waist, his coat open, ready for action. Fabe slowly began to walk toward the zoo. He heard Ortiz say, "It's all here, at least the first three kilos are pure," then DiNardo: "What about the money?" and Ortiz assuring him that he would take care of the money.

"This is it, then," Roland said, smiling at Ortiz, wanting to blow him away right now, but the park was getting too crowded. Jesus, the yuppies had made the park a safe place to be again. Instead he said, "Let's get the fuck out of here," and he hefted the flight bag with the drugs over his arm. He heard Ortiz call his name.

"The drugs are mine," Ortiz said, pointing the mini-Mac at Roland with his right hand, the left holding the suitcase with the money.

"We had a deal!" Roland shouted, looking around, wondering how the guy could be crazy enough to shoot him in front of four witnesses, not counting Falletti, who was now nowhere in sight.

"The drugs, and the money both, they are mine. I cannot afford to do business with a man like you any longer." He started to smile then, the first time Roland had seen it, but stopped when the woman pushing the baby buggy screamed. Ortiz turned, which gave the wino time to start running, a pistol in his hand now. The jogger reached into her top and came out with a gun and shouted "Freeze!" at the top of her lungs, still running, then she was on top of Roland, knocking him down, holding the pistol under his chin.

Francisco Ortiz looked at the woman screaming, heard the other woman, the running one, yell "Freeze!" and, confused now, he turned to look, which gave the couple time to reach into the buggy and pull out sawed-off riot shotguns and point them at Ortiz. Now they too were shouting for him to freeze, and the old man, the smelly one who had been carrying the shopping bags, was on top of Ortiz, and before he could pull the trigger on him the bastard had him by the throat and was running with Francisco's neck in his hands, turning him, and Francisco heard a crack in there somewhere and a bright and terrible pain before he tumbled to the ground, his hands going to his neck.

Fabe had walked to the washrooms by the snake house and picked up the public phone outside the men's room door. He asked for Angelo when the other party answered.

"Yeah?" Tombstone said when he came on.

"It's done," Fabe said.

"Hey, no shit?" Then Tombstone hesitated. "Already, huh?" Another pause, thinking about something. Then he said, "Look, Fabe, how about, I mean you did such good work, you really got to come to work for us. Maybe take Roland's place?"

He didn't even ask if DiNardo was dead or under arrest.

"No, thanks, Angelo," Fabe said, and hung up. He walked into the men's room and got into a stall and sat there with his pants up, locked in, and smoked one Pall Mall after another. It took four cigarettes, but at last Jimmy Capone came in and called out to him.

"It's light," Jimmy said accusingly.

"Doral cut up a kilo. I had to make things even, man."

"Had to round out your take, you mean," Jimmy said, smiling, though, not pissed off. Hell, Fabe figured he'd just pulled off the biggest bust of his career.

"I'm a few grand over, matter of fact," Fabe said.

"You'll find a way to spend it."

They were silent for a while, in the toilet of the men's room at the zoo. At last Fabe said, "I don't know how to say it."

Jimmy said, "Then don't. Just get going. But I'll tell you one thing: I'm getting your season tickets, the Bears' home games."

"You got into my safe."

"So what?"

"What were you looking for?"

"Evidence of drug dealing." Just like that, no apology or even a hesitation. "And I'd've found any, we wouldn't be talking now."

"How'd you get my combination figured?"

Jimmy Capone sighed, shook his head. "All you wise-asses," he said, "think you're smart. And every goddamn one of you uses your birthday for your safe combinations. Christ."

"DiNardo?"

Jimmy Capone had been waiting patiently, figuring Fabe would ask, not wanting to bring it up himself. He smiled inwardly, his moment of triumph at hand.

"Fabe, DiNardo and Ortiz are looking at fifteen apiece on the drug charge. Ortiz another ten, federal, for carrying an automatic weapon. Four cops in the park, every one of them ten-year veterans, another three in the van, they got it all on videotape, with sound effects and everything. Don't worry, you moved far enough away."

"Then there *are* six guys in the department you trust."

"That's right. And every one of them is willing to swear in court that we got an anonymous tip, we set it up all by ourselves. Any smart lawyer wants to know why I didn't use any of my own squad on it, I got the perfect out. Everybody knows that Narcotics guys take Christmas Eve and Christmas off. I got the best reason in the world not to use them; I couldn't reach them in time."

Fabe was shaking his head still.

"I sent a call to Homicide. The bullets in Washington match the bullets come out of a stud pulled out of the Lake yesterday. We put the gunman at Doral's, named Lloyd Cassero, with the stiff, they did time together in the joint." Making conversation now. Trying to stall saying good-bye. "You're free, Fabe," Jimmy told him. "These cops, they'll swear up and down it was just DiNardo and Ortiz. Just to get them. Finally. So you'd better get the hell out of here."

"That many on the force you can trust?" Still on it. Jesus Christ.

"And more, if I need them, goddammit." Jimmy got mad then, hot, a little red in the face. "How many fucking guys you know you can trust, huh?" And Fabe turned to Jimmy, looking shocked that Jimmy even had to ask, the pain of the realization there in his eyes.

Fabe said, "Just one."

Tatum O'Neal was searching the zoo, looking for the boss. Christ, they were going to need him once they got these characters back to the squad room, the press were going to have a field day on this one. He found his commander in the men's room in the snake house, hugging a guy back there by the stalls.

Tatum backed out quietly, and swore he'd never mention it to anyone, ever. Jimmy Capone had shown him already once today how he got even with guys who pissed him off.

Sally Evans listened to the tape on the machine in her bedroom as soon as she got in the door. As she listened she got higher and higher, felt better and better. God, when he'd said to her in the restaurant, "Go and check your messages," she'd almost died, thinking he'd gone to her house and Jacobs had left a message on the tape or something, and Fabe had figured out that she was a cop.

She took a leisurely shower, since she had a few hours to set things up. The press would be involved, certainly. So she had to look her very best. She soaped herself sensuously, enjoying the feel of her hands on her skin, turned on now, eroticized

237

at the thought that she'd pulled it off. And *how* she'd pulled it off, that was the best part.

God, she'd been a clerk in the Chief's office, typing and filing, and was grateful to be out of a squad car, happy for the assignment, because most cops hated it, were put there only when they were under investigation for something. But not Sally, she loved it. Because it freed her time so she could go to school.

She'd never planned to stay a cop forever, anyway. The fact that she had been a working cop would look good down the road, though, after practicing law for a while, then getting into something bigger.

The thing was, you had to know when to take your shots.

Dozens of superior officers had come on to her over the three years she'd been on the force. And she'd weighed the offers, gone out with the ones who could do her the most good. Like, for example, getting her out of a squad car and letting her ride a desk straight days, five days a week, while she went to school. The best ones were the married ones looking for a little action outside the house. They never made silly demands or wasted her time talking about love.

Captain Abe Jacobs, though, he had been the jewel in the crown. He had seen her typing one day, and she'd crossed her legs, giving him a shot, looking up at him from under raised brows. They'd got to talking, and he'd said that maybe the OPS could use a lady who had a degree in drama from Northwestern, before she went on to pre-law. And he'd made her prove her acting abilities, by God. Acting like she was enjoying that little cock of his inside of her, yechh. But he'd come through. Got her assigned to his department, undercover. She was to serve food twice a week to a cop she was supposed to prove dirty. Jacobs took it very personal, too. Tried to get her to wire the booths, for God's sake, as if they sat in the same booth every time. After the first few weeks, though, she knew it would be just a matter of time until she was put back in the pool. These two guys never said anything about anything else but football or something like that.

But the extra money was nice. She got to keep her tips and wages, on top of her regular pay. After today, she'd get promoted to plainclothes, maybe she'd even ask for Vice, where the real action was for a woman. Put her right in a city council seat.

Too bad about Fabe, though. God, what a lover he was.

When he'd called, she'd been surprised and even a little disappointed. It wasn't him she was after. But when she'd told him to call back and she'd called Jacobs at home, getting the "Who *is* this?" treatment from his little princess of a wife, turning all the charm on then, saying, "An associate," and Abe had come on the line, saying, "Christ, I told you not to call me here," and she'd told him, why, he'd gone apeshit. "Hell, *yes*, go out with him," he'd told her. "The guy's a convicted *felon;* God knows what he might tell you." So she had, and then, after feeling the gun in his pocket, hanging all over him to see if he was carrying, she'd called Abe from the phone in Water Tower Place. He'd said to her, "God, he's a *thief*, they don't carry guns," telling her something really important had to be happening, find out whatever she could whatever way she could, and did she get his meaning. And God, looking around just as Fabe was walking out of the bathroom, checking his fly, looking around for her, she'd played it straight, called Abe a made-up name and shot the shit with him about school until Fabe came over to her. And she'd had her back to him and so he'd never know that she was talking to anyone besides a girlfriend from school.

It wasn't easy, being an undercover agent.

And Abe, he'd been so in a hurry to find out if she'd found

out anything that he'd called her and left a message on the machine. God, when she'd heard his voice, she was so terrified that she'd just shut the machine down, gotten undressed and poured the sex appeal on Fabe, in case he'd heard it coming from the bedroom. Not give him time to think. But it had all worked out okay. He'd come into the shower for seconds, hadn't he? Left her his car and everything, given her cab fare.

And then the real kicker. The message on the recorder. A couple of million, cash, and ten times that in cocaine. It would be the biggest bust this year. And she'd be the star. Big promotion, nice raise, and she could kiss Abe Jacobs off and set her sights a lot higher.

She dressed carefully, in colors that would go well with the television cameras. Then she sat down on the bed and called Abe at home, and wasn't this her lucky day, the Dragon Lady answered again. Putting all she had into it, she said, "Is Abe there?" a bit of laughter in her voice, finding it amusing that she was talking to her boyfriend's wife, sexy, sultry, voice low and husky, and the bitch threw the phone onto a table or maybe the floor, and Sally heard her shouting, "Abe, goddamn it, Abe, it's *her* again!"

"Sally . . ." A warning in his voice. But she was ready for him, had the tape run back to Fabe's message, and so she turned the knob, holding the receiver next to the speaker, and let Abe listen to Fabe's voice.

"Christ in heaven, it's better than I ever hoped."

"Abe, it'll be your bust, I understand, you did the masterminding, but I *am* going to get full credit, aren't I." Not a question, a statement, letting him know that if she didn't get full credit, some of his bosses were going to hear about how he picked women for his undercover assignments. And his bitch of a wife, too.

240

In the lobby of Fabe's apartment building, a dozen of Abe Jacobs's headhunters were standing around while Abe talked to his star. Sally detested the OPS guys—condescending, self-important little pricks. Playing politics, kissing ass and busting their own brothers to get ahead. God, she hated them. They were dressed up in suits and ties, knowing they would be on television later. They'd probably try and steal the whole show. Which was what she and Abe were talking about at the moment. Telling him if he gave her any shit, she'd back out, and without her there was nothing they could do. They couldn't go in without a warrant, couldn't get a warrant on the evidence obtained illegally, a private conversation left in her home on a recorder. Abe reasoned with her, assured her she would be the star of the show. Okay.

A bunch of them crowded into the elevator, three of them going into the fire stairway, in case Fabe tried to take off. She had her keys, but the door was unlocked.

"Fabe?" Sally called. Nine guys on her side of the door, and she had to act as if she wasn't confident. Thank God for drama school. "Fabe?" Get a little fear in there, the way an actress would play a waitress who was about to run away with a drug dealer. "Fabey, honey?" Into the bedroom, the bathroom, but he wasn't here, she was wasting her talent.

She walked to the door and threw it open. "Come on in, guys," Officer Sally Evans said.

Abe Jacobs was furious. Somehow, he'd snookered them. Only one person could have told him that they were coming, and she was such a ladder-climbing bitch she wouldn't have told Fabe if the man was her brother. Goddammit. If Fabe Falletti was carrying a fortune in drugs and cash, then it stood to reason that James Capone knew about it. Get Falletti in a room alone, offer him immunity and relocation if he'd work for Jacobs, go undercover against Capone and the rest of the goddamn rogue cops. But he was gone.

Now what?

One of his men, Paulie, came toward him with a white face and a ghost of a smile. He was carrying a manila envelope, standing there like he didn't know what the hell to say.

"What is it?" Abe asked.

"Sir, we got a real problem here."

"I'm waiting, Paulie." Anger there, controlled, remind the guy who the boss was.

"Uh-sir, I already called for the commander on call."

"You *what*?"

"Sir, we have evidence here implicates you in a shakedown with Officer Sally Evans—"

"You *what*!?" Grabbing for the envelope now, the son of a bitch pulling it away.

"I'm sorry, sir, the commander told me to keep all evidence away from you, to inform you that you were to be detained in the apartment until he got here."

"This is fucking ridiculous, I'm your *cap*tain!"

Paulie was outright enjoying it now, he may not have been the star of the big bust, but he'd certainly hooked himself a big one here, a captain, and Jacobs bet he was ever so glad he'd worn a red tie so it would show up better on the ten-o'clock news.

"Who's the commander on call today?" he demanded, trying to get his dignity back.

"Commander James Capone, sir . . ." And Abe felt his belly sinking.

18 The letter read: "Officer Evans. People like you and Abe Jacobs should be put in prison. As an ex-con I have no choice but to leave, as I cannot pay the million dollars you demanded from me to keep myself from getting set up in a cocaine deal. When you told me Jacobs was involved, I nearly went to Jimmy Capone, but he hates drugs so much he would arrest me himself, just for being implicated in it. I am leaving town on an afternoon train for good. I have signed the title of the Cadillac over to you, and the deed to the apartment, along with a real estate contract selling the apartment to Jacobs, for the price of one dollar each. May you rot in hell."

There was no signature.

Probably wouldn't stand up, but it would wreck any chances the two of them had for promotion and advancement, that was for sure. As Jimmy Capone led the two of them out of the apartment for questioning on Christmas Eve, he thanked God for Fabe's suspicious nature, because if Fabe hadn't listened to the girl's recording machine the night before, Christ knows what would have happened today.

And maybe they'd get lucky. Maybe he could railroad these two head-hunting assholes right into Joliet. Then he could use his time for real police work, instead of having to watch his back twenty-four hours a day, not trusting half his crew. Either way, this was a hell of a Christmas present his old buddy had given him.

Fabrizzio Falletti had left Jimmy at the zoo and gone directly to the Jefferson Street apartment. The lock was a piece of cake, as was the one on the fifth-floor door. He had gone immediately to the recording machine in the bedroom and set the tape back to where his message began. It had been a risk, but it paid off because she hadn't taken it with her to try and get a warrant. But she'd want to use it for evidence if his plan got her in any shit. He hit the "record" button and "rewind" at the same time, erasing the tape, right back to where Jacobs' voice was asking Sally if she'd learned anything, not leaving his name or anything, but who else could it be but a cop? When Jimmy had told him that he'd been warned against a deep-cover OPS agent working to get him, well, it was easy to figure out then.

He had left the apartment, and left the car right there in front, keys in the ashtray. He'd taken his satchel and walked toward Michigan, found a pay phone, made a call. Listened to Sally's message singing at him.

At the beep, Fabe said, "Okay, bitch, I'm clean, but I'm leaving the car and apartment for you and Jacobs. Leave me alone now. By the time you hear this, I'll be halfway to Florida, where maybe the cops let a guy live down his past." And he hung up.

Hell, he owed a ton of money on the apartment yet. No big loss. The car had been paid for, but Angelo Paterro would have his goonies out looking all over for it. It would do him no good.

Tombstone hadn't bullshitted him. No one sets up a made mobster and lives to tell about it. Especially a thief, a home invader who might one day talk to the wrong people, let them know that DiNardo had really been set up by Campo. And so

Tombstone would have to have Fabe killed. He might not lose too much sleep searching for him if Fabe stayed out of state. But if he hung around Chicago, sooner or later he'd catch his lunch, and he wasn't ready for that yet.

Fabe caught the airport bus in front of the Westin. There were maybe a dozen holiday travelers got on with him, adults, drinking champagne in the back of the bus, partying, and Fabe watched the bus driver stare at them warily, wondering if she should say anything.

They were singing Christmas carols now, and Fabe thought, not now, but maybe next year I'll be ready to join in without feeling like a fool. He had a million dollars. What he'd set out to get in the first place. Three sets of identification, and the take. Time to start over. Anywhere he felt like going. He decided he'd get on the first plane boarding, no matter where it was headed, see what happened.

He'd miss Jimmy, though. The apartment, the car, the furniture, the clothes, he could replace all that. He wished he had his Leonard-Hearns tape, though.

But Jimmy was one in a million.

The revelers were singing "Silent Night." It had been Fabe's mom's favorite song.

And Doral, he'd miss the hell out of Doral. Big bullshitting son of a gun, but if the chips were down, Doral would be there for him.

But that was it. Almost forty and there were only two people in the whole goddamn world he cared about, and one of them was dead.

Well, had he deserved better? Doing what he did when he'd been a cop, without any thought or anything, just plowing right in there, blinded by injustice he'd mostly imagined. Hell, Jacobs *had* caught him with his hand in the till.

They were finishing up now, wrapping up "Silent Night." Fabe, sitting on the airport bus with a million dollars in a black leather satchel on his lap, thought, the hell with it, now or never, and softly, so no one could really hear him, he sang, "Sleep in hea-ven-ly pe—eace . . ." And it felt really good singing, Christ, used to sing it every year a thousand times with Ma before she died.

Thinking maybe Doral had been half-right all along. Life's a bitch, and then you die.

But sometimes you caught a break.

"Sle—eep in hea-ven-ly peace," louder now. He joined in the clapping.

There. That wasn't so bad now, was it?

Getting up, taking them up on their invitation to join the happy crowd, Fabe thought, yes, sometimes you get lucky.

About The Author

Eugene Izzi was born and raised in Chicago and, except for the two years he spent in the army, has lived in the Chicago area all his life. He had taken jobs as a steelworker and a construction worker prior to devoting himself to writing full time. His short stories have appeared in several magazines. He now lives in a suburb of Chicago with his wife and two children. *The Take* is his first novel.